Finding Y

A novel

By
Kari Rimbey

Finding Y
A novel

© 2022 Kari Rimbey

Published by Fischer Publishing: https://www.fischerpublishing.net
Publishers note: This novel is a work of fiction. All characters are fictional and any similarities to real people are purely coincidental.

ISBN   9798810932758 paperback

Cover design by:
Heather Wilbur

Cover includes Shutterstock images.

Dedicated to the memory of
Tim Farmer and his older brother, Mike.

Conditional Probabilities

CHAPTER 1

Every print and pattern stripped from her bedroom, on the advice of a sleep specialist, brought Ava Roberts no relief. Blank walls, printless comforter, and vacant dresser top only provided an empty canvas on which her mind could wander. Pillow punched, she sat on the edge of her bed, head low, shoulders tight. As if her small frame doubled in weight over the last four hours, she stood and shuffled to the window. A six-inch gap slowly slid open; cool air drifted over her face. Long hair brushed away from tired eyes, she breathed in the earthy smell of fallen leaves and damp soil, but the change in sensory input failed to stave off an endless volley of mind bombs.

Hand on the windowsill, she rocked in a steady sway from heel to toe. "Timothy Gray, go away," she whispered, "You're not my problem." Window closed, she flopped back on her bed.

Well past two in the morning, Ava tapped the lamp on her nightstand. White noise from the air filter afforded her a measure of cover for middle-of-the-night meanderings. She tiptoed to her closet, slowly slid the door open, and pulled a tablet out of her backpack. Something boring that required a lot of attention, that's what she needed. Anything to quiet her mind. Experience told her to turn off the mental chatter or she'd have a whopper of a headache. Or fall asleep in class again. Or both.

Her precalculus program open, she read ahead into the next chapter: Bayes' Theorem on Conditional Probabilities. Eyes on the blank walls in her bedroom, Ava pondered what she might use to test the theorem. How about the probability that Timothy Gray would get help if conditions didn't change? Tablet tossed on the floor, she ran both hands through her hair. "This is impossible. Why can't I get him out of my head? It's not like I can do anything to help him."

With a slow creak, her door opened. "Ava . . . everything okay?" Lola, her mother, asked, leaning into her bedroom.

"Sorry, Mom. Did I wake you?"

Lola waved off the question. "Trouble sleeping?" Her mother moved to her side and sat on the edge of the bed, smile soft and patient, knowing eyes already collecting clues to the obvious.

"I'm all right, mom."

"You sure?"

Ava's conscience teetered between tell and don't tell, still uncertain if what she witnessed leaned more toward active imagination or probability.

"Mom . . . have you ever thought someone wanted to hurt themselves, but you couldn't do anything about it?"

"Ava, what happened?" Lola leaned in close, a hand on Ava's arm. "One of your friends?"

"No," she replied with a smirk. "He doesn't even know me. Anyways, it's really none of my business." A thumbnail in mid-chew, she felt a sliver of relief by stating the facts. Not her business. Time to let it go.

"He?" Her mother asked with an extra hitch of concern in her voice. "You know you can trust me. Did you see someone with drugs?"

She met her mother's intense stare. "No, Mom, it's not like that. I'm not even sure what I saw."

"Tell me what's bothering you, sweetheart. Sharing your worries might help. You need your sleep." Her mother swept a hand over Ava's forehead, lingering as if checking for a fever.

Ava considered a cloaked response. She didn't have to say who it was. "Do you think boys can have eating disorders, like some girls do?"

The tight lines on her mother's brow relaxed. "I suppose they can. Maybe for different reasons."

A deep breath in and slowly out, Ava tried to shake off her Timothy fixation. "It's probably nothing."

"Even if it is something, you need to get some sleep." Her mother gave her a hug, one of those back pats that suggest it isn't as bad as you think it is. Lola stood up to leave, then turned back before closing the door. "I want to talk more about this, okay? Right now what you need is rest, not worries."

"You're right. Thanks, Mom." Her mother's sage advice swam around between this *can* and *can't* wait.

More than enough time passed for her mother to retire to her own bedroom. Ava shifted from worry mode to information gathering, a healthier approach. It would be helpful if she knew more about Timothy. Besides, minding one's own business is overrated. It's 2037. Social media is an invitation to snoop. She tapped her phone and typed in a search. Suggestions from distant cities lined the screen. None of those Timothys were him. Eyes painfully dry, she turned off her phone.

"Wait." Phone back on, she did a general search, name and city, and found an address, a JV basketball roster, and a game schedule. So, Timothy played on the JV basketball team. Ava scrolled through the dates, finding his first home game scheduled for the third of December.

An offer flashed on the side of the page. For a small fee, she could open an eagle-eye search that listed access to the following: news articles, criminal records, background check, previous addresses, former employment, lawsuits, etc. One of her father's observations filtered into her own and took root. Nothing was private anymore.

Since she wasn't a creeper, she wouldn't pay the fee to do an eagle-eye search on Timothy. With a quick scan of the JV schedule, she made a mental note of home games. It wasn't such a bad idea. There's nothing creepy about a freshman girl going to a basketball game.

* * *

Ava sat on the top bleacher, tablet on her lap, a stylus in hand, and a digital notebook beside her. The band began to set up in the balcony. Clangs and clatters from music stands and instruments joined the rhythmic thud of the basketball. Soon the gym would fill to capacity with energetic fans anticipating the varsity game.

She glanced at the shot clock—6 … 5 … 4. Timothy maneuvered his way through the key, his tall, thin frame swimming in an oversized blue jersey and long, baggy shorts. He set a screen, taking a knee to his thigh and an elbow in his ribs before turning to the basket to rebound the ball. If he got the rebound, which wasn't often, he would make the quick basket every time. Not once did he try for the initial shot. In fact, it didn't seem as if he tried at all.

At the sound of the final buzzer, the visiting JV team celebrated the blowout with howls and fist pumps. A small group of hometown fans acknowledged the end of the game with robotic applause. Were Timothy's parents there? Ava didn't spot anyone that resembled him, his thin, sandy blond hair nowhere in the Colfax crowd. A dark-haired woman sat alone, separated from the other parents. She might have been his mother. The woman sat on the first bleacher ten rows in front of Ava, her face hidden from consideration.

What a bummer, a loss by fourteen points. Ava watched as Timothy glanced at the score. Chin to his chest, he headed to the locker room. His mystery struggle weighed heavy on her. Lord help me. Why am I doing this?

Playing the Crush Card

Chapter 2

The smell of barbecue tofu and cornbread grew stronger as Ava walked into the high school cafeteria. Blue and gold game posters lined the walls of the large room cluttered with the sounds of clattering trays, shifting chairs, and three hundred voices eager to be heard.

She had gone to the first JV basketball game the week before and was confident her motives remained undetected.

"Over here." Her friend, Rochelle, waved for Ava to join a table already crowded with freshman girls.

Without interrupting the flow of conversation, the girls shifted to make room for her, their latest romantic interests the current and most popular topic.

"What about you, Ava?" Rochelle asked with a playful smile. "Don't think I haven't noticed your sudden interest in JV basketball."

Ava shrugged, a long strand of dark hair twisted around her finger. Other than to her mother, she hadn't mentioned anything about Timothy. If Rochelle was on to her, Ava may have to play the crush card. "Just hanging out. Had homework to do." A lot of girls were at the game. Boys were there. It made sense.

"Whatever, Ava. You know you have a thing for Mr. Skinny Legs." Rochelle teased, then leaned in and whispered, "Can't keep your eyes off him. It's his smile, right? The guy might be skinny, but he's cuter than a tub of puppies."

"Who does she like?" a girl from across the table asked a little too loudly.

Ava looked at Rochelle with wide eyes. "Don't."

"Timothy Gray," Rochelle announced triumphantly, as if saying it aloud would magically make them a couple.

"Senior, huh?" another girl said with a sly grin.

"Did you say Timothy Gray?" another girl blurted as if she had a bullhorn attached to her lips. "Doesn't he have a girlfriend?"

Ava turned a deep shade of hide-under-the-table red and glanced across the cafeteria. She knew he couldn't hear them. To her relief, the girls shifted their attention to other topics of interest: details on the new girl from Texas and the firing of an aide in their history class.

She listened, nibbling on her half-eaten sandwich while the other girls talked over each other. Ava was content to be a part of this particular clutch of freshman girls. Two years earlier, she was the new girl in the seventh grade, and Rochelle, with her fire-red curls and unrestrained confidence, had been quick to befriend her. Ava's need to belong welcomed the connection. At first, she felt as if she didn't fit in at Colfax—like a puzzle piece placed in the wrong box by mistake. Without closer inspection, it would appear she belonged. By the time the new-girl label wore off, it became apparent that at one point or another everyone feels like a single-piece puzzle.

Most of the girls in her grade were friendly, and like most girls, they talked a lot but also talked around the things that really mattered to them, hinting at concerns while leaving out facts in an effort to protect one's self-esteem. Though she'd told Ava, Rochelle wasn't telling the other girls her father might lose his job and have to move. Recent information making the rounds on the gossip grapevine dished on Crystal, the girl at the end of the table, who had a new boyfriend pressuring her to sleep with him. Ava had her own secrets which she kept to herself. Everyone knows that the favorite thing to share is a secret.

"Are you doing anything this weekend?" Rochelle asked, pulling Ava out of her mental wandering.

"I think we're going to Walla Walla to see my grandparents," Ava replied. "Probably on Sunday."

Rochelle pulled a piece of fake meat out of her sandwich and plopped it on her tray. "I'm not going anywhere. Get to scrub golf clubs and pick up leaves. Wish it would hurry up and snow already."

For almost a year, Ava had a job. She missed doing errands for a local attorney's office, but a long stint of doctor appointments put an end to it six months ago.

A hand hovering over the food in her mouth, Rochelle asked if Ava wanted to go to a movie. "Maybe Saturday?" she added, then opened an app on her phone to see what was playing.

"I'm in," Ava replied.

They promised to text plans for Saturday night, then joined in the conversation that had circled back to the girl from Texas.

The new senior had a confident posture. She was pretty, but her hair seemed very Texan and out of place in eastern Washington. Everything really was bigger in Texas. Within a week or two, the girl's tall hair could shrink to Whitman County standards, maintain the identity of its roots, or influence the old standard, making tall volcano-shaped hair the new thing. Some of the older girls at the Texan's table appeared to be sizing her up. Was she friend or foe? Three girls were overly friendly, their laughter like honking geese and their attention on the boys at Timothy's table. Ava tried to suppress a grin as she watched the boys targeted for attention. They sat in a state of frozen annoyance, apparently waiting for the exaggerated cackling to stop.

Lunch break almost over, Ava pretended to listen to the gossip at her table while she watched Timothy. Her heart sank as he slipped away and walked toward the bathroom. Nothing was unusual about his destination, but an unsettling pattern caused her concern. Less than thirty seconds later he retraced his steps, the side of his fist tapping his chest as if to coax out a burp and dabbing at the corners of his mouth with the back of his hand. He started to look her way, as people do when they sense someone watching them. Ava shifted her eyes to her hands before he caught her. When he turned away, she saw him pop something in his mouth, a mint or maybe an antacid, before returning to his table of friends and collecting the wrappers from his lunch.

The guys at the table, some juniors, mostly seniors, showed a preference for his attention and said something that made him laugh. Ava wanted to be wrong, but every day at the end of lunch, since she'd first noticed him three weeks earlier, Timothy Gray had emptied the contents of his stomach.

"Caught you lookin'." Rochelle stood up to leave, eyebrows wiggling. "Going to the game tonight?"

"I think so," Ava said with a sheepish grin. She could go with the crush thing.

"You'll probably want to catch the JV game, too." Rochelle snickered and headed down the hall as if she had an ability to read minds. "If I didn't have to work, I'd go with you," her friend yelled over the crowd.

Ava, lips pulled into her mouth, gave her a thumbs-up. As much as she fed off Rochelle's energy, she preferred to do reconnaissance alone.

On the way to her locker, Ava shrugged off the misunderstanding. No harm, no foul. Besides, crushes were as fleeting as free candy in a crowded classroom. At her locker, she offered a tentative wave to a smiling familiar face, then turned to collect what she needed for her next two classes.

"Hey." The sophomore in her coding class strolled closer and leaned on the locker next to hers, his arm in an arc above her head. "Coming to the game tonight?"

"The game? Oh, uh, yeah." She couldn't remember his name. Trey or Trent maybe? One of the varsity players.

"So, Avery, right? Thought you might want to hang out sometime," he said as he acknowledged another girl passing by with a jut of his chin. "Did you see my three-pointer?" Hair flicked out of his eyes, he shot an imaginary ball in the air and followed up the move with a fist pump, crowd-cheering noises added for affect. He then moved far too close and set his arm on her shoulder.

Not bothering to correct him on her name, she dipped her shoulder and took a step back. "Sorry, I didn't really see . . . got lots of homework . . . and stuff. Thanks, though."

"So that's a no?" he asked with a half-cocked grin.

"Can't. Sorry. But hey, good luck on your game." She reached in and closed her locker as if it had a spider on it. "I'd better get to class."

"Okay. Catch ya later, Avery." Lover boy jogged down the hall and saddled up to his next potential conquest before Ava turned the corner. No broken heart there.

Even if her interest in Timothy wasn't romantic, he still consumed her thoughts. Why would a guy want to throw up? She had heard of wrestlers purging to make their weight class and girls desperate to look like the emaciated models in the fashion magazines, but why Timothy? She didn't know anything about him.

Divided Attention

Chapter 3

Rochelle waved for Ava to move to the student section. Within ten minutes, half the town would crowd into the bleachers to watch the varsity play.

"Were you here for the whole JV game?" her friend asked. Before the band started to pound out another jazz tune, Rochelle's bag of popcorn tilted toward Ava for easy access.

Backpack stashed at her feet, Ava nodded but didn't comment, a handful of popcorn conveniently rendering her speechless.

Rochelle asked how the JV team did.

"They lost," Ava replied with a shrug then tried to think of something to ask that didn't have anything to do with Timothy.

"You know," Rochelle said between bites of popcorn, "Timothy used to be one of the best players ever."

For that insensitive comment, Ava gifted her friend an elbow poke to the ribs. "That's not nice."

"No, for real. When he was a freshman he was on the varsity team. Before his brother died."

"What? His brother died?" Ava whispered. This was critical information; however, she didn't want to be overheard talking about it.

Rochelle grabbed Ava's arm. "You didn't know about Billy?"

"No." Ava held a finger to her lips. "Let's talk about it later."

Rochelle clamped a hand over her mouth but seemed satisfied after taking a quick inventory of the people seated around them. "Good call," her friend said. "Later would be better."

The varsity took the floor, the energy in the room like a Viking showdown. Some of the guys who also played football seemed to forget the difference between the two sports, shrill whistles sounding off as two players went at each other, their opinions of fair play not matching up with the referee's call. Students yelled. Boys were benched. Coaches waved off warnings as they complied, and the game continued.

First quarter of the game almost over, Ava noticed a trickle of JV players making their way into their usual corner, hair wet from showers, ties crooked, sports bags slung over their shoulders. Timothy wandered in and took up one of the last seats against the wall.

Rochelle, apparently not gifted with the art of subtlety, gasped as if the world's most famous person had just walked past them. "He's here, Ava. Do you see Timothy?"

"Would you zip it? I see him, okay?" Ava nonchalantly kept track of him throughout the game, his attention divided between his phone and the occasional validation of the guy sitting next to him. Whatever he was doing, he didn't look happy to be there.

* * *

Large snowflakes swirled like falling feathers around Ava and Rochelle as they walked to the parking lot after the game. As usual, Rochelle's mother was their ride home. Ava took advantage of their privacy to ask about Billy. "You were going to tell me about Timothy's brother. What happened?"

Chin lowered, Rochelle slowly shook her head. "The worst thing ever. Billy went to this party and he drank too much or took something. People in Billy's class said he wasn't into drugs. I can't really remember the details. I think Timothy was with him. Anyways, I'm not really sure how, but Billy died at the party or maybe on the way home. Everybody was so freaked out about it. When it happened, Timothy was a freshman and Billy a senior. I heard Timothy hasn't been the same since. Beyond bummer, huh?"

"Wow . . . That's terrible." Ava cleared the tightness in her throat with a cough. She now had a reason coupled with sketchy facts but wanted to change the subject before they got to the car.

11

"I heard Timothy won't go to any parties even if there's no drinking," Rochelle added. They walked another twenty feet without saying anything. "Ava, are you really into Timothy? Are we talking stalker crush, infatuation, or distant admirer? Open up that mouth of yours. Spill already. A nun on Sunday is chattier than you."

"I don't know," Ava replied, attention on the sidewalk in front of them. "He's cute."

"Come on, girl! You've got to let me in on these things. You know I've had a thing for Jase Shoemacker since—forever. The love of my life. He'll never know it, though. Got that? Never. Like I think you would say anything." She wrapped an arm around Ava's. "I trust you as much as grass is green. I'd die though, if he ever found out. Oh, hey, then he could kiss me."

"Kiss you?" Ava stopped walking, Rochelle pulled to a standstill. "What in the world are you talking about?"

"The whole Snow White dead girl routine. Oh, sorry. Bad joke timing, with the whole Billy talk and all."

"No. No apology needed," Ava assured her, their forward progress back in motion.

"I'd try it though—pretend to be dead." Rochelle continued, "If I thought I could get those lips of his coming at me."

"Yeah, but you like to keep your options open. I saw you watching someone tonight," Ava said with a nudge. "I mean, besides Jase. A Newport player? I'm on to you. It's confession time."

Rochelle giggled, grasped Ava's shoulder as if she might faint. "You mean that guy that looked like Superman, number seventeen? So gorgeous!"

"And he probably doesn't know it either," Ava added, her voice flat.

"Sure he does. Who cares? I could be Lois Lane right now." Rochelle threw her arm across her forehead, pretending to fall against a light post. "Superman, save me!" she sang out at the top of her lungs.

"Come on Lois Lane." Ava tugged on her friend's coat, "Your mom's waiting for us."

One hand on the light post, Rochelle reacted with theatrical disappointment. "Number seventeen, don't leave me!" Her antics earned her a few smirks from a passing herd of juniors and seniors, but as usual, Rochelle didn't care.

When they got to the car, her friend pulled the door open and told Ava that sweats were sexier than spandex.

"What are you two talking about?" Rochelle's mother asked.

"Gorgeous guys," Ava replied.

The Fraud

CHAPTER 4

Lunch over and tardy bell buzzing, Ava hurried into her fourth period class and slipped into one of the last available chairs at the front of the room. Three weeks into her Timothy-watching vigil, and nothing to show for it. Progress and any potential for it nonexistent. She'd been to several games, the second causing her more concern than the first. After playing a few minutes in the first quarter, Timothy had returned to the bench for the rest of the game, elbows resting on his knees and appearing as interested in the floor beneath him as he was in the game. In the third quarter, it looked like the coach asked him to go in, but he shook his head and pointed to the player sitting next to him.

While her math teacher answered a classmate's question, Ava's thoughts continued to wander.

Someone behind her tapped her shoulder. She turned back and took the tablet pressed her way, scanned the screen, marking the appropriate boxes with her stylus, and handed the tablet to the person beside her. The teacher's lecture on Bayes' theorem served as background noise while she rolled her stylus between her fingers.

"Ava, did you hear what I said?" the teacher asked, students already headed for the door.

She startled. "Sorry, Mr. Stevenson. Can you repeat the question? Please?"

He strolled to her desk, a hand on his hip, head tilted like a goat getting ready to charge. "The announcement. Did you hear it?"

Ava rubbed a finger over a spot on her desk. "I didn't."

"There's a sign-up sheet on the door for after-school tutoring. It's only one day a week. Are you interested in helping?"

"Helping? Sure." She waited until the class filed out of the room before checking the list. Two columns were divided into two-lined groups, the top space for the tutor, the line beneath it for the student. Ava picked up a pen from the table by the door and scanned down the page for the first blank, top line.

"Wait—what?" Ava stood with the pen hovering over the paper as she reread the list. She did see it. Timothy had signed up to be a tutor on Wednesdays after school.

Ava's pulse quickened as she considered her options. This was her chance! Before she could talk herself out of it, she wrote her name on the space below his, as his student, and set the pen back on the table. Timothy would be her tutor every Wednesday afternoon. No! I can't do it! She reached for the pen to cross her name off, hands shaking.

"Are you done?" a girl behind her asked. "I need to see if I have a student yet."

Ava stepped aside. "Yeah." An ache built in her gut as she walked to her next class. In two days, she'd be seated across from Timothy in the library while he spent his time helping her with something she didn't need help with. She was a fraud, or worse, a stalker and a fraud. What was she thinking! Why didn't the teacher have an online sign-up like every other teacher from this decade? She could have deleted it. That's probably why they went with paper and ink. More of a commitment. Maybe it wasn't too late to change it.

* * *

With the last class of the day finally over, Ava hurried to cross her name off the list. Pen dropped on the floor, she searched the floor and moved aside to let someone behind her look over the list.

"Are you Ava Roberts?"

Ava tried to breathe in, her throat tight. She wouldn't need that pen. "Yes," she squeaked.

With a broad smile, Timothy leaned toward her as if he had a secret to tell and tapped a thumb on his chest. "Timothy Gray." He pointed to the list. "Looks like you and me on Wednesdays."

"Oh yeah, on Wednesdays." She felt like she had cotton in her mouth and her brain.

"Don't worry, I won't be too hard on you." His friendly blue eyes sparkled as he waited for her to respond.

Currently incoherent, she forced a smile and nodded.

"See you Wednesday, Ava."

She waved, then pretended to look for something in her backpack as he walked away. *What have I done? Idiot! I'm going to die right here in the hall, and if not here, in the library on Wednesday.* She could already see the headline in the Whitman County Gazette—*Freshman Stalker Dies of Embarrassment.*

* * *

Like a sailor grasping the edge of a ship before walking the plank, Ava felt a thump in her chest. She looked up the stairs leading to the library, her grip glued to the handrail. Why was it Wednesday already? She hadn't told anyone about the tutoring session she still planned to get out of as soon as possible.

Rochelle caught up to her before Ava could work up the courage to take a step. "Hey, doing anything? Want to come over? The golf course is closed," she said with a twirl. "I'm free as a bird."

Ava knew Rochelle's high spirits had another reason besides time off from work. Her father's job as manager of the golf course was secure. Whoever logged a complaint about him threatening someone with a 9-iron was too slim on evidence to get him fired. Rochelle wouldn't be moving. Definitely a reason to celebrate.

The truth of it, Ava wanted to go with Rochelle, but she needed to deal with her present debacle alone. "I'd like to, but I have . . . I have a thing in the library for about a half hour." Ava scratched at a spot on her arm that didn't itch.

"What're you doing? I could wait 'til you're finished." Rochelle smiled and moved toward the stairs.

Ava chewed her cheek. "I have something for precal. Hey," she said in her best I've-got-a-great idea voice, "why don't I just walk to your place when I'm done?"

Rochelle agreed and took a few backward steps toward the door. "Do you want my mom to pick you up?"

"No, that's all right. It's not that far and kind of nice out."

The mid-December Wednesday warmed up to a comfortable fifty degrees, sun out, no wind, and snow from the previous week nearly gone. The half-mile walk to Rochelle's house would give Ava a chance to recover from her poorly thought out plan. One more lie and she would be free of this mess.

"Okay," Rochelle replied. "See ya in a few."

"See ya." Ava forced a smile, a seed of both relief and guilt needling her conscience. She wasn't really lying, just evasive.

Like a worm in a hole, guilt dug down a little deeper. Evasive as in shifty, secret-keeping girl about to ruin her life. Maybe she should have told Rochelle. She watched through the glass door as Rochelle crossed the street. Too late now.

This was a colossal mistake. Ava climbed up the stairs to the library, rehashing the list she'd spent the entire day making and remaking: options on how she might get out of this. *Hi, Timothy. It looks like Wednesdays aren't going to work out for me.* That's simple enough. Or, *Hello, I'm really a hypocrite that doesn't need any help after all.* Better yet, *Hi, I'm Ava, your friendly-freshman stalker, here to meddle in your private life.*

She pushed the heavy glass door open, scanned the library. Yes! Clearly a gift from heaven. He wasn't there. "Perfect. Bullet dodged." Shoulders feeling lighter, she turned to leave.

"Oh no you don't, Miss Roberts." Behind her, Timothy pulled her backpack off her shoulder, pointed across the library, and marched past her. "Come on. You're not getting out of this. It'll be painless, I promise." He set her backpack on a table in the far corner and plopped in a chair that seemed too short for his lanky frame. "Alrighty then." He rubbed his hands together as if he were sitting down to a twenty-ounce steak, "Let's do us some precal."

Ava couldn't remember anything on her get-out-of-this list except the part about her being a liar. With clammy hands, she pulled out her tablet and sat across from him. "I, um, thanks for doing this." Unable to look at him, she stared at her hands, her face about to spontaneously combust.

"Ava, it'll be easier if you sit over here." He tapped the chair to his right. "I don't bite—anymore."

"Hey Timmy," one of three older girls called from across the library. The trio strutted toward them like models on a catwalk, a

17

swirled mound of two-toned hair atop their heads. Neon plastic miniskirts fell inches above their thigh-high boots with beaded fringe that swished and clicked with every step.

Ava tucked her canvas slip-ons under her chair and took up lint hunting on the sleeve of her beige sweater.

"What are you doing up here, Tim-Tim?" The alpha of the pack shot a glance at Ava with a smile that suggested she'd just eaten something gross, Ava's existence apparently unpalatable.

Timothy opened Ava's tablet to a random page and swiped the screen. "We're working on math. You headed out?"

"We were gonna go to Pullman," the girl said, an orange-tipped pinky on her bottom lip. "Do some virtual gaming or somethin'. Want to come, Timmy?" The leader of the threesome cocked her head and smiled at him as if he'd just asked her to the prom.

"I'm sorry, Carina, I can't. But thanks for asking." Timothy looked over the page in front of him.

"Are you sure?" she whined, her bottom lip stuck out like a pouting toddler as she flicked long bangs away from her eyes in neck-wrenching twitches.

This was the out Ava needed. "You know," Ava said while trying to push away from the table, "We can cancel. You go. I don't mind at all." She tried again to push her chair back, but it wouldn't budge.

"Fabuloso! You're goin' with us," Carina ordered with a smug grin.

Looking at the floor to see why her chair wouldn't move, Ava saw Timothy's foot wedged behind one of the legs.

He looked over the open program on the table as if to suggest interrupted work in progress. Timothy tapped a finger on his chin. "You know what, maybe another time."

"Please, Timmy?" Carina pulled a strand of dyed black hair into her mouth. "Me wants youzee to come with us."

What in the world? Ava put a hand over her mouth to keep from saying anything involuntarily. Or gagging. Is this girl Timothy's type? Surely not his girlfriend. That pairing didn't add up at all.

"You know, I really can't," he replied. "Have practice tonight and some other stuff I've got to do."

"Be that way!" Carina jerked her shoulder back then morphed into her previous coy toddler routine with doe eyes and a shy grin. "Bye-bye, Timmy."

The three girls walked out of the library and waved from the door. Carina added an airmailed kiss. One side of Timothy's face hitched up in a half-smile, his hand lifting in acknowledgment of their exit. The second the girls were gone, he huffed out a loaded sigh.

"For the record, I hate being called Timmy. And what's up with the volcano hair? Is that red on top supposed to be lava?" He looked at Ava, clearly expecting an answer.

"The big hair? . . . Uh." Ava ran her eyes swiftly over his then focused on the tablet. "I think it's a new style."

"What's wrong with the old style? I like it better." He closed her screen and pushed it aside.

"I guess new isn't always better," she replied, feeling like she could finally breathe, maybe even talk in complete sentences.

"Like what?" Timothy stretched his arm across the empty chair on the other side of him and leaned back.

"I'm sorry?" She wasn't sure what he was asking and noticed his foot was no longer wedging her in place.

"Go ahead. Give me an example where new isn't always better. You said it." With a slow theatric gesture, he placed both hands behind his neck, eyes and smile playful.

"An example?" Ava rested her chin on her hand, his stare as distracting as a strobe light.

Without taking his eyes off her, he claimed she was stalling.

She pointed to her tablet. "Aren't we supposed to be working on precal? And about Wednesdays. I'll probably have to—"

"Still stalling." He crossed his arms and donned a smug grin as if his unspoken challenge was already won.

"Wine." She leaned back in her chair, assuming his posture but not his confident stare.

"That's a good one. I would have said that if you hadn't." He side-eyed her, cleared his throat, and wore a liar's grin. "I'm going to say . . . cars, like Mustangs and Camaros. The ones that run on good ol' gasoline."

Ava was starting to like this game. "Antiques," she said without hesitation. She'd left him an easy one, not that he needed it.

"Wait." He raised his eyebrows and sat up strait in his chair. "How about paintings? You know, art. Top that."

"Cheese," she said, a finger poking the table.

He slumped down, tapped her tablet. "I don't want to play with you anymore. We're supposed to be working on precal."

In an attempt to disguise a sudden rush of attraction, Ava focused on scanning the pages in her textbook program. "Can you explain how the Brute-Force Method works?"

"Let's take a look." He leaned forward and scanned the page. "Oh yeah, I remember this."

As he explained the method to her, Ava wondered if Timothy's quick game of wits was intended to help her relax. If it was, it worked. This tutoring thing wasn't going to be as hard as she thought.

Following his explanation, she asked pertinent questions every so often. She also noticed the cinnamon mint he had in his mouth and a faint clean-forest scent, probably his clothes or maybe his shampoo. His face seemed pale against his oversized, black sweatshirt, but his blue eyes were bright and when he smiled, they scrunched into narrow slits. It took some work to pay attention and continue to ask questions to which she didn't need answers.

His teeth, they didn't fit the warning signs, at least not for someone who had been purging for any length of time. They were movie-star straight and brilliant white. The warning signs she'd searched online listed discolored teeth with ruined enamel from stomach acid.

While he helped her work through the rest of the equation, Timothy cleared his throat again. That was on the list. He'd been clearing his throat every few minutes.

"Okay, that's enough." He looked at her for a second without saying anything and closed her program.

Oh, no! He can tell I'm a liar! Ava fumbled with her stylus, dropping it as a layer of clammy sweat accumulated on her hands.

"Trees," he said with a poker face.

Ava furrowed her brow. "Trees?"

"Yeah, trees. The older ones are better. You know, bigger."

The pinch in her back released. "Wisdom," she said as she began to put her things in her backpack.

"Ava Ostentatious Roberts, come on." He held his arms out with exaggerated offense. "That's a whole different level. New rule. You can only use tangible objects. And another even more important rule: Never outsmart an upperclassman, especially not a senior. You knew that, right? It's very important." He dropped his hands to the table, then patted her elbow. "Worry not, frightened freshman, thou art forgiven. Let's get out of here."

She tucked her chin and ran fingertips over her top lip as if she could actually wipe a smile off her face.

Timothy pulled her backpack over his shoulder, his arm swooping a wide arc insinuating she walk out of the library in front of him. "What did you think?" he asked as they walked down the stairs. "I thought we made some progress."

"Yeah, we did. You're a good teacher, tutor, or whatever." As comfortable as a second left shoe, she stopped on the last step and thanked him for carrying her things.

Timothy stepped past her off the stairs, still taller even with her one-stair advantage, and handed over her backpack. "You're welcome. So, Wednesday after Christmas break. Same time, same place."

She started to wave but stopped before embarrassing herself. "Thank you."

Timothy took several long strides toward the exit then turned back as he pushed the door open. "See ya later, Ava."

* * *

With a light, energetic step, Ava walked to Rochelle's house, replaying the half-hour she'd spent with Timothy—every word, gesture, and flirtatious grin. It wasn't so bad. Her inner critic again called in the mental sparring squad. Not so bad? Don't kid yourself—he's amazing! Easy, this isn't a crush thing; it's a mission. What if it's both? It's not! Don't let a crush screw this up.

She kicked a clump of snow melting on the edge of the sidewalk. Easier said than done. She couldn't help but like him. What was she going to tell Rochelle? Very little. Nothing.

CHAPTER 5

For the first time in her life, Ava was glad to see the end of the Christmas break. She wanted to return to school. On Wednesday, she hurried up the stairs to the library for her second meeting with Timothy. Still uncomfortably aware of Timothy's lunchtime routine, Ava was able to deal with it, even smile at him when he caught her eye on the way back to his table. This was only temporary, she reminded herself. The plan for his rescue had to progress one careful step at a time but must remain the main objective. Every day he continued to purge moved him that much closer to irreparable damage.

Rather than fret over an elusive next step in the process, Ava built an inventory of what she'd learned that she didn't know a month ago. Timothy wasn't lacking when it came to attention, especially from girls. She noticed he had a smile for anyone that talked to him, even if he wished they'd stop. Other than his disdain for being called Timmy, and his dislike for volcanic hairstyles, nothing seemed to bother him. He rarely complained. A light-hearted easiness about him suggested confidence and contentment. He was genuinely friendly, but she *knew* something in him was broken. If it was grief, he kept it well hidden.

Ava arrived at the library before Timothy and pulled the necessary items out of her backpack. Thankful that the second floor wasn't nearly as cold as the classrooms downstairs, she unzipped her coat and checked the clock, wondering what might have kept him. Over the Christmas break, the guilt that nearly incapacitated her during their first session had been whittled out of her conscience, justified by the fact that their meetings served a higher purpose.

"Look who's ready to get to it," Timothy said as he approached the table, looking as if he'd heard something funny.

With a new measure of confidence, Ava felt comfortable enough to question him without having a panic attack. "You look amused. Gonna let me in on it?"

He plopped down next to her without saying a word. Maybe he couldn't say anything through the giant grin he seemed unable to contain.

"What?" She looked at his contagious expression and smiled back.

Still not saying anything, he started to put her things away.

She had no indication why. "We're not doing precal today?"

"Nope. Are you hungry?" He zipped her backpack, slipped a strap over his shoulder.

"Hungry? Why?" Was he asking her to go somewhere? With him? A flutter built in her stomach. She didn't want to read too much into the question.

"I want to get some pizza. Wanna go?" He waited for her response, still grinning from ear to ear.

"What's going on? Does pizza make you this happy?" Ava followed him out of the library and down the stairs. "Well, are you going to answer me?" she pressed.

Timothy looked at her as if she already knew the plan. "I think we can take one Wednesday off. It shouldn't hurt your grades any. Do you want to go?"

"Sure." She pulled her phone out of her coat pocket, hoping her mother wasn't already on the way to pick her up, and tapped out a quick message.

"Before you put that away, can I see it?" Timothy pointed to her phone. "Why don't I enter my number, in case something comes up. You know, if you can't make it on Wednesday or something like that. Okay with you?"

Ava handed it to him. "Good idea." Was that the only reason he wanted it?

He gave her phone back. "Can I have *your* number?"

After entering her information in his phone, she handed it back to him. He slid next to her, leaned in close, and told her to smile.

Before she realized what he was doing, he had already taken the picture.

"I wasn't ready," she protested. That was a surprise. A picture of the two of them—together—on his phone. Even if it was only a contact ID, he had it. The flutters in her stomach suddenly multiplied, filling up her lungs as well.

He inspected the picture. "It's perfect."

Ava wanted to see it but she didn't ask.

Tucking his phone in the pocket of his coat, Timothy pushed the door open and held it for her, his long arm reaching over her head like a tree branch. Afraid he'd be able to read her enthusiasm over his sudden interest, she kept her eyes on the icy ground and followed him through the parking lot. "Where are we going?"

"Main Street Pizza," he replied. "There's a bunch of kids already there."

So that was it. He didn't necessarily want to take her but felt obligated because of their session. She would be tagging along so she didn't feel ditched. The flutters in her stomach instantly transformed into a pile of rocks.

"This is me," Timothy said, tapping the frosty hood of an ancient blue Dodge pickup. He opened the passenger door, moved a sports bag behind the bench seat, then stepped back for her to get in.

Ava thanked him and slid onto the cold seat, not telling him she already knew this was his pickup.

"Man, it's freezing." He started the engine and turned the heater on high. "I don't want you to get too cold on my watch, so let me know if you need to snuggle." Pulling his sweatshirt sleeves over his hands, he faced her with a mischievous smirk, waiting as if she hadn't responded to a legitimate offer.

"I'm good," she replied, looking out her window long enough to hide a flattered grin. Was he really flirting with her or just being funny?

Timothy dropped his head in mock disappointment. "Can't blame a guy for tryin'. Be back in a second." He grabbed an ice scraper from under the seat, then hopped out to clear the windshield.

Something was going on, but she didn't have a clue what it was. He'd never acted like this before, at least not around her. Silly, yes, but not this. The reason for his flirtatious mood was probably already sitting at a table at the pizza place, waiting for him to get there. Ava was certain his interest in her was merely temporary—the privilege of sharing in his excitement granted for the simple reason that she was the only person available at the moment. Lucky her. Ava blew out a what's-going-on-here huff. Was she going to get stuck in a corner by herself while he hung out with whomever it was he really wanted to see? She still wasn't sure who his girlfriend was. Hopefully not Carina.

Timothy jumped back in the pickup and tucked the scraper under the seat. "According to my mom, who keeps tabs on all notable Colfax news past and present, this pizza place was a hangout a long time ago. Used to be Chinese food, then a bistro forever that just closed to remodel and add a pizza parlor. Kind of a vintage thing, I guess. Got everyone excited to give it a try. Awesome, huh?"

Ava replied with a nod.

"You're a newbie, Miss Ava, to our quaint little town that has not changed much since the dawn of time. So that newsflash was *mucho importante*."

"Thank you for that." Fiddling with her sleeve, she shied away from his inviting smile. "I feel dully informed." Apparently, he was informed as well. Had he asked someone about her? Maybe in a town this size, everyone, like his mom, knew who the newbies were.

Timothy pulled out of the school parking lot and headed toward Main Street, driving past grain elevators over a hundred feet tall and a new three-story apartment complex—a skyscraper for a town the size of Colfax.

As they passed a farm supply store, he asked her what kind of pizza she liked.

"I like anything. Oh no, can we go back? My cash-card is in my locker. It'll only take me a second to grab it."

"You don't need it. It's on me." He turned left at the grocery store.

Her lungs grew tight. This wasn't a date; it was charity.

"Besides, you're tiny. Can you even eat two pieces?" He gave her that same challenging grin she'd seen before.

Waiting for the light to change, Ava crossed her arms, brow furrowed, trying not to smile. "I'm not tiny. I'm five-five, almost."

"Almost? What, like five-four and two-thirds?" He tried to laugh with his mouth closed but his effort produced a snort like a grunting pig.

Both of them lost it, his grunt laugh hilarious.

"I'm pretty cool, huh?" He pulled over to the curb and cut the engine, his face flushed.

Ava held a giggle-stifling hand to her mouth.

"Don't make me do that when we're eating or pop'll shoot out my nose."

If she was merely a tag-a-long she no longer cared. She'd take what she could get. Ava grabbed the door handle and tried to resist the goofy grin claiming her face.

"Wait. I'm a gentleman. Kind of old school. Ava, I know you're perfectly capable of pushing that door open, since you're almost five-five, but I'd like to get it for you." He paused, apparently waiting for her to approve of his chivalry.

As if the handle were suddenly hot, she pulled her hand back without looking away from him. In response, his eyes scrunched into those delighted, narrow slits. He jumped out and skirted the front of the pickup in three leaping steps.

This was a first. Ava thanked him as she stepped out onto the sidewalk, her usual observation skills completely jumbled. Soon enough, she'd know what this was all about.

They walked around the corner, both holding their coats tight to their necks, his hand beneath her elbow. A gust of freezing January wind peppered them with ice crystals. Through the big picture windows, Ava could feel eyes on her but resisted looking inside. She hurried through the door Timothy held for her, the smell of fresh bread and pepperoni encouraging her appetite. Before the door closed behind them, Ava heard what she'd expected.

Surprises

Chapter 6

"Timmy, over here," Carina sang from the far end of the pizza parlor, pushing the girl next to her, who obediently shifted over to free up space. "I saved you a seat."

He offered a single wave then stopped at a closer table to greet a group of friends vying for his attention. A dozen kids sat crowded at the table, most of them senior boys and a few juniors. Two guys had their girlfriends with them, tucked snugly under a we're-together arm.

Ava stood behind Timothy, wondering if she should sit down or keep standing behind him like an idiot. Maybe they thought he was trying to shake her off; the nice guy stuck with one of those leech types that are hard to detach.

"This is Ava." Timothy pulled her in front of him, his hands resting on her shoulders.

Like the new girl in kindergarten, she waved at the older kids. "Hi."

The group returned the greeting, staring at her with wide eyes and surprised smiles, then passed glances between them as if they had questions they could hardly wait to ask.

She expected Timothy to clear up the obvious misunderstanding, but he offered no excuses for his freshman sidekick.

"Timmy," Carina called again, her voice sounding a touch screechy, "Over here."

The girl was persistent. Timothy smiled at Carina then tactfully shook his head without saying anything. Ava pretended not to notice the jilted girl's jaw drop. Carina pulled her friend over to fill the empty space next to her, spearing Ava with a death glare.

"You didn't tell me what kind of pizza you like," Timothy said, pointing to a small table by the window.

She sat in the chair across from him, still processing the fact that this was a him-with-her situation. "Anything without green peppers, but I can pick them off if you like them."

The waitress came over with menus, told them to help themselves if they wanted anything to drink. When they walked the twenty feet to fill their glasses, Ava felt like they were on center stage.

"I like these old pop dispensers." Timothy pulled a plastic lever to fill his glass. "Can I fill yours for you?"

She thanked him, noticing with a quick look behind her that they were indeed the floorshow.

"What would you like?" he asked.

"The same thing." She pointed at the raspberry-ginger cola.

"Timothy Gray. Ladies' man," one of his friends teased, followed by quiet snickers.

On the way back to their table, Timothy flashed a toothy grin. "Warner, that's gonna cost you."

"My bad," his friend said with a chuckle, obviously loving the attention.

By the time they sat down, a cold northern chill drifted toward them from Carina's table.

Ava faced away from the crowded room and whispered, "I don't think Carina is very happy."

Timothy leaned in even closer. "I don't care what Carina thinks. I held her hand once in the seventh grade and I'm still paying for it."

Well, that solved the Carina mystery. Apparently, Timothy had two stalkers, each with very different motives.

To her relief, Timothy carried the majority of the conversation. She continued to ask him questions, struggling to stay in the shoes of Ava-on-a-mission rather than Ava the girl who is distracted by the shape of his jaw, the high bridge on his nose, his full lips, and the sandy blond curls wrapping around the edge of his ears. His thin hair was longer than usual. The curls at his temples and the base of his neck would likely fall prey to a pair of scissors within a few days.

"What do you do during the summer?" she asked, before taking another bite of pizza.

He told her about his job driving a truck for harvest and that he used to pull the bankout wagon until his uncle bought a driverless, GPS-guided model that moved remotely on the three-dimensional grid. She asked him if he'd saved up to buy his hotrod Dodge Dakota. When he told her his grandfather gave it to him his freshman year, Ava noticed Timothy cut the story short, his thoughts seemingly focused on the past as he watched a few cars go by in the fading sunlight.

"Have another piece." He spun the tray around so she could pull one of the few remaining slices onto her plate.

"No, thank you. I'm good," she replied, spinning it back.

"You only ate one piece. How do you expect to reach five-five if you don't eat anything?"

She narrowed her eyes. "I'll wear heels. Besides, those are big pieces."

After a few seconds of silence, she asked him if his father was a famed Whitman County farmer.

"No. A contractor. You know that new complex going up on Main Street?"

Ava nodded. "Next to the hotel?"

"Yeah. He's the general on that project." Timothy fiddled with the pizza pan on the table, then slid another piece onto his plate. "I work for my uncle."

"Do you like farming better than construction?" Ava thought the question neutral enough to ask but noticed Timothy's jaw flex before he answered her.

"Construction isn't really my thing, at least not right now." He forced a smile, his humorless eyes suggesting unspoken reasons for his preference. "What about you? Have a job?"

She put her pizza down and adjusted her plate and napkin. "I had one, but . . . some things came up and I had to quit."

"Fired, huh?" he said with a chuckle. "Drunk on the job?"

"You heard about that?" she teased, her hair pulled under her chin.

His stare so attentive it made her blush, he proclaimed her number one on his people-I-love-to-talk-to list. "But really, what happened with the job? Still waiting for your day in court? Extortion? Embezzlement? Helped yourself to the stuff in the employee fridge?"

"Nothing that interesting. I had a job running errands for an attorney. A good job. I liked it. Run to the bank, make copies, run to the post office. That kind of thing. My bank account tops out at around four hundred dollars, so I don't think I'm a flight risk."

He sat back with a slump. "Rats. I had you pegged as secretly loaded. Blows that theory. Even without the money, I think there's still a potential for chemistry between us. Right?"

A hand over her mouth, she ducked her head and cleared her throat. Chemistry?

"Uh-oh. Need the Heimlich?" He asked. "I've always wanted to try that."

Head tilted, she pushed a hand at him. "I'm good."

Timothy drank down a few glugs and slid another piece of pizza on his plate. "You said some things came up that made you have to quit your job? What kind of things?"

She really didn't want to tell him about her problems with headaches and fatigue. "Just some health stuff. Trouble sleeping. Boring things." This conversation needed a U-turn. "I have a question for you."

"Fire away," he said, leaning closer. "If I don't know the answer, I'll make one up."

"A farm question, from the Gazette last week." She waited a second for the topic to register.

"Bring it, I'm ready."

"What's the deal in the news between our farmers and the Russians?" Ava had heard her dad complaining about the article and hoped Timothy knew what she was talking about, since she didn't.

That appeared to be the magic question. With bright eyes, he held his hands up, a few inches between them. "Do you want the non-farmer's explanation," he asked, then stretched his long arms out. "Or the farmer's?"

"I'm not in a hurry." In all honesty, she could listen to him talk all day.

Timothy put his pizza down, an index finger hovering in the space between them while he drank a few swallows of pop, tapped a fist on his chest, and cleared his throat. "The Palouse has been in the national spotlight for nearly a year over the hard-red wheat originally brought to the states by Russian immigrants. Some Russian scientists made this doofus claim that our farmers were reaping the best crops in the world because we're propagating grain the Russians hold the patent for. But, after a bunch of interference from the U.N., the university found some stored samples of hard-red that were a genetic match and older than the patent. Score one for Palouse farmers and a big, fatty zero for Russia."

"That's crazy," Ava said. "I didn't even know there was such a thing as a global patent." She routed her attention from his eyes to the table and back, appreciating his zeal.

"Like Russia isn't trying to propagate *our* patented grain." He cleared his throat again, shifted in his chair, his long fingers drumming on the edge of the table, then struck a frozen pose. With one eyebrow cocked, he held her gaze for the longest three seconds since the creation of time. "You don't really want to hear about this, do you?"

"I do. I think maybe farming is your thing. Is it something you're interested in doing? I mean, not just right now, but for a real job." When he smiled at her, Ava stuttered to reframe the poorly worded question. "Wait . . . not that it isn't . . . it's already a real job. I meant, like, as a life profession." Ava ringed her fingers around her wrist. If he would stop looking at her that way, she could remember how to talk.

He tilted his head, flashed his signature broad grin. "Why? You looking for a man with a good job?"

Ava pulled back in her chair, her face instantly hot. "What? I didn't—ask—say that."

He chuckled and spun the pizza tray around. "Last piece."

She shook her head. "I can't."

Looking over the lone slice, Timothy blew out a long breath then finished off his sixth piece. "I did not have room for that." He emptied his drink then tapped a fist on his chest. "Be right back."

A dark, sinking feeling moved over Ava like a thick fog. He could be going to the restroom for the same reason everybody did.

31

Her inner voiced pleaded with him: *Timothy, please don't do it.* She knew he would. He turned out of sight down the hall. In less than a minute, he'd send everything he just ate down the drain.

Without thinking things through, she pushed her chair back and followed twenty feet behind him. Since the restroom was a unisex, one-person-at-a-time setup, it might make sense for her to follow him. The tiny hairs on the back of her neck stood up, the rhythm in her chest thumping like a bass drum. She had no idea what she was going to say or do to stop him. What if he just needed to go to the bathroom?

CHAPTER 7

Ava walked through the narrow hall past ancient video games. Timothy saw her before he shut the door, stepped back into the hall, and fumbled with something in his pocket. It slipped out of his hand, a U-shaped clear-plastic tray making a tick, tick sound on the tile floor at his feet. He appeared not to notice.

Ava picked it up, handed it to him.

"My retainer," he said without looking at her. "Supposed to be wearing it." Timothy shoved the tray in his pocket and stepped away from the door. "Ladies first."

She noticed his eyes shifting, avoiding hers.

"That's all right," she insisted. "Go ahead."

He pushed his hands deeper in his pockets and kicked at some unseen thing on the floor. "Uh, Ava, well, I don't really want you going in there after me. It could scar you for life."

"Maybe I need you to go first," she said, fiddling with the handle on a pinball machine.

"No, Ava. I can't take care of business with you standing right here." He walked behind her, his arms folded.

She hadn't thought this through very well or at all. Ava closed the bathroom door and turned the faucet on, her reflection staring back at her. She screwed up. What was she going to do? To complete her charade, she yanked out a paper towel and tossed it on top of a crumpled mound overflowing onto the floor. That was it! With the top of the paper mound now in the toilet, she pressed the lever. Satisfied with the thick mess lodged in the drain, Ava pulled the door open.

"You don't want to go in there. It's clogged." With her best embarrassed shrug, she apologized, hands clasped behind her, eyes on the floor.

"Maybe I should have gone first," he teased. "Don't worry about it; I can wait. Ready to go?"

They retrieved their coats, and he paid the check. Timothy waved a quick goodbye to several friends agreeing to see him at practice. Ava was never so glad to step into frigid winter air. Her whole body felt like a furnace. She licked her top lip, tasting salt deposited by several rounds of jangled nerves.

"Where do you live?" Timothy asked as he reached for the door handle.

"Up in the Heights." As they hurried toward his pickup, she pointed to the far left on the top of the hill. "At the end above the tree line. You can't really see it from here. By the cemetery. Those colored lights and that blue star, that's our backyard."

She noticed he'd moved behind her, his six-four frame blocking the majority of the freezing wind. Timothy's closeness affected her. Why? She'd been close to him before, but this was different. A self-sacrificing gesture which seemed to be his nature. He pulled the pickup door open and stepped aside. Ava allowed herself one harmless indulgence, a hand on his forearm as she stepped into the pickup. He had a coat on. It wasn't a big deal.

Timothy rounded the front of the blue Dodge and hopped in, started the engine, then rubbed his hands together. "Need a little hug to warm you up?"

Maybe her indulgence wasn't so subtle after all. "I'm good," she said with a reprimanding grin. Her stomach tightened. She wanted to shout *Yes!—I'm near death. Wrap your arms around me*! "Thanks for the pizza."

"My pleasure. It was fun. You are a bit of a mystery, Ava Roberts."

Timothy cleared the inside of the windshield with his sleeve and leaned forward to look up the steep hill, the view growing darker as the sun drifted behind the other side of the valley.

"A mystery? Is that a good thing?" she asked.

"Of course it is. You show up to do precal looking like you're going to pass out, then you turn around and school me at my own game of wits. You're not easy to read. Sneaky isn't the right word, but I wouldn't place any bets against you in a poker game."

She dusted the dashboard with the palm of her hand. "Sneaky? I don't even know how to play poker."

"See," Timothy said, "That right there. Some kind of subliminal thought-shifting ninja move. You do a lot more thinking than talking, don't you? I'm on to you. This shy girl thing. It's a cover, isn't it?"

Whatever he was up to, she was having fun with it. "A cover for what?"

"Yep. There it is again, another question. You're a real pro at this. I saw it on this spy movie. A double agent that answered every question with a question."

"A spy movie?"

Timothy threw his hands up. "See! You just proved my point."

Ava giggling at his antics.

"Alright, agent Roberts, okay if I take you home?"

Eyes locked with Timothy's, she blew on her cold hands, certain that she wasn't the only one not saying what they were thinking. "Sure."

"How long have you lived up in the heights?"

"Just over two years. We moved here from Seattle. Moved around a lot before that for my dad's work. Dad lived in Colfax when he was in high school. Now, with everything going on in the cities, he wanted to come back to a small town. Said Colfax was only one stoplight bigger than when he was here before."

"That's our claim to fame." Timothy deftly checked his teeth in the rearview mirror, prompting Ava to send her tongue on a spice search over her own teeth. "We're now a four-stoplight town," he added, "Busting into the big time. Next thing you know, movie stars and drug lords are gonna start buying up farmland. By the way, I'm glad you moved here." He pulled away from the curb and waited for the light. "Even if you're not a movie star. Not a drug lord, are you?"

"No," she replied, hands in her coat pockets. "Considered it, but I'm not the salesman type. And then there's the jail time."

"Yeah. That's a real deterrent. That and the whole getting-shot thing. I wouldn't want that for you."

A wave of this-is-heaven warmed Ava's face. She asked Timothy where he lived.

"You know the development past the ball fields?" He glanced at her as they turned south onto Main Street.

"Eagle's Nest, along the river?" She already knew he lived there but, being a low-level stalker, didn't know which house was his.

"Yeah. I live over there."

They talked for a few minutes as he drove up the hill, both mentioning places they'd once lived. She'd moved from Vancouver to San Diego, then to Seattle, then here to Colfax.

"A world traveler. No wonder you're so smart."

She looked at him with an I-don't-think so grin but appreciated the vote of confidence. Timothy told her he'd moved from Spokane twelve years ago then quickly changed the subject, seeming more interested in the fact that the heater was finally blowing warm air.

"Right here is good." Ava slid her backpack over her shoulder, a hand ready on the door handle.

"Ava, I'm not going to dump you off in the middle of the road." He did a U-turn, pulled in front of her house, and shifted into park.

"Would you like to use the restroom?" Ava offered, her attention on the street leading down the hill. "Because, you know, at the pizza place?"

"No. I'm good. Want to ask you something, though." Timothy paused for a moment, a thumb brushing over the top of the steering wheel.

She swallowed hard, her mouth suddenly dry.

"Honestly," he said, pausing as if carefully choosing his words, "is the tutoring really helping you? You don't feel like I'm wasting your time, do you?"

"Not at all. I mean, it's not wasting my time. It's good." She wondered what gave him that impression. Did she come across as bored? Nothing could be further from the truth.

Her father's dark-grey sedan drove slowly past his pickup and pulled into the driveway.

"Who's that?" Timothy continued to watch the car through his rear-view mirror.

"My dad." Ava reached for the door handle. "He's home early." Her new and immediate goal: let Timothy leave ASAP.

"What does he do?" Timothy sat up a little straighter, both hands on top of the steering wheel. "CIA? FBI?"

"Dad's a real-estate broker. He usually gets home after six."

Ava would have liked to sit in Timothy's pickup all evening, getting to know him better. He was easy-going, easy to talk to, and even though he was very thin, easy on the eyes.

She opened the door, reluctant to say goodbye but in a hurry to leave. "Thanks for the ride—and the pizza."

"No prob—"

Ava's father appeared by Timothy's door, the streetlight casting the man's expressionless face in eerie shadows. Mr. Roberts tapped on the driver's side window and stepped away from the pickup. It was obvious he wanted the young man—with his daughter—to exit the vehicle. Timothy nodded in compliance and pushed his door open while Ava jumped out and jogged around the front of the pickup.

"I don't think we've been properly introduced," Ava's father said without a trace of humor. Her father pulled his tie loose as if it had been choking him all day, the cold wind whipping his dark hair into jagged tufts.

"Dad, this is my *friend*, Timothy. Timothy, my dad, Eric." Ava tried to telegraph a plea to lighten up, but her father ignored her.

Timothy put his hand out. "It's a pleasure to meet you, Eric."

Her father shook his hand slowly, staring at Timothy like a boxer getting ready to defend his title. Though an inch shorter, her father outweighed Timothy by fifty pounds or more. "The pleasure is mine. You can call me Mr. Roberts."

"Yes, sir." Timothy smiled nervously and seemed at a loss for words.

"You two spending some time together, are ya?" her father asked.

Ava pulled the collar of her coat over her chin. Was he really trying to sound like that old actor, one of his favorites, Clint Eastwood? "Dad—we're *just friends*."

"Well, why don't you be *just friends* in the house? Come on inside, Timothy." Her father turned and walked toward the front door without waiting for a reply.

Ava wanted to hide in the frozen shrubs. "I'm sorry," she whispered, "You don't have to stay."

"It's okay. I have a few minutes." He pushed his hands deep in his pockets and followed her inside.

"Hello," Ava's mother said with uncommon friendliness, like a used-car salesman sizing up a promising customer. "You two look absolutely chilled to the bone."

"Mom, this is Timothy Gray. Timothy, my mom, Lola Roberts."

Timothy bent down and offered her mother his hand. "It's nice to meet you, Mrs. Roberts."

"Please, for heaven's sake, call me Lola." She shook his hand, her wide smile broadcasting the fact that Ava had never, ever brought a boy home. "Can I take your coat?"

"Mom, he's just dropping me off. Timothy has basketball practice soon. Like right now."

"Oh? Well, okay. Would you like to stay for dinner?" her mother offered.

Ava palmed her forehead.

"Thank you," Timothy replied, "We just had pizza."

Her father strolled back into the living room after putting his coat away, his arms bowed out from his sides as if his biceps needed room to breathe." Pizza, huh? Where did you go?"

"Main Street Pizza," Timothy offered, fidgeting with the zipper pull on his coat. "They remodeled the cafe. Put in a pizza oven. I guess the name, Main Street Pizza, kind of, you know, explains all that. I thought Ava might like–"

Ava stepped between Timothy and her father in an effort to stop a potential showdown. "There were a bunch of kids there," she blurted.

"Sounds fun." Her dad walked past her, sunk into a recliner, hands behind his head. "Have a seat, Timothy."

Timothy looked at his wet shoes, then sat in one of the nearby dining room chairs.

Ava's father asked how they knew each other, his full attention on their guest. "Have any classes together?"

Timothy shook his head. "No classes together, but I'm her tutor on Wednesdays. We skipped today and went to pizza instead."

Her father sat up strait. "Tutor? For what class?"

A warning jolt shot through Ava. "Dad—he has to go to practice."

"I still have a few minutes," Timothy assured her and turned back to her father. "I help her with precal."

Ava went pale, dropped onto a chair across from Timothy. This was going to be the end of everything she'd accomplished and the most embarrassing moment of her entire life.

"Precal? Ava doesn't need help with precal." Her father had that look; one that suggested they'd better come up with a better answer.

"Eric, honey," her mother chimed in, like one of those vintage television housewives that live in their aprons. "Can you help me with something in the kitchen?" She was a terrible actress. "We don't want to keep you, Timothy. It was so nice to meet you. Please, come back soon—anytime."

"Lola," her father protested, "Can it wait a minute?"

"No." Her mother grabbed his hand and pulled him into the kitchen.

When Ava gathered enough courage to peek at Timothy, she was surprised to find him staring at her with a suppressed grin, his lips tucked into his mouth and eyes bright.

"What?" she asked.

Timothy shrugged, still staring at her. "Nothing."

"What's so funny?" This liar's reveal was not a laughing matter.

"I better get going." He stood up to leave and moved toward the front door.

"Wait." Ava jumped up and took a few steps closer, running her hands down the sides of her hips. "I'm sorry about . . . about my dad."

"Sorry for what? He's watching out for you. Doesn't want you running around with some psycho. You worry too much." He smiled at her and pressed the door handle until it clicked.

"About precal. You know, the tutoring." Ava looked at the floor and swallowed hard, the end of each sleeve pulled into her grip.

Timothy took a step toward her, closing the distance between them. "Were you going to tell me you were acing the class and *never* needed my help?"

She jerked her head up, her involuntary ability to exhale suddenly disabled.

His brows rose clear to his hairline. "Yep. Busted. Checked your grades this morning to see if our sessions were helping any. That's why we went to pizza. You don't need help with precal, do you?"

Ava couldn't form a single word, the small bits of air she managed to breathe in apparently shuttled off to every organ except her brain. She shook her head and assumed her need to floor-gaze, the weight on her chest expanding up her throat.

For a split-second, Timothy glanced toward the kitchen, then bent down very close to her. "I'm flattered," he whispered, his breath warm on her ear.

She sneaked a quick look at him. "I guess I'm the psycho."

He put a hand on her shoulder. "You're not a psycho. And I thought, you know, since we're used to our Wednesday schedule and all, we could still get together and do homework. Maybe you could do some of mine." Gently pushing her shoulder, he clearly wanted her to look up at him.

She avoided his eyes as tears started to build in hers. "I know you're just being nice. This is so embarrassing."

"Ava, for a secret ninja agent, you don't know anything," he whispered.

He had her full attention. She looked up, surprised to find him almost pained. No teasing this time.

"I wouldn't have said we were *just friends*." Timothy locked eyes with her for an intense second, then pulled the handle and slipped out the door.

As if bolted in place, Ava stood there in shock. This wasn't happening. Why did he have to say that? She was in deep now, way too deep. No! No! No! This wasn't the plan. I'm not helping him, I'm making things worse!

CHAPTER 8

"Dad, why can't you be nice instead of acting like an interrogator?" Ava slunk down on the other end of the sofa, head back against the cushion.

Her father reached over and patted her knee. "I know what I'm doing. You wouldn't understand, babe."

She folded her arms. "Yes, I would."

"Ava, protective daddy needs to be the first impression a boy has of your father. I know you're getting older, but you'll always be my baby. My daughter. And players can't play when daddy's on defense. Mr. Nice Guy can show up later, after I've vetted any potential kiss collector."

"Dad—players? That's so old school. And please, don't give me the buy-the-cow, free milk speech. We're not a thing." She pulled a knee up on the sofa, fingers brushing through her ponytail.

"You're not dating, but he's helping you with math you don't need help with and taking you out for pizza. Ava, do you think you're talking to a tree stump?"

"No. It's hard to explain. Timothy didn't lie to you, Dad."

"Listen, babe, I like him. He could use a few pounds, but as far as first impressions go, I'd say he's a good kid. Don't tell him I said that. He needs to be afraid of me for at least a month or two. That should be enough time to see if your shiny new apple has a rotten core."

"Dad, he's not rotten. He's good." More like amazing, she thought, her thumbnail carving lines in the nap of the sofa cushion.

Her father reached over and covered her hand with his. "I didn't ruin your life. You don't need to worry. It's obvious the kid likes you."

She did need to worry, now more than ever.

"However, Ava, I do wish you'd slow it down a little. You guys are young, and your dad's ticker isn't ready for this. How old is Timothy?"

Ava forced a week smile. "He's a senior."

"A senior?" Her father closed his eyes, slowly dropped his head back, and called for her mother. "Lola! . . . Lola, it's an emergency."

"What do you need, Eric?" her mother called from the kitchen.

"A stiff drink."

"A what?" she asked, walking into the living room with a half-peeled potato.

He looked at her as if fate had dealt him a cruel blow. "Make it a double."

"Eric–you don't drink." She looked at Ava. "He never has."

He pressed a hand over his heart. "I do now. Timothy is a *senior*."

Lola rolled her eyes. "I think you'll survive, dear." She smiled at Ava. "And I think Timothy is a wonderful boy."

They were both right. He was both good and wonderful. And she was in trouble.

* * *

A few minutes before ten, Ava heard a light tap on her bedroom door. "Come in."

Her mother slipped in, leaving the door open just enough for the hall light to filter into her dark room, and sat on the edge of her bed. "I thought you might still be awake. Honey, is Timothy the boy you thought might have an eating disorder?"

Ava sat up and slowly smoothed a crease on her comforter. "Yeah."

"Did you talk to him about it?"

"No. I just wanted to help him." Her throat began to tighten, the pitch of her voice edging higher. "Now everything is messed up."

"Ava, sweetheart," her mother took her hand. "If he does have a problem, it's not up to you to fix it. Don't you think his family already knows?"

"They probably do. How can they not? I don't get how he can be so happy, as if nothing's wrong, but still want to hurt himself." She waved a hand in front of her face, taking a few seconds to gain her composure. "He lost a brother."

"A brother?"

"Billy." Ava pulled a in a deep breath and sat up against her headboard. "Rochelle told me his brother died three years ago. Billy was a senior. I don't know how, exactly, but he took something or drank something and died at a party. Timothy was a freshman when it happened. Rochelle said Timothy hasn't been the same since. He's never said anything about it, not to me anyways. It's not like I'm someone he'd confide in."

"I know you want to help him, but, Ava, honey, you can't shoulder that kind of responsibility. He needs more help than you can give him. You can be a friend, though. That's important."

Ava pulled in a lungful of air and slowly exhaled. "What would you do if you were me?"

Her mother brushed a hand over the comforter covering Ava's leg, her head tilted. "I don't know. I'd pray about it. I might take a direct approach. Simply ask him if he's throwing up."

"Whatever!" Ava tossed her hands up then slapped them down on the bed. "Mom, no way. That's crazy."

"Don't accuse him; just ask if he's feeling okay. When he realizes you noticed, he'll have to say something about it."

Ava pulled her knees to her chest. "I can't do that. If I did, he might try even harder to hide it."

"You can't control that," her mother said. "You might say something to the school counselor. They're equipped to handle things like this."

Ava leaned away from the headboard, fingers working around a clump of hair. "I'd feel like I was telling on him."

"But it could help him, right?" her mother pressed.

"Or make him mad."

"What's worse, Ava, being mad or permanent damage?" Lola stood up and turned toward the door. "Sweetheart, the longer you stew about this, the harder it's going to be on you."

"I know."

"Love you. Try to get some sleep."

"Love you, too. Night, Mom."

As soon as her mother shut the door, Ava reached for her phone, then stopped short of it and pulled the comforter to her chest. It wouldn't hurt to pray for him. "Lord . . . I'm sorry I don't talk to you more, so it's not really fair for me to ask for things, but can you please help Timothy? If there's anything I can do for him, will you show me what it is? I know you care about him even more than I do. Please, Lord, whatever it takes, please help Timothy."

We Need To Talk

Chapter 9

The sun wasn't up when the alarm sounded on her phone. Ava turned it off, feeling like she'd fallen asleep only minutes earlier. Feet encased in invisible cement, she dragged herself out of bed, pushed tangled hair away from her face, and trudged to the bathroom.

"Good morning." Her mother said, leaning into the hall, concern evident in her half-smile. "I made some crepes. Can you eat something before you take a shower?"

"Sure." Ava sat on a barstool, picking at her crepe. She didn't feel like eating, but her mother took the trouble to make her favorite breakfast.

"Do you have room for two?" her mother asked.

"No, thank you. One's enough." Even if the food felt like lead in her stomach, she'd eat it so her mother wouldn't worry about her.

"Did you get any sleep last night?"

"Yeah," Ava replied. Maybe four hours when she put it all together.

Her mother looked at her, mouth twisting with thoughts unspoken. "Do you want a cold lunch today? I had soup in mind."

"I can make it," Ava offered.

Her mother insisted she could make it while Ava took her shower. "We might need to leave a little early today. It snowed last night."

"Is Dad gone already?"

Her mother rummaged through a cupboard, a lidless container in one hand. "He left an hour ago."

Ava hopped off the stool. "Do you think school is canceled?"

"Not so lucky. I already checked."

Ava put her plate in the dishwasher and headed for the bathroom.

"Would you like chicken noodle?" Her mother called down the hall.

"Sounds good. Thanks, Mom."

Ava let the hot water fall over her face. If only she could wash her worries away. Done with her shower, she tied her robe and wiped the mirror with a hand towel, her reflection revealing puffy eyes with dark circles. "It's the living dead," she quipped, concealer dusted over her face until it reflected the same color of pale. It was going to be one of those days, the ones you wish you could skip but end up remembering forever. She wound a band around sopping wet hair. Feet still heavy, she shuffled back to her bedroom and riffled through the hamper in her closet, nearly falling in it while looking for her comfortable jeans. A baggy, well-worn sweatshirt completed her ensemble.

"Ava," her mother called from the kitchen, "ready to go?"

"Coming." She grabbed her phone and dragged her backpack on the floor behind her.

"Do you have any plans after school today?" her mother asked.

"No. I don't think so."

"Well, call me if you—Ava?" Her mother looked at her as if she were still in her pajamas. "This may not be your best day ever, but if you feel like you look bad, it's going to make you feel even worse."

"Mom, thanks a lot."

"Spare me the offended routine. You know I'm right." Her mother pulled her back into her room and opened her closet. "Here, put this sweater on."

"It's not going to make any difference." Ava took her sweatshirt off and pulled the purple sweater over her head.

"Bathroom."

"Mom!"

"You don't have time to argue. Pull that band out of your hair." Standing in front of the bathroom mirror, her mother plugged in the hair dryer. "Put some blush on."

She complied, swiping a faint rose-colored line across pale cheeks while her mother tugged at her hair.

"There. Now you can put it up without having it drip all over you."

Band around damp hair, Ava turned away from the mirror.

"See?" Her mother said. "Beautiful. Now, let's go."

"Whatever happened to natural beauty?" Ava protested, as they got in the car and waited for the garage door to open.

"Are you telling me natural beauty was what you were going for?"

"Not really." Ava stared out the window as they drove down the hill. Frost glittered on bare tree branches in the morning sun, but not enough to brighten her mood.

"It'll be okay, sweetheart. You hang in there."

The phone in Ava's coat pocket buzzed. She pulled it out, tapped the screen. "Oh."

Her mother glanced at her. "Get a text?"

"Yeah. From Timothy." She chewed her bottom lip and sat up straighter, reading the short message several times.

"So?" her mother asked.

"Nothing important." Ava selected the flashing-star icon so he'd know she agreed and would reply later. "He wants to get together at lunch. Probably wants to tell me he saw dad on the FBI's most wanted show."

Her mother gave her that look, the one mothers give when they're saying you know better. "Along with every other father that loves their daughter."

They pulled into the school parking lot swarming with students in a hurry to make it to class on time.

"Have a good day. Love you," Her mother said as Ava hopped out of the car.

"Love you too. Bye, Mom."

Ava jogged to the entrance, bone-chilling cold nearly freezing her damp hair. By some miracle, the auto sensor approved her temperature for entry. Just past the breezeway, her phone chimed as she reached the metal detector. She fished around in her backpack, found and dropped her phone. Apologies offered as she inched between two boys, she dragged her bag on the floor with one hand while retrieving her cell with the other.

"Backpacks open. Sports bags open. ID cards ready," the security guard repeated in a slow, monotone voice as impatient students waited for a quick inspection.

Ava checked her phone. The text was from Rochelle wanting to know if she was there yet.

"Your bag, miss."

"Sorry." Ava held it open, pulled out a carabiner with her ID, scanned in, and tucked her phone in her pocket.

When she got to her locker, Rochelle was waiting for her. "Ava, finally! I just heard about last night. At pizza? When were you going to tell me?"

Bag in her locker, Ava pulled out a folder and her tablet. "What did you hear?"

"That you were with Timothy and you're totally going out with him. Why am I the last to know this?"

Dodging oncoming students as she and Rochelle walked to class, Ava resisted the rumor. "We just went to pizza. We're not going out. It might have looked that way." Lucky for her, with classes starting in less than a minute, they didn't have time to hash out the details. She would wait to tell Rochelle about his text. Lunch . . . what did he need to tell her?

Rochelle leaned close to her ear. "I heard Crystal's older sister told him you had a crush on him."

Ava grabbed Rochelle's arm. "What? When?" Oh, no! Ava pressed her coat collar over her mouth.

"I don't know, but it looks like cupid landed a direct hit." Rochelle grinned from ear to ear and turned to go into her first class. "Third period. I want to hear all about it."

Ava forced a smile. Could things get any worse? With only seconds left before she was late for chemistry, she hurried around the corner. It looked as if someone might be waiting for her.

"Ava . . . we need to talk," Carina said, waving her over with one finger to the lockers across the hall. "You know Timothy and I are together, right?" The senior girl cocked her head and tilted her chin, bright red lips pursed tight like a suckerfish.

"I'm going to be late for class." Ava turned away from Carina, hoping the girl didn't clock her in the back of the head.

"I want you to stay away from him," Carina called after her, gaining another face-to-face with Ava. "Timmy is way out of your league. Way out like the stars. You can see 'em, but you can't touch 'em." Her smile faded into a sneer. "Got it?"

Ava smoothed an eyebrow and breathed out through her nose. "He doesn't like being called Timmy, and we don't always get what we want." Ava instantly regretted the comeback. What was she thinking? Carina's mouth hung open, her Cleopatra eyeliner framing eyes that threatened to pop out of their sockets. That's all I need. Why not add a jealous senior girl to this colossal mess.

The teacher gave Ava a reprimanding stare as she slid into a chair at the front of the class. The door sensor, no doubt, read her ID and recorded a tardy. Head on her hands, she wished she stayed home. Her mom was wrong; it didn't make her feel any better being at school. She'd get through it. Everyone had bad days. Apparently, it was her turn.

Confession Time

Chapter 10

After slogging through her first two classes, Ava took her usual seat next to Rochelle. Their third period teacher reminded Rochelle that she could visit after class, so Ava managed to avoid more probing questions, at least for the time being. Rochelle grinned at her as if they had cause to celebrate. Yay, I'm a loser. She and Timothy were not a thing.

Ava waited until class was over to send Timothy a text letting him know she was on her way to lunch and asking if he was already there.

Rochelle met her outside the classroom door. "So, you and Timothy? When did this happen?" She tugged Ava away from the stream of students. "Tell me everything!"

The lockers keeping her upright, Ava sifted through potential confessions. "It's not like that. Sorry to say, you've got it all wrong. The pizza place just happened to be open on the same day Timothy just happened to be helping me with math. Then rumors went from one pair of dumb lips to another and now I have senior girls threatening me." She held up her phone, Timothy's text highlighted. "He wants to talk to me in the cafeteria." Her chest started to heave with deep breaths, a gloss blurring her vision.

"Oh, Ava, I'm so sorry. It's not that bad." Rochelle hugged her and stepped back, a hand on her shoulder. "All this will be forgotten before you know it."

Ava pushed off the locker. "Yeah. Maybe."

"Or," Rochelle added, "things might *just happen* for a reason. Could be a good thing."

Ava offered her a tired smile. "I better go. Don't want him to think I ditched."

Rochelle walked with her to the hall outside the cafeteria, leaving Ava to her task with a thumbs-up, her sunny-day friend lightening her load even though Ava hadn't been completely honest with her. Or honest at all. In fact, she hadn't been honest with herself. Someone with functioning brain cells wouldn't be in this mess. To know when to quit isn't a bad thing. Maybe a short let's-get-this-over-with talk with Timothy will put this all behind her. People have survived worse. Maybe Rochelle was right. By next week, all this would be old news.

At the door to the cafeteria, Ava scanned the lunch crowd, then checked her phone when she didn't see Timothy.

"Looking for someone?"

She spun around to find him leaning against the wall by the stairs.

"Want to have lunch with me?" He smiled at her, but something about him hinted at uncertainty.

"Sure. Is it okay if my dad sits between us?" Just the mention of the previous night's events brought heat to her face, leaving her with the need to inspect her shoes.

Timothy chuckled, walked toward her, covering the distance between them in silly, giant steps. "I like your dad." He pointed to an empty table in the corner. "Over there?"

Ava's gut tightened. What did he want to tell her?

"I like your sweater. Purple looks good on you." He smiled and looked away, a shy smile replacing his signature broad grin.

She picked at a loose thread by her wrist. "Thank you." Why did he look so nervous? She felt a thump gaining speed in her chest as they sat down, both of them focusing on the contents of their lunch as if an inventory of each item required their full attention. She should get this over with and apologize. No real explanation needed. He could be back at his friend table where he enjoyed his life, and she could go back to minding her own business. It needed to be done. One deep breath in, she leaned in and faced him, his eyes searching hers as if trying to read her thoughts.

He tapped the table in the space between them. "Saw you at a few of the JV games. Do you like basketball?"

Ava fiddled with the lid on her thermos, almost spilling her soup. "I, uh, I do. I had some homework . . . I like to watch—the game. But I'm no good at it, at all." It would be great if she could talk like a normal person.

He took a bite of his sandwich, leaned back, and stretched his long legs past her chair. "How do you know?"

Was he really going to lay everything out there just like that? How did he know what she knew? Her mouth suddenly dry, Ava took a sip from her water bottle. "Know what?"

"That you're no good at basketball." He crossed his arms as if settling in for a lengthy explanation.

Her gut relaxed and airways again accepted needed oxygen. "In P.E." She shrugged, the end of her ponytail in a constant twirl around her finger. "I wasn't very good."

"That's it? You've only played in P.E.?" He leaned forward, an elbow on the table.

Ava worked the edge of her bottom lip into her mouth. Why did he look at her like that? And so close! "I guess it's not my thing. Some people are good at it. Some aren't." She stirred the spoon in her soup, her apology on hold until it felt right to throw it out there. At least he was talking about basketball even though he hadn't appeared to have a great love for the game—not anymore.

"Why don't we shoot some hoops after school? Just for fun?" He leaned back, took a bite of his sandwich, his raised brow encouraging agreement.

Of course, he didn't want to hash over the misunderstanding in the middle of the lunchtime rush. She'd give him credit for cutting her loose gently and privately. The pinch between her shoulder blades relaxed. "Take my word for it, basketball is not my gift."

"Don't want to hang out with me, huh?"

Hang out with him? "What? No! I mean—not *no* I don't want to hang out." Ava searched his face for the humorous glint he so often wore. It was there, just not as obvious as usual. "I'll go, but I can't shoot. At all. Isn't it open gym? Your friends will be there, right?"

"I'll help you. Come on, it'll be fun." He pointed at her thermos. "Better eat."

"This is coercion," she said, attempting and failing to glare at him. Apparently, they'd part ways as friends.

"Maybe." He met her failed glare with a grin. "You'll thank me." He finished the last few bites of his sandwich. "Be right back." Timothy pushed away from the lunch table, his routine still as predictable as the clock.

Ava dropped her head to her hands. He could already have permanent damage. A thump gained speed in her chest. Did she want to help him or not? This was it. Her last chance. If she really cared, she had to say something.

Less than a minute later, Timothy slid back in the seat across from her and took a long drink of water.

Rubbing sweaty palms over her thighs, Ava forced words out of her mouth that could override any potential friendship. "Are you all right?"

"Fine. Why?" He rolled a mint around in his cheek and gulped down the rest of his water bottle.

Her arms and legs felt electric. "You just threw up," she whispered, as if this one instance was all she had in mind.

"I'm sorry." He put two more mints in his mouth. Shifted his gaze around the room.

She put her hand on his forearm, hoping his sweatshirt was thick enough to mask her trembling hand. "Are you sure you're not sick?"

He avoided looking at her. "Let's head to class."

Without saying a word, they gathered their things together and threw wrappers and empty bottles away. She felt his hand on the small of her back, gently nudging her for a quick second to walk in front of him. Ava wondered if he was processing a response or wanting to drop the subject without one. She couldn't let him get out of it, so she maneuvered beside him in the crowded hallway.

"Do you feel okay?" she asked, as quietly as possible.

He didn't reply.

"Timothy—" She stopped in front of him, grabbed his arm, pulled him close to the lockers. "What's wrong?"

He rubbed the back of his neck, still avoiding her gaze. "I have this thing."

"Thing?" She couldn't see or hear anything but him, her senses fine-tuned to take in his every word.

"Yeah." He waved a hand up and down in front of his gut. "It's a problem with my . . . digestive system. It's why I'm so skinny." He glanced at her, took a step back, and quickly looked away.

She released his arm. "I'm sorry." Ava moved close enough to see the tiny beads of sweat forming on his forehead. "Didn't mean to put you on the spot." Ava felt like she'd been hit with a two-by-four, her thoughts a logjam of rapid-fire realizations.

"Really, I'm okay. It's kind of like acid reflux. I can tell when food isn't going to stay down, which is most of the time." He shrugged. "It's no big deal. I'm used to it, but I'm sorry if my breath smells like puke."

"No, it doesn't. I . . ." How could she have been so wrong?—about everything—the whole time!

"What were you going to say?" He asked, his smile more of a grimace.

All of her worries, for nothing! Wait. This is freedom. Freedom to be a girl who likes a guy. It's that simple. She sucked in a deep breath, her insides rolling with excited flutters, the crowded hall starting to move like waves. She touched his sleeve. "So, when we went to pizza, you didn't feel good before we left, did you?"

He shook his head. "Knew better, but I ate too much."

Ava grabbed both his arms. "Timothy, I stopped you. You should have said something. I'm so sorry!"

"Don't worry about it. Come on, we need to get to class." He didn't look at her.

Ava, more than willing to change the subject, asked him how he was at chemistry. "I could use some help." Blinking to hold back happy tears, she tried to swallow past the lump building in her throat.

They stopped at the base of the stairs, students swarming past them.

Timothy turned to go up, then hesitated, a gleam in his eye and the corner of his mouth tilted. "I can help you with it, but are you talking about your homework—or us?"

She bit her lower lip and pushed his arm.

He laughed and took a step back. "Don't have an answer for me? Not even a question?" When she didn't reply, his eyes grew wide then scrunched into that smile she loved. "See you after school." He spun around on one heel and walked up the stairs.

Ava didn't hear a word said in her last two classes.

CHAPTER 11

She may be the worst basketball player in the world, but Ava couldn't wait to get to the gym. She sent a quick text to her mother and hurried down the hall, the sounds of shoes squeaking and basketballs thumping on the wood floor growing louder.

"Ava—there you are." Rochelle clutched her arm and looked at her with an expectant grin. "Well? Are you going to tell me *anything*?"

"I'm sorry." Ava quickly sifted through several careful responses, but she no longer had anything to hide. She blew out a long, cleansing sigh. "Timothy is so amazing."

Rochelle held her fingertips over her bottom lip and bounced on her tiptoes. "And?"

"I think I'm the luckiest girl in the world." It was true, and somehow, saying it made Ava feel as if she were floating, all the worries that had weighed her down now gone.

Rochelle squealed, reaching to give her hug. "I knew it!"

Ava gave her a tight squeeze. "I'm going to the gym. Timothy's waiting for me." She pulled away, taking several backward steps.

"Okay." Rochelle waved at her but didn't leave, fingers twisting an earring.

A pang of guilt needled Ava when she waved back. Rochelle had always been there for her, but now her friend was the odd man out.

"Do you want to go to a movie?" Ava asked. "How about Saturday night? Maybe there's a new chick-flick we haven't seen."

"Yes! Text me." Rochelle turned and walked to the exit with a bounce in her step.

About to cross the point of no return, Ava slipped inside the gym door. She stood there for a decade-long twenty seconds—a fish out of water. At the far end of the court, Timothy tossed the ball through the net with ease. She knew he went to open gym most every day after school. Watching him make basket after basket with minimal effort, she wondered why he didn't take those shots during a game. No more worries, she reminded herself, hands in her pockets as she walked along the front of the bleachers.

"Hey." Timothy jumped sideways to retrieve the ball. "Ready to show me how it's done?" He dribbled to the sideline, dropped his thin frame on one of the few bleachers pulled away from the wall, and blew out a few winded breaths. Half of a water bottle emptied, he snapped the lid shut, eyes on her while she waited, then dropped the bottle in his sports bag.

Ava sat next to him, her hands rubbing together. "You know I'm going to embarrass myself."

"Come on." With a tug on her arm, he held the ball out until she took it. "Try a free throw."

She tried to hand it back, noticing several guys watching them with smirky grins, but Timothy pointed to the basket.

"You go first." She pushed the ball at him.

He titled his head as if she deserved his pity and took the ball.

"Stand here," he said, pointing at the free-throw line.

Resigned to get this humiliation over with, Ava complied and moved into place. Timothy showed her how to stand, how to hold the ball. After making a few shots himself, he handed the ball to her. She tossed it toward the basket. Watched it bounce off the rim.

"It's a lost cause," she claimed. "Besides, this sport needs more fans than players. I'm happy being a fan." She wandered off the court while he went after the ball.

"Ava—get over here. I'm not letting you give up that easy." He waved her back to the line.

"Take the ball." Timothy repositioned her hands. Reminded her to bend her knees. "Try to get a higher arc. You know, instead of shooting straight at the basket."

Ava blew out an exasperated breath and launched the ball. After a few more attempts, she finally sent one through the net.

Timothy celebrated, pumping a fist in the air, no doubt to bolster her confidence. "See—nothing but net." He grabbed the ball and jogged back. "Try again."

"Maybe it was a lucky shot." She took the ball from him.

"Are you doubting my coaching skills?" He snatched the ball out of her hands.

Ava stepped back, her mouth open. Timothy dribbled around her, weaving and taunting, daring her to try to get the ball. She set her jaw. Swiped at it a few times. "How am I supposed to get it? Your arms are seven feet long."

Timothy held it within her reach. "Try harder."

She turned away from him as if giving up. When he took another step toward her, she grabbed the ball.

"Oh yeah? You little cheat." Timothy wrapped an arm around her waist, pulled her against his chest, and stripped the ball away from her.

"Mr. Gray—a little too handsy there," a teacher called from the other end of the gym. "I'd hate to write you up when you're having so much fun. A little more social distancing, please."

Timothy loosed her from his grip, guys she recognized from the pizza parlor hooting and snickering. Ava fanned her warm face. He was flirting with her and she loved it.

"Sorry, Coach." Timothy faced her with a full-faced grin. "See what happens when you cheat?"

"Me?" Lips pressed tight together, Ava glared at him, stepped to the line, and held her hands out for the ball.

He handed it to her then whispered close to her ear, "Careful. If you shoot the ball without concentrating you'll screw up."

"I thought you were helping me?" she scolded, her eye on the basket in front of her.

"I am. You need to learn to shoot with distractions."

She tried not to look at him. Lined the ball up the way he showed her. "You're definitely a distraction." She shot the ball and watched it fall short of the rim.

"Can't stop thinking about me, huh?" He chased after the ball. Jogged back. "Sorry. I'll be nice this time."

They stayed in the gym for another fifteen minutes. At some point along the way, the tension that came in with her had left her alone to enjoy the company.

"My dad played basketball in high school. And college," she said with a shrug, not claiming any kind of hereditary skill.

"Really? You didn't want to play?" He tucked the ball under his arm as they walked toward the bleachers.

She sat down, not in a hurry to leave. If she had superpowers, she'd keep the clock from ticking. "Just didn't." Ava remembered leaving an elementary day camp in tears, her father assuring her that even the pros forget sometimes, and shoot at the wrong basket. Since then, other than P.E., she'd stayed off the court, her father eventually easing up on trying to convince her of the sports appeal.

Timothy sat down an arm's length away and stuffed the basketball in his sports bag before slinging it over his shoulder. He side-eyed her, then slid closer, bumping into her arm. "I better take you home before you show me up." He moved his hand in a wide circle. "I think this is your thing."

"You think so?" she asked, mirroring his cocky grin.

He landed his spinning hand on his chest. "Yeah. This is your thing."

She pushed her shoulder into his. "That's entrapment."

"So." He held her gaze, then pushed a loose strand of hair away from her neck, his eyes softening. "Come on. I'll take you home."

* * *

"You were right; that was fun," Ava said, putting her backpack on the floor in front of her, then hooking her seatbelt.

"See?" Timothy said, "You can trust me."

He drove out of the parking lot, acknowledging several classmates and a teacher.

"Are you sure?" She bit her lip, her smile purposefully mischievous.

"Better be careful," he replied, glancing at her with one brow lifted. "That kind of talk can get you in trouble." His smile grew wider. "I'm not about to conjure up the wrath of dad, so, Miss Roberts, don't try to get *handsy* with me."

Ava burst out laughing. Unable to restrain herself, she clamped a hand over her mouth, but Timothy's wide-open grin made it impossible for her to stop laughing.

"Miss Roberts, get a hold of yourself!" He teased, prolonging a sheer joy she'd never felt before.

If this was love, she couldn't get too much of it. She wiped her eyes, not interested in concealing her infatuation. "My stomach hurts."

"I wonder why? I've never seen you laugh like that. Aren't you full of surprises."

All too soon, Timothy parked in front of her house and cut the engine.

Ava took a few deep breaths. Blew out a contented sigh. "Okay . . . I think I've got it together now."

"I'd be happy to join you, since I'm done driving." He smiled at her, his eyes soft, a hint of color spreading over his face.

She swallowed hard. More than anything, she wanted to hold him. Wrap her arms around his neck, but she wouldn't make the first move. She couldn't. She sat frozen, starring at him. At his clear blue eyes and his—

"Oh, no!" Timothy blurted. "Get out! Hurry!" Timothy threw his door open and jumped out.

Ava jerked the handle, leaped out onto the sidewalk. "What?"

Timothy walked around the pickup, reached through her open door, grabbed her backpack, then pushed the door shut. He wrapped a long arm around her shoulders and pulled her toward the front door. "A fire," he replied with a smirk.

"Where?" She grabbed his hand, looked behind her.

"It's okay. We got out just in time." He drew her in tight to his side. "I'll see you tomorrow, Miss Roberts." Pulling his arm away, he walked backward a few feet and put a hand on his chest. "Ava, you're not good for my heart." He shook his head and smiled at her before spinning around and jogging back to his pickup.

Standing on the porch, Ava waved as he drove away. "You're good for mine." She didn't deserve this perfect life, but she was glad to have it. Wouldn't trade it for anything in the world.

Anticipation

Chapter 12

After dinner, Ava's phone buzzed on the kitchen table. She pushed her homework aside, pressed her thumb on the screen to accept the live-cam call. Yes! Timothy!

"Hi." She could see he was closing a door to what looked like his bedroom.

The picture screen filled with teeth and nostrils until he pulled it back to reveal a sheepish grin. "Cute, huh? Busy?"

"Not busy." She stood and walked over to the sliding glass door.

"Hey, have anything going on Saturday night?" he asked, his voice laced with a hint of uncertainty. "I have an away game in Newport tomorrow, but I'd like to see you, you know, maybe get together on Saturday?"

"I'm not busy," Ava replied, a delighted sense of vertigo encouraging her to lean against the cold glass. "Do you leave early tomorrow?" An internal alarm announced that she could no longer hear the program her father was watching.

"We're leaving before lunch," he replied. "It takes forever to get to Newport, and coach takes our phones."

"What do you want to do?" Oh, no—Rochelle. She forgot all about their plans. Not wanting him to read her expression, she switched the camera off, held her phone to her ear.

"Already tired of my face?" he asked.

"No. I can hear you better on private-call. My dad was watching TV."

"Makes sense. Anyways, I thought we could go to Moscow and go ice-skating and then maybe get a burger. Or we could do something else if you want. You know, whatever."

Could anything sound more fun than that? Ava bit her lip and tapped a fist on the dark glass. Wouldn't Rochelle understand? "Can we go next weekend? I just remembered I told a friend—Rochelle—I'd go to a movie with her. But I could easily call her and change it. She probably wouldn't mind. I mean, she wouldn't mind. Really, it's not a problem. She'd be fine with it."

"No, don't change your plans. I need to earn points with your *amigas*. What if I grab a friend and crash your party? You know, double the fun?"

"She'd be good with that." This would be even better. Ava paced around the kitchen island, a hand on the edge to steady her balance.

Timothy offered to drive his mother's car so they could all ride together.

"Perfect." Ava started to add something, but the steely glare coming from the dad-shaped statue standing in the hallway caught her off guard. "Can you come a little early? My dad is going to want to have a *friendly* chat with you." She watched her father for a sign of approval.

Maintaining a constant poker face, her father, Eric, turned and walked away.

"No problem. How about 5:30?" Timothy asked.

"That would be perfect."

After the call, Ava sashayed into the living room to sweet-talk her father. "Dad, it's a double date; Rochelle is going, and Timothy is coming over early to talk to you. I can go, right?"

Her dad didn't look happy. "I'm not making it easy for him. He'll have to agree to a few things, or you're not going anywhere. And, I need to talk to him alone. No interference from little miss starry eyes."

"Okay. But can you—"

He pushed a hand at her. "Ava, no but-can-yous."

She sat in a chair across from him, bouncing her legs. "Thanks, Dad."

"Don't look at me like that," her father said as he scrolled through news channels.

"Like what?"

"Like you just won the lottery. Makes me nervous."

Ava jumped up, leaned in, and kissed his cheek. "Didn't Mom win the lottery with you?"

"Here we go. What else have you got in your work-dad-over playbook, kid? You might consider pursuing a career in sales."

"Dad, I'm not working you so you'll let me go. I'm just pointing out that all guys aren't bad. Like you. Right?"

Her dad turned off the TV monitor. "Wrong. All guys are bad. Every one of them is a pervert."

A hand on her hip, she leaned against his chair. "Then did Mom marry a good guy?"

"Of course she did, but me and your mom, that's a whole different ball game. There's no comparison there. In fact, I think I hear your mother calling you. She probably wants to celebrate while I sit here and age ten years."

"Love you, Dad," Ava sang as she danced down the hallway."

After replaying Timothy's call with her mother, Ava called Rochelle who seemed as excited as she was. Rochelle wanted to come over early on Saturday to plan and obsess over every possible detail; what to wear, how to do their hair, and things they could talk about that wouldn't annoy the boys. More than happy to indulge her, Ava agreed.

* * *

On Saturday, the rotation of the earth seemed to slow down as Ava watched the clock in the Kitchen, every second a minute, every minute an hour. She picked at her lunch, too excited to eat, and stared at the landscape beyond their backyard. Sunshine reflected off frost-covered rolling hills, a patchwork of bright-green sprouted winter wheat and tilled-brown earth. To the north, she could see the top of Steptoe Butte rising above the frozen fields. Everything about the day idyllic.

When Rochelle arrived at four and took over the wardrobe planning, Ava relaxed a little. Sifting through the closet, her friend compiled a collection of potential first-date outfits.

"You don't want to look like you're trying too hard. How about this?" Rochelle held up a red sweater and a wide leather belt.

Ava pursed her lips. "I don't know about the belt."

"Oh, wait. I've got it. This looks really good on you. Rochelle pulled out a teal blouse with a pleated collar.

"Yeah, I like that better."

"And these black boots with . . . these matador jeans. What do you think?" She asked, holding up the stirrup pants with a narrow strip of Spanish embroidery down the side of each leg.

"Mission accomplished," Ava agreed, appreciating her help as nervous energy made her stomach gurgle.

"Now, for hair and makeup." Rochelle marched to the bathroom, her long, red curls bouncing with each determined step.

"Getting her all lined up?" Lola asked, leaning on the open door.

"What do you think?" Rochelle directed the question to Ava's mother. "Hair up or down?"

"Down," her mother replied. "As much as she likes it tied back, it looks so pretty down."

"Do I have a say?" Ava asked.

"Only if you want it down," Rochelle ordered, charging the curling iron.

"I don't really like the ringlet look. It's perfect for you, but it's not me."

"I know that." Rochelle lifted Ava's dark hair away from her face, adding a loose curl to each side. "You should leave your hair down more."

Ava scrunched her nose and informed Rochelle that she didn't like her hair in her face.

"Yes. Now for the face." Rochelle squinted at her as if she were a blank canvas.

A hand up, Ava told her she wasn't interested in the painted look.

"No," her friend replied, "We're not going for circus clown."

Rochelle dusted her cheeks, brushed a thin layer of mascara on her eyelashes. "I have some lip sheen in my purse that will complete this masterpiece. Be right back."

Her mother inspected the work in progress. "You look very nice. This might be Rochelle's calling."

Ava chewed her lip. "Is it too much?"

"No," her mother assured her. "She's highlighted your natural beauty. Not overdone at all."

With lip sheen tried and approved, Ava talked to Rochelle while her friend fussed over her own hair and makeup. Timothy and friend would arrive in fifteen minutes. They still didn't know the identity of Rochelle's mystery date. Ava added another layer of antiperspirant and fanned her face with her hands.

A car pulled into the driveway. She turned to Rochelle with wide eyes. "He's here." Hands trembling, Ava walked to the front door, pulling it open as soon as she heard a tap.

"Hey."

"Hi," Ava said, voice quiet and breathy as if intending to keep his arrival a secret. "Come in." She stepped back, giving him room to walk past her, and checking the sidewalk for his friend but didn't see anyone.

Timothy stepped inside, hands deep in his pockets and eyes on her. "You look—" he scanned the room and then leaned closer. "You look really nice."

"Thank you." The intensity of his stare affected all her senses. She twisted a strand of hair around her finger, shuffled her feet. "Rochelle's already here and—"

"Good evening, Mr. Gray." Her father sounded like a judge greeting an offender before handing down a sentence as he strutted into the dining room.

"Hello, Mr. Roberts, how are you?" Timothy shook his hand.

"Fair to middling. Why don't we sit outside while the girls finish getting ready?" It wasn't a question.

Timothy smiled at Ava and followed her father out onto the back deck.

Not a Player

Chapter 13

"Did he give you the third degree?" Ava asked after Rochelle slid into the back seat of his mother's car and shut the door.

"You might say that, but he didn't leave any marks," Timothy grinned at her then shook his head as if recalling one of her father's threats.

"What did he say?" She prodded.

"Uh, stuff . . . about respect. You don't need to worry about it. One question, though. Fair to meddling—what does that mean?" He reached in front of her to open her door.

"Fair to *middling*, kind of like in the middle, or average. It's something his grandfather used to say."

"Okay, yeah, that makes more sense. Your dad's pulling out the ancient lingo to mess with my game."

"You're not a player, are you?" Ava asked with narrow eyes. "Dad warned me about those."

"Not guilty," he replied, throwing up his hands. "My every intention is most honorable."

"Good to know." she flashed a satisfied grin and pulled her door shut.

After Timothy got in and closed his door, Rochelle asked who was going with them.

Timothy turned, draped his long arm over the seat. "Do you know Jase Shoemacker? He's a senior."

Ava covered her mouth, eyes on Rochelle. Wide-eyed and jaw dropped, Rochelle grabbed the front seat. She did know Jase. She'd admired him from afar and had told Ava in confidence that she had a forever crush on him.

Timothy started the car and turned up the heater. "I think you'll like him. Jase is a lot of fun."

"Yeah," Rochelle said, "I like him. I mean, I'm sure he's fun to hang out with, or whatever." Rochelle's face took on a fresh flush of warm pink.

"Thanks for letting us crash your party," Timothy said as he backed out of the driveway.

"No—this is awesome. Thank *you*." Rochelle primped her hair and looked at Ava with bright expectant eyes and an even brighter smile.

They drove to the south end of town, up the hill, and into the Fairview apartment complex past the hospital. Jase walked out the main entrance as Timothy drove up the circular drive, then slid into the backseat next to Rochelle with a bounding plop, instantly infusing the mood in the car with high-octane energy. Timothy wasn't kidding when he said Jase was a lot of fun, but Jase wasn't just fun, he was loud. He talked loud and laughed loud, which quickly influenced Timothy to do the same, only not at the same ear-splitting decibel.

Ava exchanged glances with Rochelle as they rode to Pullman, entertained by the guys as Timothy and Jase competed for attention. This was a side of Timothy Ava hadn't seen before. She liked it. Clearly both boys were enjoying their captive audience as they took turns telling embarrassing stories about each other. They'd both been caught papering Coach Thatcher's house and had to remove twenty rolls of toilet paper from the trees in his yard.

"Coach sat in a lawn chair and drank iced tea while we cleaned up the mess," Timothy added. "And laughed when his dog got into the pile of paper and spread it all over again. When we got it done, coach took us down to the river to go tubing. Sometimes crime does pay."

Jase bobbed his head in agreement. "That was awesome. We did some crazy stuff in junior high."

Ava noticed all of their comical adventures happened before high school. Had his brother's death changed everything for Timothy? Why did he play on the JV team if he no longer wanted to play? She pushed melancholy thoughts aside. This was a night to enjoy.

* * *

"I think Rochelle and Jase had a good time," Ava said as Timothy walked her to her front door.

"Were they with us?" he teased. "What about you, Miss Roberts? Did you have a good time?"

She clasped her hands behind her. "I did. A really good time." She couldn't recall if the movie was good or not. If it were an endless loop of furniture commercials, she still would have loved every second. While Jase and Rochelle were off in their own world, the people around them shushing them every other minute, she and Timothy shared a bag of popcorn. He'd slouched down in his chair and leaned against her arm, whispering about how much popcorn she was taking and clearing it from her hand. He would then overfill her hand and challenge her to eat it without spilling. Since she wasn't up for the challenge, he attempted it and failed on purpose. Their whole evening was a back and forth of silly challenges, getting to know each other, teasing, watching Jase and Rochelle feed off each other's antics.

Timothy tugged on the side of her coat sleeve. Cleared his throat. "How about just you and me next time?"

Ava told him she'd like that, a handful of hair pulled under her chin.

The porch light flickered, but it didn't have anything to do with the bulb or the electricity.

"I better go in before my dad comes out," Ava said with an apologetic smirk.

Timothy held her gaze for a long, silent second, then turned to leave. "See you Monday, Ava."

"Thanks again," she called after him. "I had a good fun—I mean time. A good time." She chuckled, a hand on her face.

He turned, looked at her with a satisfied expression. "Me too."

She watched him walk to the driveway, waved when he reached the car and looked back.

Ava felt dizzy when she turned to close the front door. Who wouldn't be dizzy after all of that?

"How'd it go?" her mother asked, tying the belt on her robe.

"Amazing. I feel light-headed from the whole thing. Cloud nine for sure."

"I'm glad you had fun. Now your father can stop acting like he's going to have a heart attack."

"Whoa." Ava reached her hands out to steady herself, the floor rolling beneath her feet.

Her mother grabbed her arm. "Are you all right?"

"Yeah, just a head rush. I think I forgot to breathe for a second . . . or a maybe a minute." She giggled, a hand to her chest. "A little overwhelmed maybe. If he would have tried to kiss me, I probably would have passed out."

Her mother cocked her head, gave her that look that signals an incoming offering of unsolicited advice. "You save your kisses for later. Enjoy getting to know him. Why rush the romance?"

"How many dates did you go on with dad before he kissed you?"

"That's different," her mother protested as they walked down the hall.

"So how many dates?" Ava pressed, the floor no longer fluid.

Her mother pushed a hand at her. "I don't remember . . . for sure."

"Are you a hypocrite, Mom?" Ava asked, leaning on the wall outside her bedroom.

"Okay, the second date. But we were already in college and got married six months later." Her mother pointed a finger at her. "You don't have that option, missy."

"So, dad's not really a practice-what-you-preach kind of guy?"

"Maybe he knows how difficult it would be for Timothy if you start kissing on him now," her mother said with a hand on her hip, one brow lifted.

Ava looked at her, newly enlightened. "Oh. I didn't think about that."

"I'm glad you had a good time, Ava. I didn't say there was anything wrong with *wanting* to kiss him." Her mother patted her hand. "Good night, little miss dreamy eyes."

"Night, Mom."

* * *

An hour after she went to bed, Ava's phone buzzed in her backpack. It was almost midnight, but she was still wide awake. She quietly slid her closet door open, pulled her phone out, and pressed her thumb on the screen. Timothy sent her a text.

An animated teddy bear handed her flowers next to a message that said, "*Can't stop thinking about you. Good night, Ava.*"

Sliding back under her warm comforter, she started to tell him how much she missed him already but deleted the message, replacing the text with a simple reply: "*That's so sweet. Good night, Timothy.*" She added a happy animoji hugging itself and twisting from side to side before turning her phone off to keep from checking it all night. It sat there by the clock within easy reach. She shouldn't message him again. Maybe he wanted her to. No, she shouldn't. He needed his sleep as much as she did.

Timothy Gray . . . I can't stop thinking about you either.

The Invitation

CHAPTER 14

"What do you think about coming over to my house for an early dinner on Wednesday?" Timothy asked Ava after school as they walked to the parking lot. "My mom wants to meet you."

"Am I going to have to have a talk with your dad?" she teased. "Tell him what my intentions are with his son?"

Timothy rested his arm across her shoulders, one brow cocked. "He doesn't get home until after I leave for practice, so go ahead, tell *me* your intentions."

Ava bumped him with her elbow. "I assure you they're honorable."

"But of course, Miss Roberts. I would expect nothing less."

She jabbed his ribs. "You better stick to farming. I don't think you have a future in acting."

"What?" He held a hand to his chest. "I am seriously offended right now. Didn't you know I was a lead in the school play?"

"No, you weren't."

"I was. How dare you doubt me, fair maiden."

Ava stepped in front of him, her hand on his arm. "What part did you play?"

"Do you really have to ask? The prince, of course." He grabbed her hands and pulled her closer.

"Which one?" She tried to appear unaffected but loved every silly minute of it.

"Charming. I could show you the final scene," he teased, his eyes playful.

Her face felt warm, but the air was cold. "No. I believe you," she replied with a sudden fit of the giggles.

Shoulders slumped with dramatic disappointment, he released one of her hands and pulled her toward his pickup.

"Is there a home game tomorrow?" Ava asked. "I didn't see it on the schedule."

"No. We're supposed to get freezing rain for two days, so the game is cancelled. It's against Freeman. Shouldn't be too hard to reschedule." He leaned on the driver's side door and claimed her free hand. "You sure I can't give you a ride home?"

"I'd like that, but I told Rochelle we could work on homework. We're doing code for our fake website in graphics. She's driving us home."

"She's driving?" Timothy asked, eyes narrow.

"Yeah. Just got her license."

"I don't want to sound like one of your parents, Ava, but I wouldn't want to ride with a new driver on these roads."

"Rochelle lives on the flat. The roads are clear. Other than whiplash at the one stop sign, the potential for risk is minimal. She's a good driver." Ava released his hand, took a backward step, Timothy's gonna-miss-you smile melting her insides. "See you tomorrow."

Palms up, he reached for her in a stage-worthy pose. "In case I don't ever see you again, Ava . . . my love, maybe I could show you that last scene."

"Nice try, Prince Charming," she replied as she reluctantly turned to walk away, a bounce in her step.

* * *

"School's cancelled," Ava's mother said with a tap on her bedroom door. "You get to sleep in."

Bummer. Ava wouldn't go back to sleep anyway. Back of her hand rubbing an eye, she pushed out of bed, pulled on a pair of sweats, and shuffled into the kitchen.

Her mother scooted a cup of hot chocolate toward her. "You don't seem too happy about a free skip. I wonder why?"

Ava grinned, clearing tangled hair away from her face. "Did I tell you Timothy invited me over for dinner tomorrow? It's early, before practice. He wants me to meet his mom."

"What about his dad?"

"His dad won't be there. I think he gets home late." Ava sipped her mega vitamin poorly disguised as hot chocolate.

"Well, I hope they sand our hill so you can get down there. Your father called. Said he slid halfway down to Main Street. We're not going anywhere today."

Ava walked over to the dark sliding glass door and turned the deck light on. A thick blanket of ice encased the cedar planks. Frozen spikes hung from the railing.

"How can Dad drive to Spokane in this?"

"I've been watching his GPS." Her mother showed her the app on her phone. "It's taking him a while. Must have left right before they closed the highway."

Ava watched the slow-moving dot on the map. "Looks like he's a few miles from Rosalia. Why did he even go?"

"He's meeting a developer buying an office building by Riverfront Park. It'll be the biggest sale he's ever brokered. The buyer flew in yesterday. They're supposed to have a meeting at ten this morning."

"They couldn't live-cam it?" Ava scoffed, as if adults should know better.

"Your dad is kind of old fashioned. Live-cam isn't anything like meeting in person. Would you rather live-cam with Timothy or be with him in person?"

Ava smiled at her. "Good point, but not at all the same thing." She took a few more sips of the now tepid cocoa. "What's in this? Tastes like seaweed."

"It's not very good is it? They can't sell anything these days unless it has a nutritional additive. Want to make cookies today?"

"Yes," Ava replied, "With pure sugar and butter and lots of real chocolate. You don't have to work?"

Her mother told her she had a logo to tidy up and a few brochure designs to send off—nothing that couldn't wait until later.

Ava checked her father's progress on her mother's phone. "Looks like dad is stuck on the highway."

"Let me see." Her mother studied the still screen, lower lip in her mouth. "Voice command . . . Call Eric's car."

"Mom, put it on speaker." Ava held her breath, waiting for her father to answer.

"Hello. You're watching me, aren't you?"

When they saw his tired smile, they both released a loaded breath.

"You weren't moving," her mother replied.

Ava could see consistent flashes of light reflecting off his face.

"I'm stuck behind an accident. It doesn't look too bad, just a fender bender, but they're blocking the road. Hey, after this meeting I'm going to come right back home. The highway should open up again by noon."

"Okay. Drive safe," her mother said. "Love you."

"Love you, Dad." Ava added, relieved to know he was all right.

Surprise Visit

Chapter 15

Mixing bowl in the dishwasher, Ava took a teeth-only bite from a hot chocolate-chip cookie and checked her messages. Rochelle forwarded several funny video clips and a text bemoaning the fact that she wouldn't see Jase today. Timothy sent her a selfie of himself taking a drink from a milk carton, with a caption that read, *"Don't tell anyone."*

Expanding his picture, she admired his skewed hair. Ava replied to both messages, saving Timothy for last in hopes that he'd call. It wasn't ten seconds before the caller ID flashed his picture.

His phone was on private-call setting. She couldn't see him, which was fine since she didn't want to scare him with her messy hair. He asked if she was doing anything, then told her his father was acting like a caged animal because he couldn't go to work. Timothy wanted to get out of the house. He assured her he could make it up her hill, then told her he had a surprise and she needed to bundle up. They were going to play outside. Ava wanted him to come over but warned him again that the hill up to her house was solid ice.

"I can make it," he insisted. "Be up there in twenty, thirty minutes tops."

Ava ended the call, a surge of electric energy travelling through her. He's coming over! She paced the hallway to soothe twitching legs. "Mom, Timothy's coming over." She tried to sound casual. No big deal. Just Timothy coming over to hang out—with me!

Lola thanked her for the warning and went in her room to change out of pajama pants. Ava dressed and pulled a brush through hair that fought off every attempt to tame it. Panic attempted to infuse her anticipation, but she resisted its theft of her excitement. Why fuss with her hair? She'd be wearing a hat anyway. Hair in a ponytail, she headed to her closet in search of thick gloves, hat, and scarf. By the time she was ready, Ava thought she heard a motorcycle pulling into the driveway. She opened the door to find Timothy parking a four-wheeler with chains on the tires and a tote with two hockey sticks strapped on the back. He waved, his face covered with a ski mask, and wearing a loose, black snowsuit and thick, black mittens.

"You made it," Ava said as she tried to get to him without falling.

He pulled his helmet and mask off. "Ready to play?" Timothy seemed elated to see her, his hair sticking up and wide grin claiming most of his face.

"Yes, I'm ready." Ready for anything he had in mind. She would be happy to sort gravel as long as she could be with him.

Timothy loosened the straps on his plastic tote before walking confidently toward her, his steps steady on the ice.

"You're not sliding around?"

He lifted a foot, revealing a grid of spikes strapped to the bottom of his boot. "I brought some for you, too." Taking her arm in his, he helped her walk to the four-wheeler.

"Maybe we should skip the hockey and go for a walk," he teased, pulling her closer.

She pressed tight lips together and pointed at the hockey sticks. She could tell his flirtations were all in fun, as if he were testing her reaction to every jest. Testing the water before committing to the plunge. She didn't mind the process. In fact, she wanted to jump all-in, but a constant internal reminder nudged her to be careful, protect them both from hasty decisions. He seemed content to do the same, to keep everything in the slow-moving safe zone.

Timothy rubbed his gloved hands together. "This'll be fun." After strapping spiked grids to the bottom of her boots, he handed her the shorter stick. "These haven't been used for a while," he said, wiping a layer of dust off the handle.

Ava asked him when he played hockey.

"We played when we were in grade school. I wasn't sure we still had these."

Ava noticed he said *we*. He still hadn't mentioned his brother. She worked over several things she could ask him without souring his playful mood.

"Where did you play?"

"A junior league in Spokane. These sticks are gonna be a little short." He looked at the stick she was holding and chuckled. "Yours is long enough."

She scowled at him. "Jerk."

He grinned while staring at her for several playful seconds. "You can't intimidate me; you're too cute."

"Keep your mind on the game, Mr. Gray."

"Oh, yeah, the game."

They carried the tote to the sidewalk and pulled out two orange cones and several pucks. Since Ava lived on the end of the street, they didn't have to worry about traffic. After a few minutes of coaching, Ava was able to push the puck across the icy road, switching the stick back and forth to guide it toward the orange cone.

"This would be a lot harder on skates," Ava said as she pulled the puck toward her.

"You ready to play?" Timothy picked up one of the cones and moved it another fifteen feet down the road. "This is my goal. You have to hit this cone."

"With the puck?" Ava asked sarcastically.

He shook his head as he walked toward her. "Some people are so hard to coach."

A foot on the puck between them, he reminded her she had to tap her stick three times. "Don't cheat."

She grinned at him, her stick tapping the icy pavement. "I'm ready."

They played for close to a half hour, taking advantage of opportunities to grab an arm or a waist, leaning against each other when they got close to a cone.

"I think we have an audience," Ava said, pointing down the sidewalk.

A little boy, maybe eight years old, watched them over the hood of a parked car.

Timothy waved him over. The young boy slid his boots along the ice towards them, his ears and nose red from the cold.

"What's your name?" Timothy asked him.

"Jeffrey," the boy replied, looking at the hockey sticks like a dog looks at bacon.

With a pat on the boy's head Timothy asked Jeffrey if he had a hat.

The boy replied with a nod.

Timothy lowered to a squat and told the Jeffrey he could play if he put on a hat. They watched the young boy scoot across the ice, his arms pumping as he hurried to comply.

"I think we have a third player," Timothy said with a chuckle.

"I call him for my team," Ava said pushing his arm. "I'll be the goalie."

"You call?" Timothy scoffed. "Is that supposed to be some magic phrase that makes your wishes come true?"

"Isn't that how it works?" Ave challenged.

"I call you wrap your arms around me and give me a big kiss." He looked at her, brow raised and hands out.

"It doesn't work like that!" she squealed, jumping away from him. "There are children present." She pointed at their new player eagerly sliding his way toward them.

Timothy went over the rules with Jeffrey and handed the new player his stick. Ava traded with him, giving the small boy the shorter one. Ava and Jeffrey played for a few minutes until Ava insisted Timothy play. She thought she'd get somewhat steadier on her feet, but she'd fallen several times for no apparent reason. The last time Timothy helped her up, he asked if she was doing it on purpose, told her she didn't have to be so dramatic just to get his attention. Though not true, she went along with his accusation. The truth, she was a bit of a klutz. More so when she got tired, like anybody not used to doing the sports thing for more than twenty minutes.

She sat on the sidewalk, watching Timothy help the little boy make a goal. Although the air was cold, Ava felt warm clear to her toes. Timothy shifted into coach mode, giving Jeffrey detailed pointers he hadn't bothered going over with her. It wasn't long before a few more potential players lined the sidewalk. Ava didn't mind sharing Timothy. It gave her an opportunity to see another side of him. She liked what she saw. Patient. Friendly. Drop-dead gorgeous.

After appointing Jeffrey the new coach, Timothy sat on the sidewalk beside her. He watched the kids play, calling out an instruction every once in a while or a reminder to keep the sticks down. He seemed winded but clearly was having fun.

"Do you want something to drink?" Ava offered.

"Sure." He stood up and reached for her hands. "You guys take turns," he ordered as he helped Ava to her feet.

When they got to the door, Timothy reminded her to take off the spikes. They went inside, leaving boots and a pile of coats, gloves, and hats inside the door.

"Ava?" her mother called from the den.

Ava waved for Timothy to follow her down the hall.

"Hello, Mrs. Rober—Lola."

Ava's mom looked up from her computer. "Hi, Timothy. Help yourself to the cookies on the counter. We just made them this morning."

"Thank you. Sounds good."

"We needed a break," Ava said, combing her hair back with her fingers. "Hockey is a popular sport."

Her mother said she'd seen them all playing. Told them as they turned to leave the room that it looked like everyone was having fun.

Ava poured Timothy a tall glass of milk while demanding that he not touch their milk carton with his mouth, and set a plate of cookies in front of him. "I'm glad you came over." She sat beside him and nibbled on a cookie, wishing the day would never end.

"Me too," he said, trying to talk around the cookie in his mouth. "Because these are awesome." He eyed her, a sly smile creasing his cheek.

"Funny." She inched the plate away. "Can you stay for a while? We can make some lunch and then reclaim your hockey sticks. Now that the sun's out, it's not so cold. We could go for a walk." Not paying attention to what she was doing, she brushed a fingertip over his wrist then pulled her hand back.

"That's a tough choice." He pulled the plate closer, leaned into her shoulder. "It's a great day for a walk."

* * *

After eating leftovers from last night's dinner, Ava and Timothy put their coats on and headed back outside. Their melting, makeshift hockey rink was now swarming with a dozen kids fighting over two coveted sticks.

"It's a good thing you chose the walk. Our rink looks a little busy. We could go up there," Ava said, pointing to the cemetery less than fifty yards up the hill. "It's a nice view from the top."

Timothy looked up the hill, his eyes trained on the north end. "I don't really want to go up there."

"Are you scared of ghosts?" she teased, waving her hands toward him.

"Not scared," he replied, voice flat and expression serious. "Let's play hockey instead."

What was she thinking? She wasn't thinking; that was the problem. "I'm sorry."

He assured it was nothing, his smile forced.

Within a few minutes, half the kids began retreating into warm houses, called inside for lunch or a need to thaw frozen fingers. Timothy and Ava took turns playing with the kids until Ava insisted she'd rather watch. While the kids were celebrating a goal, her father pulled up and stopped at the far end of their rink.

Timothy called the kids back from the road while he moved the cone so the car could pass through. Her father drove slowly past the impatient players, parked beside the four-wheeler, and got out of the car.

"Mr. Roberts, I can move that," Timothy pointing at the four-wheeler as he jogged toward it.

"That's all right. Leave it," Her father replied, casually leaning against the trunk of his car. Eric's attention shifted to the kids in the street, several pleading for Timothy to come back and play.

Ava joined her father, trying not to make it obvious that she was watching her dad watch Timothy. She pulled her gloves off, the sun's reflection adding a measure of warmth on the dark car.

Her father laughed when a young boy fell on his rump. The boy then tried to reach for the puck before it hit the cone. "Aggressive little guy. Where did the hockey sticks come from?"

"Timothy brought them." She pointed at the four-wheeler.

Eric glanced at it, then turned his attention back to the players in the street. "Oh—the little fighter almost had it."

Jeffrey returned to the scene, mouth full, a half-eaten sandwich in hand.

"That was our first recruit," Ava informed her father.

He chuckled, watching as the returning player shoved the rest of his sandwich in his mouth and asked if it could be his turn. Timothy let a little girl go first, promising Jeffrey he would get a turn soon enough. Ava noticed her father nodding in approval as he tucked his hands under his arms. After a few minutes, her dad claimed the need to let her mother know he was home and went inside.

Timothy joined her, tired but happy. "I don't know how I'm going to take those sticks away. These kids could play forever."

"I can keep them for you, if you want to leave the stuff here," Ava offered.

"Good idea. I better get going. I want a rain-check on that walk, though," he said, pulling her into his side.

* * *

The kids in the street protested as Timothy turned out of the driveway and down the road. Ava listened to the fading pop, pop, pop of the four-wheeler then turned to look up the hill toward the cemetery.

With the spikes still strapped to her feet, Ava hiked up the short trail packed down by bicycles and boots. Having walked past the hundred-year-old, weather-beaten tombstones on the south side of the cemetery, she headed to the north end. Fingers of light reached beneath pine trees lining the road at the top of the hill. Twenty yards in front of her, sparrows pestered a hawk perched on a low branch. As she drew closer, the hawk flew away, the angry chatter subsiding. After working through several rows of newer graves, Ava found it, the ice on the inscription melted away by the sun.

William Nicholas Gray
"Billy"
11-7-2017 — 1-28-2035
Son, Brother, Friend
"Blessed are they that mourn,
for they shall be comforted."
Matthew 5:4

That night, with sweats and thick socks on, Ava climbed into bed, her covers pulled snug to her neck. She hadn't noticed the chill until well after Timothy left. Content and tired, she replayed the events of the day, reliving every minute. Timothy was good with kids. He'd make a great dad. Careful, girl, it's way too soon to start thinking that way. If only they were five or six years older.

Soon, she'd meet Timothy's mother. Though it made Ava somewhat nervous, she looked forward to the introduction. Some mothers were known to be possessive of their sons and not too quick to grant approval. Now that Timothy was Mrs. Gray's only son, his mother might be particularly difficult to win over. Ava wanted Mrs. Gray to like her.

Pictures of Billy would likely hang on the wall next to Timothy's. She knew better than to mention Billy. It seemed abundantly clear that Timothy wasn't ready to talk about his brother. Maybe his mother would.

The Truth

CHAPTER 16

Wednesday morning offered clear skies as Ava's mother drove her to school, a day full of promise complete with slivers of golden light peeking over the eastern side of the valley. At the end of the block, kids lined up on the corner to board the bus coming up the hill. White-tailed deer dotted the hillside, helping themselves to sprouted winter wheat in the field beyond the graveyard.

"Are you going straight to Timothy's after school?" her mother asked.

"That's the plan. Kind of nervous, though. I hope his mom likes me."

"Of course she'll like you. You don't have anything to worry about."

* * *

Ava and Timothy planned to have lunch with friends since they would be together after school. He'd teased her, asked if she was getting tired of him, then interrupted her retort with an agreement that they shouldn't ditch their friends. That didn't mean they didn't notice each other during lunch. It was almost as much fun catching him watching her as it was sitting next to him—almost.

Rochelle asked her if everything was all right between them. Ava assured her things couldn't be better.

"I don't want to be one of those ball and chain girlfriends." Ava glanced across the cafeteria. They weren't just friends and it felt good to admit it. She caught his eye again and smiled. Timothy was talking to the guys at his table, but he was looking at her.

"He needs to hang out with the guys too," she told Rochelle. "Don't want him to get bored of me."

"Looks like it doesn't take much distance for the heart to grow fonder," Rochelle teased.

With her face growing warm from the attention, Ava tented a hand over her mouth to hide a full-faced grin. She couldn't wait to spend the afternoon with him.

* * *

"Here we are," Timothy said as he opened his front door.

Ava walked past him, snapping and unsnapping the pocket on her coat as she noticed the high entry ceiling and crystal chandelier. A large leather bench flanked a short wall topped with dark wood and ornately carved molding. Beyond the wall, she admired a dining room with a dozen high-back chairs around a polished table.

"Mom, we're here." Timothy took Ava's coat and dropped it on the leather bench along with his own.

"Hello there, Ava," his mother said with a tender grin as she joined them in the entry, her hands clasped together at her chest. "It's so nice to meet you." She smiled at her son, her expression a mixture of pride and gratitude.

Timothy rocked from one foot to the other. "This is my mom, Grace."

"It's nice to meet you," Ava replied as she took the woman's outstretched hand.

Ava recognized her. She had seen Mrs. Gray at Timothy's games but hadn't realized this woman was his mother. Grace, a foot taller than Ava, didn't pass her dark hair color on to her son, but her blue eyes were clearly the blueprint for Timothy's. The faint lines around her mouth and eyes suggested decades of smiles.

"Come on in, Ava. I hope you like meat loaf. Oh dear, you're not a vegetarian, are you? I forgot to ask Timothy about that."

"She's carnivorous," Timothy assured her, then turned to Ava. "I requested the meat loaf."

Ava looked at him with a self-conscious grin, then turned back toward his mother. She thanked Mrs. Gray for having her over and offered to help. Grace assured her the only thing left to do was wait for things to finish cooking. His mother then suggested Timothy show Ava the eagle's nest.

After Mrs. Gray went back to the kitchen, Ava asked Timothy if his mother was talking about a real nest.

He grabbed their coats and held hers while she put it on. "Yes. The celebrated nest; it's our claim to fame. Want to see it?"

"Sure."

They left the house and walked hand-in-hand a few blocks toward the narrow river winding through the middle of the impressive complex. Ava admired the houses with their grand porches and tall entries. She knew it was one of the newer developments, but the security gate and the tall iron fence at the entry had discouraged any potential sightseeing.

Timothy pointed toward the river. "That fenced area over there, see the nest?"

"Oh, yeah. It's big."

As they walked, Timothy told her it had been there for decades but had become a target for idiots, so a wealthy conservationist bought the property to protect the nest. Tall junipers stood between the road and the iron fence, blocking the view for a quarter mile.

"We get nature photographers in here every spring. They always want pictures of the eaglets."

"Sounds like you know what you're talking about. I'm impressed."

He bumped her with his elbow. "Don't be. If we don't use approved *eaglish* our commune fees will double."

She chuckled at his quick wit, asked him if the fence was there before the houses.

"I think so. There were four or five houses already here when we built ours. My dad thinks the conservation thing was just a ploy to manipulate the land purchase, but he usually thinks everyone is trying to get away with something."

The sun dropped behind the tall rocky hill on the west side of the valley. A bone-chilling wind pushed past them. Timothy wrapped an arm over her shoulder, pulled his coat tight to his neck. As they headed back to the house, the wind blew harder, first bending the tops of the trees, then mingling with frozen drops of rain.

"That came on fast," Timothy said as he quickly pushed the door shut behind them.

His mother met them in the entry with an apologetic frown and fussed over the ice in their hair and their cold hands. "Let me take your coats. I'm sorry I sent you two out there. Twenty minutes ago it was lovely outside."

"It's okay, Mom," Timothy said as he took Ava's coat. "We would have crawled back for meat loaf."

"Speaking of crawling," his mother said, "The neighbor's cat got up in the attic over the garage again. Could you get it down before your father gets home? I'm afraid it will meet its end if he has to get it out of there."

"There's too many cats around here anyways," Timothy replied as he wiped a sleeve over his wet forehead.

"Timothy, Ava can visit with me. It'll only take you a minute." His mother nodded as if he'd already agreed to de-cat the attic.

Ava nudged his arm with her shoulder. "Be nice to the kitty."

While Timothy complied with his mother's request, Grace led Ava into their family room. Imitation orange and red flames danced in a large fireplace on the far side of the room. Digital frames in various sizes lined a wide granite mantel.

"Are those Timothy's senior pictures?" Ava asked as she stepped around an elaborately colored carpet to get a closer look.

"They are." Grace pointed to the one in the middle and slid through the images in the digital collage. "This is my favorite. He's always had such a beautiful smile."

Ava blushed. Somehow, admiring Timothy in front of his mother made her self-conscious. Noticing a large frame prominently displayed on the right side of the mantel, Ava didn't have to wonder if the boy in the letterman's jacket was Billy. Timothy looked a lot like his brother—the same wide jaw, Roman nose, sandy blond hair, and bright eyes. Billy's face was fuller, and his hair was thick with curls.

"I tried to get Billy a hair cut before he had that taken, but he was always so busy." Grace tilted her head, the back of her finger trailing under her chin.

Ava inspected Timothy's picture again. "They look a lot alike."

86

"They were a lot alike. Even though Timothy was three years younger, Billy always let him tag along. His death was especially hard on Timothy, but he's coming around."

Mrs. Gray must have assumed Ava knew about Billy's death. She pulled her younger son's picture closer. "Just look at that smile."

"He has a movie-star smile," Ava said with admiration. "His dental work sure paid off."

"We got lucky there," Grace replied, "He didn't need braces. Those are God-given pearly whites."

As if flames licked out at her from the imitation fireplace, Ava stepped away from the mantel. "Grace—" Her conscience screamed for her to be careful, to weigh every word before speaking it. "How long has Timothy had . . . problems with digestion?"

"I'm surprised he told you about that." Mrs. Gray pressed her lips together and looked behind her. "Would you like to sit down?"

Worried that she might have said too much already, Ava sat on the edge of a leather chair across from the fire, waiting for Grace to take over the conversation.

"He's much better. After his second surgery he finally realized how much damage it was causing." Mrs. Gray turned and looked behind her again.

"How does he keep any food down?" Ava asked, partially relieved. Maybe there was an explanation for the retainers. She might have misunderstood him at the pizza parlor.

Grace looked at her with a deeply wrinkled brow. "What do you mean?"

"Are some foods more likely to stay down? Too much pizza doesn't agree with him."

"Ava—" Grace pulled against the arms of her chair, leaning closer to Ava. "Is he still purging?" his mother whispered.

Ava sat frozen in place, sudden panic pumping through her veins like water breaching a dam.

Grace got up, took a slow step toward her, put a hand on her shoulder. "Sweetheart," she said, voice breathy and trembling, "you need to tell me if Timothy is throwing up at school. Please—before he gets back."

It was too much. Ava couldn't hold the tears back. Her chest tightened, her lungs failed to offer enough air to speak. All she could do was nod. He'd never speak to her again.

With quivering lips, Grace fell back in her chair, a hand on her head. "Ava—" she said, her voice broken. "Thank you for telling me." His mother took a few deep breaths. "He has to stop. It'll kill him if he doesn't."

Ava stood up, her thoughts a jumbled mess. She took a step toward the entry. The room began to spin. She had to get out of there. "I need to go."

"Ava, no. I know this is hard. Sit down, sweetheart. Please sit down."

"I can't." Every sound, tap on the window, creek in the floor was Timothy coming back. He'd regret ever meeting her. He'd hate her. An invisible belt tightened around her chest as she considered her options. She didn't have any options except run for the door.

"Ava, stop! No, please don't go!" Grace yelled, launching out of her chair.

Ava threw the door open and ran toward the gated entrance, frozen rain stinging her face and arms. She wiped her eyes with the back of her hand, stepping into the shadows as a car approached the gate. After the car passed, she slipped out, the gate closing behind her.

The sky drew darker as she ran down the road against the rocky hillside, lungs burning, hands growing stiff from the cold. Behind her, lights grew brighter as a car rounded the corner. Ava pushed through a patch of wet shrubs bordering an icy bike path. One, maybe two miles to Rochelle's house. Running might keep her warm. The lights behind her stopped. She turned, shielding her eyes with her arm.

Why This

Chapter 17

"Ava!—what are you doing?" Timothy sprinted toward her, thrashing through the tall grass, arms swinging wildly as if pushing through flames.

"I'm sorry!" Ava pressed her hands toward him, willing him to stay away.

"Sorry? Are you kidding me? What are you thinking?" he yelled, nostrils flaring, eyes ablaze. "Why this?" He thrust both hands at her, continuing to close the ten feet between them. "Can't you see how stupid this is? Get in!" A deep breath sucked in and held, he grabbed his hair, then exhaled a quick hiss through clenched teeth. "Ava—get in. I'll take you home." He grabbed her arm, pulled her toward his pickup.

"I can call my mom." She said through quivering lips, seeing for the first time the disdain he would always have for her.

"How? You don't have your phone!" he barked, jabbing a finger at the truck. "It's in there!" Timothy released her, pulled on his neck with both hands, then squeezed his arms tight to his head. Arms dropped as if they were too heavy to bear, he kicked a foot into the wet ground. "Don't be stupid, Ava. Get in," he said, his voice shifting into an unnatural, slow, cold, and mechanical tone. "If you don't get in, I'm going to pick you up and put you in myself. Just . . . please, Ava, get in."

Ava stepped away from him and ran to the pickup, her entire body shivering, fingers numb, unable to feel the door handle. She got in and closed the door, pressed against it to distance herself. The pain in her heart felt a hundred times worse than the icy needles pricking her cold fingers.

Timothy jumped in the door he left open, then slammed it shut, his chest heaving as he sucked in deep gulps of air. She didn't need to see his face to sense the anger rolling off him. He started to say something, then stopped, shook his head.

Ava buried her wet face in her hands. "I'm sorry," she stuttered, through muffled sobs.

"What if something happened to you? Ava, did you think of that?" He pounded the steering wheel.

Startled, she jerked her head up. Faced him. The anger in his voice didn't match what she saw. "Timothy!" She reached for him, but he pulled away.

He closed his eyes and held them shut for several agonizing seconds as if to block out an ugly view. "That would be on me—Ava—on me," he choked out, tears pouring down his face. Sweatshirt pulled off, he pushed it at her, then yanked the gearshift and punched the gas, fishtailing onto the road.

She slid her arms inside the warm fleece; held it tight to her chest. Timothy didn't say another word until he stopped in her driveway. The engine running, he shifted into park and pulled her backpack out from behind the seat.

"Ava—" He swallowed hard, pulled the front of his t-shirt into a clenched fist.

She took her things and pushed the handle. What could she say? The least she could do was listen.

"I shouldn't have yelled at you. I'm sorry." He stared down the hill, his hands trembling on the steering wheel.

She slid out of the pickup, took a few steps, and turned back. Timothy drove away without looking at her. If he never wanted to look at her again, how could she blame him?

* * *

At 11:12 p.m., Ava's mother slipped into her room.

"I'm all right," Ava lied.

Her mother sat on the edge of her bed and tucked the comforter over Ava's shoulders like she'd done when Ava was in grade school. "It'll get better. I promise."

"Mom . . . yesterday everything was perfect; now it's all gone. I want Timothy back." Ava closed her eyes, too ashamed to admit how she'd run away from him, making everything worse.

"As hard as this is, it might be the best thing for him. He needs help. You said it yourself, sweetheart."

"I know, but why do the *best things* have to hurt so bad. It's the worst thing ever."

Her mother brushed Ava's damp hair away from her eyes. "I believe it's called love."

"Love? Feels more like hell." Ava draped an arm over her face. "He hates me." What she wanted most she'd never have again.

"I'd be willing to bet he's upset with himself right now, not you. I'm sorry, honey. It'll take a while to work through these feelings. Give it time. This too shall pass. You could pray for him. Maybe knowing that God wants what's best for him will help you as well." She kissed Ava's forehead and slipped out of the room.

*　*　*

Ava stared at the ceiling, her empty stomach gurgling and cramping as she tried to think about how she should pray. It didn't feel right asking God to give Timothy back to her, so she prayed for his parents, that they would know what to do, and that he would be able to accept Billy's death and regain his health. Enjoy life again, even if she wasn't a part of it.

The next time Ava opened her eyes it was 6 a.m. She'd slept better than she had in over a month, but her head felt heavy as if full of sand. She pulled her robe on and shuffled into the kitchen. Both her parents stopped talking. They looked at her with that smile parents have when a toddler loses a favorite blanket. No other blanket will do, and they know it.

"How are you feeling, babe?" Her father set his coffee down, walked over, pulled her into his shoulder.

"I've been better," she mumbled. "Did Mom tell you Timothy lied—about the purging?"

"She did." He released his arm and pulled a chair out for her. "It's a tough thing, but his parents need to know the truth."

Ava sat down, her head supported in both hands. "Dad, don't be mad at Timothy."

"No. I'm not mad at him."

"What do I do now?"

"Do what you have to," her dad said. "You need to take care of yourself. Do life, even if you don't feel like it." He kissed her cheek. "Hang in there, babe. I gotta go. You may think this is the end of the world. It isn't; it's just real life. Sometimes life has some nasty road bumps, but we get over them and keep on going."

After her father left for work, her mother poured a glass of orange juice and set it in front of her. "You should go to school. I know you don't want to, but it would be harder to stay home and stew over it all day."

Ava stared at the glass as she turned it on the counter. "I'll go. I want him to see that I'm all right." What if he didn't want to see her? Maybe he wished he'd never met her.

"Remember, Ava, Timothy is responsible for his own decisions, not you."

"I know." She raked a hand through tangled hair.

"You go get ready. I know you can do this or I wouldn't ask you to. Would it help if I sang *I will survive*?"

"No, mom. I'm going." Ava pushed away from the counter.

Her mother grabbed a wooden spoon and sang, "Go on now go, walk out the door."

"Mom, not helping." Maybe it was, just a little.

Hasty Words

Chapter 18

Ava, unable to pay attention in class, pulled at the edge of her sweatshirt sleeve until she worked a hole into the cuff. In third period, Rochelle assumed a typical breakup and tried to distract her with humorous stories. Appreciating her efforts, Ava pretended to be consoled, until they walked into the cafeteria.

Sitting across the room with his usual group of friends, Timothy looked at her the second she saw him. He held her gaze for a long two seconds then bowed his head.

Rochelle grabbed her arm and steered her toward an empty table. "Let's sit over there today." Her friend moved a chair, facing it away from the rest of the room. "Don't even look over there."

Ava sat down, pulled her sandwich into pieces, ate a few carrot sticks while Rochelle talked and pretended not to look across the room. The closeness to him was unbearable at first, but the longer Ava sat there, the more she relaxed. That changed when Rochelle's eyes focused on a moving object behind Ava, then suddenly grew wider. "Oh. Oh, no. He's coming over here."

"Ava—"

She startled, her insides jumping as if someone screamed, but the voice was quiet. His voice. Her heart leapt into overdrive. She turned in her chair to face him, her neck on instant hot and hands clammy. "Hi."

Ava could hear Rochelle saying something about her locker, but Ava's attention was trained on Timothy. Not looking at her, he pulled a chair over and sat down. She tried not to stare, but she couldn't help noticing the dark circles under his eyes and the heaviness in his posture as if he had a hundred-pound weight tied to each shoulder.

"I didn't mean it," he said, his voice raspy. "I just . . . lost it. I won't bother you anymore, but I'm sorry I lied to you. It was easier than telling the truth, I thought." He leaned forward and pressed his hands on the table to get up, but he paused.

That was her cue. He wanted her to say something but gave her an out if she didn't want to.

Not caring that her hands were shaking, she slid them over his. "I'm not mad at you."

He sat still, his pained gaze on her hands. "You should be."

"No. I understand. I care about you. I didn't think you'd want to talk to me."

He wrapped his hands over hers. "Why did you run off like that?"

"I was afraid . . . It was stupid, wasn't it?" She looked at his hands, wanting them to wrap around her, for everything to be all right.

He leaned toward her, his eyes searching her face. "Why were you afraid?"

"Because I thought what I did would hurt you. That you would hate me."

His brow furrowed. "Ava, why would I hate you? I'm the one that lied to you."

"Your mom was so upset. I didn't know what was going to happen, and I panicked." She squeezed his hand. "I'm sorry. I should have stayed there."

Timothy blew out a lungful and leaned back in his chair, keeping one of her hands tucked in his. "Can I see you after school? For a few minutes?"

She nodded and smiled at him, partially relieved of the burden she'd been holding ever since she ran out his front door.

* * *

Having already sent a text to her mother to pick her up fifteen minutes late, Ava tossed her books in her locker and checked her phone. Timothy was waiting for her in the courtyard behind the school. She told Rochelle they were working things out and gave her friend a thumbs-up as she hurried out the door.

When she rounded the corner, Ava saw Timothy leaning against a brick column, holding the coat she'd left at his house.

"I thought you might need this," he said with a cautious smile.

She took it, tucked it under her arm. "Thanks. I'll bring your sweatshirt tomorrow." She wanted to touch him, to have his arm on her shoulder or hold his hand.

"No rush," he replied, watching his feet as he kicked at a pinecone.

Ava hugged the coat to her chest. The courtyard was shaded and cold, but private. And he was here. With her. They could work this out.

"I have an appointment in Spokane tomorrow," he said as he smoothed his hair behind his ear. "My mom isn't wasting any time."

"That's good though, right?" Ava wanted to be careful. She wouldn't ask him anything that might make things worse than they already were. If he trusted her, he would tell her what he wanted her to know.

"Did you get the cat out of the attic before your dad got home?" she teased.

He looked at her and smirked. "Yeah."

Ava nudged his elbow. "You saved its life."

"Lucky cat this time. Ava . . . your dad's gonna kill me."

"He's not," Ava assured him. "He knows all I ever wanted to do was help you."

Timothy cocked his head, brow furrowed. "Help me?"

Ava's pulse quickened. Why was he looking at her like that?

He pushed off the brick wall. Stood up straight. "What's that supposed to mean?"

She wanted him to understand. What could she say? "Timothy, it's okay now."

"What?" Color spread across his cheeks. His eyes grew cold.

Ava saw a blood-filled vein instantly double in size as it climbed up his neck.

Timothy's eyes grew wide, his mouth open as if she'd stabbed him. "You already knew!"

She grabbed his hand. "Wait—let me explain."

He let go as if her hand were a hot coal. "I'm a fool . . . You've known all along. At pizza, you tried to stop me. Isn't that what you said? It is! You tried to stop me."

"Timothy, please listen," she pleaded, but he jerked away as if she'd slapped him.

"Just friends. You said that, too. You meant it, didn't you?" He closed his eyes for a few seconds, hands over his ears.

"No, that's not true!" she reached for him, but he pulled away.

"The tutoring—everything—" He smirked at her and shook his head. "I thought you were into me. Bet that was funny? The crush memo. That was a low blow. Was that part of your secret mission?" His lips were tight, beginning to quiver.

"What are you talking about?" She grabbed his wrist, but he yanked it free.

A glaze began to build in his eyes. "When I was *helping* you with precal, Crystal's sister told me you had a crush on me."

"I didn't have anything to do with that!" Panic-driven energy shot through her body like a bolt of lightning.

Timothy took another step away from her. "I can't believe this. I got it all wrong. Looks like I'm a liar and a chump."

"Stop! Please!" Ava lunged for him, dropping her coat, and pulled on his sweatshirt, but he twisted away to free her grasp.

"Mission accomplished, Ava. I don't need your help anymore." He turned away from her and ran across the parking lot.

Ava wanted to cry, but her head began to pound. Wincing at the sudden, sharp pain, she pressed her hand over an ear and scanned the parking lot for her mother's car but instead saw Timothy get in his pickup and drive away. Leaning against the cold brick wall in the courtyard, she closed her eyes as a wave of nausea slowly overwhelmed her gut. This was her reward for not minding her own business.

* * *

"Ava, are you okay?" her mother asked when she slowly got in the car.

"A migraine." It wasn't a lie, but it wasn't the whole truth either. Afraid that her parents would be angry with Timothy, she kept this latest disaster to herself.

"Maybe you should have stayed home. I think I'll take you up to the doctor."

"No. It's only a headache. I want to go home." Ava closed her eyes and laid the seat back. "Please, Mom, just take me home."

Rumored Assault

CHAPTER 19

Barely able to stay on her feet, Ava spent Friday at home in her bed, her lights off and blinds closed a good share of the day. Several times she'd rushed to the bathroom, nausea twisting her stomach, but found no relief. The painkillers she'd taken hadn't helped at all, and the pink tablets on her nightstand made her feel worse. Her mother called their family doctor who advised rest as her best option for recovery from a stress-induced migraine.

Ava didn't know what time it was when she woke to the phone ringing in the kitchen. She heard her mother answer with her usual friendly greeting, but Lola's voice quickly grew quiet and muffled. Moving slowly, Ava sat on the side of her bed before standing, then leaned on the headboard until she no longer felt too dizzy to walk. Her mother told whomever it was on the phone that she was sorry and thanked them for letting her know. Letting her know what? To steady herself, Ava kept a hand on the wall as she walked to the kitchen.

"Thank you, Grace. We'll be praying for him as well."

"Who was that?" Ava asked, leaning on the refrigerator.

Her mother seemed to ignore the question, insisting on fussing over her until she sat down.

"Was that Timothy's mother?"

"It was, and I'm sure you want to know what she said, but I really want you to take a break from worrying about him. You have this nasty migraine because of stress."

The kitchen lights as bright as the sun, Ava tented her eyes with her hands. "It's going to be worse if you don't tell me what she said."

Her mother sat next to her and stared out the sliding glass door, the back of her fingers brushing her chin.

"Mom?"

"The doctor told Timothy he had two weeks to show signs of improvement."

"Or what?" Ava pressed.

"Or be admitted to a treatment facility. If he keeps purging, he'll burn another hole through his esophagus. He also has an ulcer that is days away from perforating his stomach. The damage he's already done to his vocal cords could be irreversible."

"How was he able to hide that? He had to be in a lot of pain. Other than being thin, he acted like nothing was wrong."

"I don't know how he did it," her mother replied, "If nothing else, honey, you need to realize he's getting help. That's what he really needs right now."

"I wish knowing that made me feel better." Ava shook her head and pushed away the saucer her mother slid in front of her, the cheese and crackers not at all appealing to her. "Did his mom say anything else?"

"Grace wanted to know if you were all right. She told me what happened; that you ran out of their house. Grace knows it cost you to help her son. She's sorry for that. Said the present struggles and hurts are worth Timothy's life. His parents thought he'd stopped." Ava's mother took her hand. "I know you miss him. If he doesn't know how much you care for him now, he will when he looks back on all this. It'll mean a lot to him. Right now, he's ashamed. And all he has to cover it with is anger."

That could have been the case if she hadn't ruined everything; *all I ever wanted to do was help you.* A few careless words. One hasty sentence had cost her everything. She'd always remember the way he looked at her, as if she were the sole source of his pain.

* * *

By Monday morning, Ava's debilitating migraine subsided. In its place, a manageable headache and sensitive eyes. She ate half her breakfast. Got ready to go as if on autopilot. When she arrived at school, she didn't remember the drive there.

Ava promised her mother she'd call if she needed to come home early, swung her backpack over her shoulder, and headed toward the high school entrance. Before she got through the door, Rochelle had her by the arm.

"Ava—I've been trying to call you for three days! I heard about the fight. Forget about him." Rochelle took Ava's backpack and opened it for the security guard.

"I was sick." Ava said, scanning nearby students for curious eavesdroppers.

"I don't blame you for staying home," Rochelle said in a huff. "He's such a jerk!" Her friend flipped a red curl over her shoulder. "And, we don't have to eat in the cafeteria. If you don't want him staring at you, we can eat in the tech room. I got permission."

"Who said we had a fight?" Ava whispered when they got to their lockers.

Rochelle looked behind her then anchored a hand on each hip, lips tight, eyes narrow. "Carina told Crystal's sister that she saw Timothy push you into the wall by the courtyard. She said you hit your head and Timothy laughed at you."

Ava grabbed her arm. Pulled her close. "Rochelle—that's not at all what happened!"

"Do not cover for him. Do not! I don't care how much you like him. I will not let him smack you around. Will not! It's called assault!"

Both hands up, Ava shook her head. "Rochelle—listen to me. Timothy did *not* hit me. He would never do that."

"I want to believe you, but battered girlfriends usually lie to protect their jerk boyfriends." Rochelle crossed her arms. Scowled at her with dagger-ready eyes. "The next time he wants to talk to you, I'm not leaving," she added, curls flinging as she jerked her head back and forth. "I'm gonna stand there and stare at him like I'm a serial killer."

"No. No serial killer stares," Ava demanded, "Except for Carina. I take that back. Not even for Carina."

Rochelle's jaw dropped open. "Did Carina make all that up? You said she was jealous."

Ava shook her head. "Timothy and I were talking by the courtyard, but he didn't hit me. He was upset. After he left, I started having a migraine so I grabbed my head. If Carina was watching us, she might have thought she saw something else."

"Oh . . . well . . . okay. I'm glad he didn't hit you. Timothy wasn't at school on Friday either, and Crystal said she heard he got arrested, so I just thought . . . you know."

Ava put a hand to her forehead. "What a mess. This is just between you and me."

Rochelle nodded and stepped even closer, her ear almost touching Ava's nose.

"Timothy had a doctor's appointment on Friday. That's why he was gone."

"What?" Rochelle pulled her chin back. "How is that a big secret? Did you hit *him*?" She covered her mouth, scanned the hallway. "Was it self-defense?"

"Unbelievable. No!" Ava shoved her backpack in her locker. "I have to get to chemistry. We can talk about this later, but it's not a big deal. Really. See you third period."

* * *

Ava sat through her first two classes, wondering if Timothy had heard the ridiculous rumors. She couldn't stop thinking about him. Love was really more of a torment than anything else. Someone should really change Valentine's Day to October 31st.

At lunch, Ava assured Rochelle she wanted to eat lunch at their usual table even though several of the girls might pry for information. Rochelle took on the role of self-appointed conversation police and diverted any attempt to ask Ava about Timothy. At one point, Rochelle had taken her role so seriously that Ava chuckled, until she noticed Timothy heading for the restroom.

Apparently operating on his own autopilot setting, he startled when he caught her eye and looked confused, as if he forgot something or didn't know where he was going. He scanned the cafeteria, then returned to his table.

What just happened there? Was he practicing self-control or was he ashamed that she knew what he was doing? It didn't matter. It was his choice, and he stopped. A small victory but a victory nonetheless.

* * *

By Friday, Ava realized she'd almost made it through a week of classes with her will to survive still intact. Life would go on after all. Timothy wasn't far from her thoughts, but every minute of her day was no longer filled with obsessive regret. Rochelle asked her if she wanted to go to the home game that night. *Do life,* her dad had advised her, so that's what she'd do. Timothy didn't play in the Varsity game anyways.

The plan was to go to Rochelle's after school and from there to the game. Things gradually settled into Ava's new normal, and Timothy hadn't taken a purging break all week.

Ava hurried to fourth period and took her seat. When her teacher asked the class to turn in their homework, she realized she'd left her tablet in her locker. After a considerable amount of pleading, her teacher agreed to let her get it. She hurried through the empty hallway, turning to cut past the senior lockers, and then froze. It was Timothy at the end of the hall. She stepped behind a shadowed column and watched him fiddle with something in his pocket. He looked around before taking a few slow steps away from his locker, not having opened it, then beelined for the restroom by the exit.

Not giving it a second thought, Ava sprinted down the hall, threw the bathroom door open. "Timothy—don't do it!"

"Ava! What the heck!" He tossed his hands in front of him, as if she planned to tackle him to the ground.

"Please, no!" she shot out, struggling to catch her breath.

"Are you crazy? You can't be in here!" He took her by the arm and dragged her toward the door.

Grabbing the paper towel dispenser, she pulled against him. "No! I'm not leaving! I won't let you puke your guts out anymore!"

"Is this your idea of an intervention?" He released her. "Ava—get out of here."

Setting her jaw, she stepped further into the bathroom and crossed her arms. "I don't care if you hate me."

"Go back to class before you get us both expelled," he said through clenched teeth, finger jabbing at the door.

She widened her stance, arms crossed, heart racing.

Timothy pushed a hand through his hair. "What do I have to do to get rid of you?"

She didn't say a word. Getting rid of her wasn't an option.

"This is messed up! Can I please relieve myself in private, or do I have to do it with an audience?"

"I'm not stopping you from relieving yourself, and you know it." she shot back.

He looked at her with raised eyebrows and unbuttoned his pants. "Do you really want to do this?"

Ava's heart thumped even harder, her chest beginning to ache. He was going to win this battle. "Stop it!" She lunged forward and locked her hands around his neck.

"Ava!" Timothy pulled at her arms. "Ava—let go!"

"No! You have to stop!"

Gritting his teeth, he yanked hard on her arms. She landed on his foot, her ankle twisting to the side as she threw her arms out to catch herself. Timothy grabbed for her, but he was too late. She fell hard, hitting her head with a solid thud on the edge of a urinal. Eyes closed tight, she pressed both hands over the sharp pain, pulled her knees in.

"Ava!" Timothy knelt down beside her. "Ava, let me see."

"I'm okay," she squeaked, her head beginning to pound, warm blood spilling through her fingers.

"No! Crap! Ava—you're bleeding!"

Eyes clamped shut, she could hear the rustle of paper towels, the sound of running water. Timothy knelt down beside her, pulled her hands away, and pressed damp paper towels over the cut.

"Look at me. Ava, look at me."

Eyes forced open, tears spilled down her face, but pain hadn't conjured these tears.

"Oh no, Ava." Face pale and brow pinched tight, Timothy leaned in so close she thought he might kiss her but he stopped short and dabbed her cheek as if she were made of butterfly wings. "I'm so sorry, Ava." He wrapped an arm around her and carefully helped her to her feet, then led her to the sink.

She attempted to wash a hand while keeping pressure on the back of her head.

"Here, let me. Keep pressure on that." One at a time, Timothy took each bloodstained hand in his, rubbed soap over it, and rinsed it.

A shoulder up to swipe a tear from her chin, Ava sniffed as he patted a towel over her hands and replaced her makeshift bandage.

"I'm taking you home. Your mom will want you to see a doctor." Timothy pushed the bathroom door open and held it for her, a hand on her elbow.

"We can't just leave." She moved past him and stood in the empty hallway, her palm pressing the towel on the back of her head.

"Really? Now you're worried about the rules?" He kept a steady hand on the back of her arm and walked her toward the office.

"There's a game tonight. If you leave, they won't let you play."

"Can you hear yourself right now? You might need stitches. I'm taking you home." It wasn't a question.

* * *

"You could go either way," the school nurse said as she wrapped a thick gauze bandage on the back of Ava's head and took a close look at her eyes. "Even little cuts on the head bleed like the dickens. It's not too bad; maybe one or two stitches, but I think it will heal up fine without any." The nurse eyed Timothy. "I need to call your parents, Ava."

"They're not home." Timothy said, looking out the window. "I tried to call them. Neither one picked up."

Ava looked at him, but he didn't face her.

One hand on her hip, the nurse informed Timothy that Ava had an emergency contact.

"I don't think Rochelle's mom is home today," Ava told her.

The nurse pressed her lips together. Shifted her weight from one hip to the other. "Tell me again how this happened."

"I was running in the hall and fell against the locker," Ava blurted.

"That so? And this boy here just happened to be passing by in the middle of class?" The nurse shook her head. "I'll sign you out. I don't know why. You're both good kids but today you're both liars." The nurse pointed an accusing finger at them. "We've got cameras in these halls, you know. I could go take a peek for myself."

"Thank you, Mrs. Jackson. You can trust us," Timothy promised as he rushed over to help Ava to her feet.

"A hen's tooth I can." The nurse said with a hint of understanding.

* * *

Ava didn't say another word until they walked up to her front door. Timothy pressed the handle. "Do you have a camera code? It's locked."

"My mom's usually home. Probably went to the store. The key's in that fake rock." Ava pointed to the flowerbed along the front steps.

"You still use a key? They still make those?" Timothy said with nervous sarcasm as he slid the key out of the secret compartment and opened the front door.

"My mom's not really a fan of all things digital. Why did you lie about calling my parents?" She asked, as he put the key back.

"I needed to take you home . . . myself." Holding her arm, he shuttled her into the house, closed the door, and helped her into the living room. "Your mom's not here, so maybe it's only a half lie," he added with a smile that didn't reach his eyes. "Want some water?"

"Sure. The glasses are to the right of the sink." Ava sat down and leaned back against a cushion on the sofa, instantly regretting it. She squeezed her eyes shut until the wave of pain subsided.

Timothy returned with a glass of water, set it on the table in front of her, then sat next to her on the sofa, a noticeable distance between them. "Ava, I'm really sorry."

"No. It was my fault. Timothy . . . if you tell me why you do it, I promise to leave you alone." She kept her eyes closed, hoping it would somehow make it easier for him to answer.

For a long five seconds he stayed silent. Ava resisted the urge to look at him.

"I can't be like my brother. Billy was strong . . . good at everything, responsible. It was my fault Billy died. Everyone kept telling me it wasn't. I knew it was. My dad can't forgive me. He knows it was my fault."

Eye's open and pulse quickened, Ava forced herself to keep a steady stare on the glass of water in front of her and keep quiet.

"I feel like I'm, I don't know, stealing his life . . . if I do what he did."

Ava felt his eyes on her. She needed to resist distracting him.

"When I, you know," he said with a roll of his hand, "throw up, it helps me. Somehow, it makes me feel better. I don't know why. Probably just stupid."

Out of the corner of her eye Ava noticed his hands clamped together, alternating a tight grip, first one hand squeezing, then the other.

"I'm making things right. You know, fair."

A glimpse at the weight of his grief, Ava rested her head on her open hands. He'd given her access into his private pain, unbearable pain that would kill him if he let it. She waited for him to continue, but he sat next to her—silent, exposed. "I never knew Billy, but if he's anything like you've described, he wouldn't like what you're doing to yourself. If he were here, he'd want to be proud of you . . . tell all his friends that you're his brother."

"If he were here." Timothy stood to leave, clearly done reliving past hurts. "Will you please text me later tonight? I need to know you're okay." His gaze held hers, his uncertain, vulnerable blue eyes heavy and troubled.

Ava replied with a nod and leaned forward to stand up, wincing as pain pulsed through the back of her head.

"Don't get up." He walked to the door and pulled it open.

Now she had to stay true to her promise and leave him alone. Leave him with grief she couldn't comprehend. If she had anything else to say, this was her last chance.

"Can you do me one favor?" She hoped and prayed her request wouldn't offend him.

He faced her, arms hanging heavy at his sides, likely burdened from all the trouble she'd caused.

"Play your game tonight like your brother's there."

Not saying anything, Timothy stood statue still for a few seconds then opened the door. "That's just it, Ava—he won't be." The door closed behind him with a quiet click.

Her ear trained to the sound of his retreat, she listened to his fading steps and the familiar rumble as his pickup pulled away from the house. When she could no longer hear it, she curled up on the sofa and cried herself to sleep.

Change in the Game

Chapter 20

He knew she wouldn't be there. Out of habit, Timothy scanned
the top bleacher. Ava would not have come to his game even if she
hadn't hit her head. If she were smart, she'd stay as far away from
him as possible. With a pasted on smile for his mother, sitting in her
usual place on the front bleacher, he shot a few easy layups, most of
his effort spent on retrieving the ball.

The JV team moved through their warm-up routine, then took
the bench. Timothy watched the starters try a new play only to lose
possession of the ball and fall behind another two points. Head
down, he tapped his fingertips together in a slow, steady rhythm,
seconds, minutes, hours wasting away while he sabotaged every
chance at a meaningful life.

Early in the second quarter, the coach paced the floor and
pointed at him. "Gray, you're in."

Less than ambitious, he pulled his warm-up off, tightened the
drawstring on his shorts, and checked in, subbing for a tall, awkward
sophomore sucking in air like a panicked swimmer.

"Eat much?" a player on the visiting team scoffed.

Timothy ignored him and took his place on the floor. Nothing
mattered to him—the taunts from the other team, this game, his
father's disappointment. If his father would let him quit, he wouldn't
even be here.

"Come on, Timothy," a man called out from the bleachers,
"Make us proud."

Timothy glanced over the sparse crowd, not expecting the
enthusiasm. He saw the usual collection of parents, one reading a

newspaper. A few rows of varsity players packed up to leave and get ready for their game. On the end of the bleachers sat a meager group of fans, most of them girlfriends of players or those that wished they were, and boys that were there because of the girls.

The only real talent on his team attempted a three-point shot that bounced off the rim. Timothy rebounded it, lobbed it in, taking a chop to the arm. Feeble applause came from the bleachers, the lion's share from his mother, while players lined up along the key for a foul shot. They were ten points behind; the other team's second-string players already subbed in for most of their starters. This game was going to be a blowout. The goal: not to be humiliated by a record-breaking point spread.

"You got this," a man called out.

Timothy made the free throw and shuffled uninspired to the other end of the court.

"That's it. Start it off now."

Timothy searched the bleachers for the overzealous fan. His mother seemed just as curious, craning her neck to scan the main entrance.

"Oh—no way," Timothy mumbled. He found the mystery fan.

Ava's father, in his suit and loosened tie, leaned one arm on the bleacher railing. Was he here to talk to him about Ava's accident? Why would Mr. Roberts cheer him on if he wanted to ice him?

A surge of nervous adrenaline pulsed through his tired body. He got the ball and quickly passed it off. Another player attempted a poorly aimed shot, shifting the game to the other end of the court.

Out of the corner of his eye, he could see Mr. Roberts now sitting on the end of the bleachers. Timothy moved into position while one of his teammates scuttled around like a confused crab, leaving his man wide open for an easy shot.

Timothy threw the ball in from the sideline and jogged up the court, his coach expressionless as he signaled the same play they'd bungled a dozen times. Timothy caught a pass several feet beyond the half-court line, waited for another player to move past a screen.

"Shoot it, Gray!" Mr. Roberts boomed like an M-80, startling everyone in the gym.

As if struck by lightning, Timothy launched the ball. For a split second, the only sound in the gym was the *swoosh* of the net as the ball fell through it.

His mother jumped to her feet and screamed as if they were in triple overtime at the championship game. The coach stood motionless. A starter from the other team subbed in.

A player from the visiting team sneered as he jogged past him. "Lucky shot, loser."

One of his teammates on the home bench started to chant, "Tim—Tim—Tim." The other team missed a shot that banked off the backboard. Timothy snatched it and drove to the other end of the court.

His team jumped off the bench. The chanting grew louder, "TIM—TIM—TIM—"

He made an easy lay-in, the gym erupting with applause, prompting the visiting coach to call a time out.

"Get him a water bottle," Timothy's coach ordered, pushing him to sit on the bench. "You got enough air in you to stay in?"

He nodded and took a quick drink.

"This is the play. If Tim's open, feed him the ball. If he's not, run number three until he is open. We practiced it. But Tim, you switch to the shooter position. If they double up on him, Ryan, you break to the basket. Make it happen." The coach grabbed Timothy's shoulders. "Let me know if you need to take a break, got it?"

"Got it." He'd stay in, but he wasn't up for being the star of the game.

Mr. Roberts clapped his hands as they returned to the court. "Let's go, boys!"

The excitement in the gym made its way into the hallway and cafeteria. People waiting for the varsity game downed their last bite of pizza as they claimed a seat on the bleachers or stood by the entrance. The locker-room door opened, the varsity team, some half-dressed for the next game, stood at the home end of the court.

Timothy's hands began to shake, his body warning him that his energy reserves were nearing empty. Six more trips up and down the court caused a major upset in the game. He sank two three-point shots, assisted on two others, moving their score ahead by one point. The entire gym pulsed with energy he wished he could tap into, but his lungs burned and his empty gut tightened. He couldn't run anymore. He had to give up.

His coach called a time-out, a wave urging the team to hurry off the court.

Timothy fell on the bench and pulled a towel across his drenched forehead. From across the gym, Thatcher, the varsity coach, gave him a thumbs-up. Thirty-one seconds remained in the first half.

"Timothy, less than a minute to go," his coach said. "Thatcher wants you to float up tonight. If you want to play in the varsity game, you'll have to sit out the last half. It's your call," his coach nodded as if he'd already agreed to it.

Timothy rested his elbows on his knees, gulped in a lung full of air. "Yeah, I'll float."

The offer would be his temporary cover. He couldn't finish this game let alone play in the next one. He'd have to tell Coach Thatcher he didn't have anything left. At least he wouldn't let his JV team down. And, not all floaters got playing time in the Varsity game. Maybe he could get through the night without letting too many people down.

The referee blew his whistle, calling the players back to the floor. Timothy pulled himself off the bench, partially recovered in the short break. The second he had the ball, three defenders crowded him as if the rest of his team were decorations on the court. He passed the ball off, his teammate making an easy lay-in for another two points. With ten seconds on the clock, Timothy stole the out-of-bounds pass, sunk another three-point shot from the far corner of the court, the gym erupting with thunderous applause.

The buzzer sounded, signaling the end of the first half. Timothy stayed on his feet until he reached the locker room, then sprawled out on a narrow, wooden bench, arms and legs like anchors.

"Nice job, bro! You've been holding out on us." His teammates covered him with congratulatory pats, ruffled his hair.

He'd been holding out on them. Instead of pats on the back, they should have been angry with him.

As Timothy watched the third quarter from the bench, he began to realize how the punishment he'd placed on himself had affected those around him, people he cared about. He looked across the gym at his mother and smiled. Her eyes were swollen from crying, but she beamed with pure joy.

"I love you," she mouthed, a hand on her chest.

"Love you too, mom," His heart hurt for her. She wasn't there for the game; she was there for him. She'd always been there for him. Maybe he should have given his dad a reason to be there. Too little, too late. Not every father is proud of his son.

Someone walked along the bleacher behind him and tapped him on the shoulder. "Hey, Timothy, go ahead and eat this."

He took a small paper bag from one of the varsity players. Asked what it was.

"Some energy stuff coach Thatcher wants us to eat before a game. Doesn't taste that great, but you'll be glad you ate it."

He thanked the player, reached in the bag, and tore open a foil-lined pouch with a picture of a runner on it. It didn't taste good, but he finished it.

Too soon, the JV game was over. The visiting team made a comeback, but not enough to win the game. With no time to stay in the gym to celebrate the win, Timothy headed off the court. He made it to his gym locker, smiling at every player that tried to stoke his confidence.

"Way to go, Gray," his friend, Jase, said with a slap on his shoulder. "Glad to have you back, bro. We're taking on Liberty tonight. I'm looking forward to meeting up with that animal, Callahan. Guy needs to be in a cage. Gonna be a smackdown. By the way, you looked good out there. Still got the moves, don't you?"

"If you say so," Timothy replied with a chuckle.

"You know it. Got all the ladies screaming for you. Tim—Tim—Tim," Jase sang in his highest falsetto, hips swaying. "Got me all jealous, buddy."

"Whatever, Shoemacker." Timothy pulled his jersey on over a white t-shirt, the uniform doing little to hide his wasted frame.

"Speaking of ladies," Jase said as he tightened the drawstring on his shorts. "I didn't see Ava in the stands with Rochelle. Heard she hit her head on a locker. Big time bummer. Hope she's okay. Everything all right?" Jase wasn't usually one to press him for info on personal matters, but when it looked like he and Ava had something going, Jase had championed the idea. Even pushed

Timothy to ask her out, though having Jase go along on a double date wasn't the original plan.

Now wasn't the time to talk about his relationship woes. Jase knew he and Ava were no longer together, as if they ever were, but Jase didn't know why. "She probably isn't up for the noise," Timothy said. "Bad headache and all. I was going to give her a call. You know, check up on her." Timothy fished his phone out of his gym bag, tapped Ava's contact ID, and hovered a thumb over the call icon. Did she even want to talk to him? What a colossal mess.

"I'll take that, Mr. Gray." The coach snagged his phone. "You know the rules. No phones until after the game." Coach Thatcher handed him a pair of varsity warm-ups. "These should fit; they have a drawstring. Timothy . . . it's good to see you doing your thing."

Timothy thanked him, then chewed the inside of his cheek. "Coach, I don't know how long I can play. I want to, but I'm not in the greatest shape." Mr. Thatcher had coached both him and Billy, and Timothy knew he'd fall far short of any expectations based on his abilities before his brother's death.

Coach patted his shoulder. "How 'bout we play it by ear." It seemed as if Thatcher had something else to say, but decided against it.

The band started to add another level of energy to the gym, drums thumping, horns blasting out a decades-old dance tune. As the team left the locker room, Timothy took his place at the end of the line. After working through a few drills, he stood at the edge of the court while the announcer called out the names of the starters, the crowd cheering for each one.

At the end of the first quarter, Timothy's nerves began to settle. When halftime was almost over, the home team was up by six points, and he hadn't left the bench. If they'd been farther ahead, he might have been subbed in. He was not in any way disappointed.

Three years ago, this was his and Billy's team. His brother was so proud when his sidekick made the varsity squad. After his brother's death, the game wasn't the same without Billy. Nothing was the same without Billy. He thought he had something with Ava, but that went south along with everything else that mattered to him. He knew his brother wouldn't have wanted him to give up—not on the team, not on anything. With no footsteps to follow in, he'd have to forge his own path, but he was no trailblazer.

Missed It

CHAPTER 21

"Honey, are you all right?"

Ava woke to her mother brushing strands of hair away from her eyes.

"I would have let you sleep, but I was worried about you." She gently touched the bandage on the back of her head.

Ava sat up, grabbed her mother's arm." What time is it?"

"It's almost nine. You've been asleep on the sofa since I got home around three."

"The game!" Ava jumped up, winced, and held the back of her head.

"Sit down, Ava. I got a text from the school, so I called the nurse. All she could tell me was that you fell and cut your head but it didn't look like you had a concussion or needed stitches. What happened?" Her mother tugged on her sleeve. "Sit down, Ava."

Ava slumped down and slapped the cushion next to her. "The varsity game is half over by now."

"You know you can't go. Besides, it would be over by the time we got there. We can watch to the rest of the game online."

It wasn't the varsity game she cared about, it was the player she'd traumatized, sitting in the bleachers.

"Are you going to tell me what happened?" Her mother fished through a basket on the coffee table.

"Later. What are you looking for?" Ava asked. "Mom, you don't need the remote. Just use voice command."

"I'm not interested in talking to a sultry-voiced-pseudo female. Maybe if the voice was more of a baritone sounding Welshman I'd

115

be more open minded about having conversations with a non-person."

"Like a Viking? Dad would love that," Ava said with a smirk.

"I know I'm old fashioned." Her mother switched the television to local-live-stream podcast and selected the game feed. "I thought Timothy was on the JV team?"

"He is, and I missed it."

* * *

"And we're back in after the half," the sportscaster said, speaking over the noise of the crowd. "The Colfax Bulldogs fought to close a seven point lead held by the Liberty Lancers, but the Bulldogs are having trouble getting their shots to drop in the third quarter."

Ave pulled a cushion onto her lap and slouched over it. Maybe she didn't want to watch the game after all.

"I kept some soup warm. You need to eat something." Her mother got up and went to the kitchen without waiting for a reply.

"Coach Thatcher, calling a time-out with the bulldogs now trailing thirty-eight to forty-seven. Coming in for Liam O'Connell and Warner Berg are senior Jase Shoemacker and senior Timothy Gray."

"What?" Certain that the announcer had not said what she'd just heard, Ava activated the voice command and told it to turn up the volume, then rewound the feed and closely studied the image on the screen. She'd heard right!

"Floating up tonight from the JV team, Timothy Gray surprised the crowd by scoring fourteen points in a matter of minutes during the JV game, assisting another six. This is Gray's first time on the varsity court . . . this year."

As the game progressed, Ava focused on the voice and image on the live-stream, desperate to catch any glimpse of Timothy and agitated that she wasn't there to watch him. Unfortunately, the JV game wasn't online.

"Here's your soup." Her mother set the bowl on the coffee table. "What's going on?"

Ava put a finger to her lips and whispered, "Timothy's playing."

"In the varsity game?"

"Mom, shush. Please." Ava looked at her with an apologetic grin.

"Berg is back in the game, and Shoemacker, going in strong—takes it to the basket! We have a whistle. A charging foul called on Shoemacker, and the Lancers will go to the line for one. That's the third personal foul for Shoemacker. Callahan takes the shot . . . and it's good, moving the score one point in Liberty's favor, the score now forty-eight to thirty-eight. Berg takes the ball up the court for the Bulldogs and sends it over to Gray. The pass goes to Shoemacker. He goes up for the shot. It looks good . . . but falls short of the net. The ball is hit out-of bounds, and possession will go to the Lancers."

Ava paced the floor during a commercial break. If only the camera would show more of the court instead of panning the crowd.

"Both teams now showing signs of fatigue as Liberty slows the pace and brings the ball down the court—and Gray!—out of nowhere—steals the ball and drives it in for two! They did not see that coming. And the Lancers call a time-out with the lead. Lancers forty-eight, Bulldogs forty."

One hand clasping the edge of the monitor, Ava pointed at the close-up of Timothy flashed across the screen for an all too brief second. "He's playing! Mom, he made a basket!"

"That's fantastic, honey." Her mother set a bowl on the table. "Why don't you eat something?"

"I will. Later."

With the game back on, Ava sat on the floor directly in front of the speaker, no longer aware of the ache in her head.

"We're in Colfax with ten seconds left in the third quarter as the Lancers and the Bulldogs return to the floor. It's Liberty's ball and Callahan brings it down, goes up for three and it's noooo gooood. Five seconds left on the clock, Berg passes it to Shoemacker, the ball goes to Gray, and . . . he scores! I can't believe I'm seeing this! A three-pointer for the Bulldogs!'

"There's some discussion on the court. Was the shot made before the buzzer? Yes—it's good! Bulldogs closing the gap going into the fourth quarter, Lancers with a five-point lead, forty-eight to forty-three."

"Mom—did you see that!" Ava slunk flat to the floor while a commercial flashed on the screen.

"That is marvelous. Can you eat now?" Her mother stood guard over the bowl of soup on the coffee table as if her mission was not complete until Ava consumed it.

Ava complied, moving to the sofa and eating half of the bowl's contents before claiming a full stomach. She searched the screen, disappointed to find Timothy on the bench.

"We're back for the fourth quarter as the Colfax Bulldogs host the Liberty Lancers. It's the Bulldog's ball and they bring it in from the sideline, senior Liam O'Connell coming in for Timothy Gray. The Lancers, working a man-to-man defense, aren't making things easy for the Bulldogs. O'Connell passes to Shoemacker, back to O'Connell. O'Connell goes to basket; the shot is . . . no good. There's a whistle, a foul called on Liberty player number three, Colby Callahan. O'Connell will go to the line for two. Looks like some trouble on the floor. The referee, having a few words with both O'Connell and Callahan, and O'Connell takes his place at the free throw line. O'Connell sinks the first shot, and the second shot . . . off the rim. Callahan goes for the rebound. O'Connell, clearing out a generous space under the basket, goes for the ball, and—Oh, my! Callahan goes to the floor. It looks like things are heating up here in the fourth quarter. A foul is called, Timothy Gray coming in for number eleven, Liam O'Connell. And Callahan will go to the line, shooting one-and-one. Liberty's coach is not happy with the call. It looks like he wants an intentional foul against O'Connell, but he's not going to get it this time.'

"The first shot is good. And Callahan . . . sinks the second shot. The score now fifty to forty-four, with the Lancers holding the lead. Gray throws the ball in. Shoemacker doesn't waste any time getting down the floor. The ball goes back to Gray. Can you believe it! Another three-point shot for Timothy Gray! And the Lancers call a time-out."

Ava resisted the urge to jump around the living room, choosing instead to drum on the floor with her hands. "I knew he could do it! I knew it!"

Her mother looked at her with that grin mothers have when they think they know something. "He is a nice kid."

Ava narrowed her eyes and pointed at the screen. "Don't interrupt the game, Mom."

"Liberty throws the ball in. Oh! The crowd is not happy. Callahan, charged with a technical foul, and Gray is on the floor."

"What?" Ava studied the picture, images of concerned students and parents floating across the screen. "Why don't they show Timothy? Nobody wants to see the crowd!"

"Timothy Gray, clearly not expecting the hit, is still down. The game between the Liberty Lancers and the Colfax Bulldogs will return after a short break."

"No! Unbelievable! What's wrong with that guy?" Ava punched a couch pillow. "What a jerk! It's just a game! Why do they have to do that? I hate that kid."

"You hate him because he's playing a physical game and he plowed over the person you like—a lot?"

Ava looked at her and scowled. "If Timothy's hurt, I hate that guy—Callahan—stupid jerk."

"What if he's not hurt?" her mother asked.

"Then I don't hate him, but he's still a jerk."

"We're back at the game between the Bulldogs and the Lancers. Senior Timothy Gray up and at the foul line for two, the Bulldogs maintaining possession. He sinks the first shot, and the score is a close forty-eight to fifty, the Lancers with the two-point lead. The second shot is . . . good, bringing the Bulldogs one point away from a tie game. Berg, in for Gray, passing the ball in from the sideline."

Ava lay on the floor and hugged the pillow she'd pummeled seconds earlier.

"I'm glad you two made up."

"What?" Ava asked, wondering if her mother knew more that she was saying.

"I really liked that pillow."

Ava rolled her eyes. "Mom, you're not funny."

Timothy stayed on the bench for the rest of the quarter. The Bulldogs won by two points, but the victory didn't matter to Ava. She continued to worry that an injury kept Timothy out of the game.

* * *

Shower on, Ava pulled the gauze bandage off her head and carefully washed the blood out of her hair until the water at her feet ran clear. Certain that she wouldn't be going to sleep after a seven-hour nap, she dried off and pulled on an oversized t-shirt and sweats, found her cell-phone in the living room, and saw that her father was home.

"Dad, you were at the game?"

"I was." He winked at her and set his briefcase on the table.

"Did you say anything to Timothy?"

"Nothing you need to worry about. I was a supportive fan. The kid can shoot the ball." Her father took his shoes off and dropped onto the sofa, stretching his long arms across the back of it.

"Did you see that Liberty player hit him?" Ava took a few steps closer, her thumbnail in her mouth.

He patted the cushion next to him. "Sit down, babe."

Ava sat next to him. He put his hand on the back of her neck, his eyes soft.

"That Callahan kid is a beast. He and our guy, the O'Connell boy, definitely had some kind of Irish temper thing going on. I don't think the Liberty kid meant to hit Timothy as hard as he did, but Timothy is maybe half his size and couldn't take a hit like O'Connell. O'Connell is built like a brick wall. I think, more than anything, Timothy got the wind knocked out of him. He'll have a few bruises in the morning, but he'll be fine."

"Did you know that your father played basketball with Coach Thatcher in high school?" her mother asked as she sat on the other side of her father and pulled his tie off. "A long, long time ago."

"Careful now, missy. You're only a couple of years younger than me." He planted a kiss on her mother's lips.

Ava rolled her eyes in mock disgust. "That's it. Goodnight."

Sitting on the edge of her bed, Ava sent Timothy a text. "*Sorry I missed your game. Really wanted to be there. Watched the end of the V-game game on live-stream. Sounded like you took a hit. Hope you're ok.*"

Ava set her phone on muted-strobe and put it on the nightstand. She didn't want her parents to hear if he called her. He might not want to talk to her, not after the attack in the bathroom. He did ask her to let him know how she was doing, but what else was he supposed to say—*don't ever call me again because you're a psycho*.

What she wanted to tell him was that she couldn't stop thinking about him, that she cried when she heard he'd suddenly taken the court by storm. If he cared to make a difference in the game, maybe he could make other, more important changes.

Every few minutes she checked her phone to see if Timothy had seen her text. Finally, at ten o'clock, she could tell he'd seen her text, but, five, ten, fifteen minutes later, he still hadn't responded.

"You have to be okay with it," she whispered as she checked the screen for the last time.

The most important thing for him was to deal with his grief, and tonight he had taken a huge step in that direction.

Her finger hovered over the power button. If she left it on, she would check it for hours. Before she turned it off, the screen flashed in her hand.

In a near panic, she swiped a finger across the screen. "Hello?"

"Good, you're still awake. Where were you?" Rochelle asked, clearly excited to fill her in on everything she missed.

Ava tried to disguise the disappointment in her voice. "I'm sorry I couldn't make it to the game, but I watched it online. Crazy, huh?"

"I don't even know where to start," Rochelle replied. "Heard your dad caused a scene at the JV game. Why was he there without you?"

Ava switched the phone to her other ear and sat up straighter. "What? My dad was at the JV game? What did he do?"

"Your dad's not shy, is he? He kind of started the whole thing. Anyways, you should have seen Timothy. This huge player smashed into him. The guy was super hairy like a bear. So gross. Everyone knew it was totally on purpose too. It looked like Timothy was knocked out cold. Ava, I can't believe you missed it! Wait . . . hold on a second."

Ava could hear a muffled voice in the background.

"Sorry, I have to get off the phone. Talk to you tomorrow."

"See ya." Ava set her phone back on the nightstand, laid her head on her pillow, and closed her eyes, willing herself to do the impossible and go to sleep. She felt herself finally drifting . . .flashes of faint light . . . stars twinkling against a dark sky—Timothy!

Ava threw her covers back and grabbed her phone flashing on the nightstand. He replied to her text.

"I know it's late, but can I talk to you for a few minutes?"

Ava sent a quick reply, *"Sure. Go ahead and call."*

"In person? I'm at your front door."

"What?" Ava jumped up, threw her phone on the bed, and pulled a sweater over her t-shirt and sweatpants. Not wanting to turn any lights on, she ran her hand along the wall and wove through the dining room furniture until she reached the front door. As quietly as possible, she pressed the handle down and pulled the door open.

"You're here!" Ava stepped out onto the dark porch and slowly closed the door.

Timothy pushed his hands in his pockets and looked at his feet. "Ava, I—"

The porch light suddenly blinded her. The front door opened. Her father stood there in his robe as if it was perfectly natural to catch his daughter sneaking out of the house to talk to Timothy in the dark.

"Evenin'. I enjoyed watching your game, son," Eric said, scratching the top of his head.

"Thank you, sir." Timothy's eyes shifted between her and her father's like a hunted deer.

"It's kind of late, isn't it?" her father said, his voice casual.

"Dad, just a few minutes. Please?"

"You two can talk inside." Mr. Roberts held the door open for them and turned the living room light on. I'll give you fair warning though; I'm coming out here in my whitey-tighties in ten minutes to join your conversation."

"Thanks for the warning, Mr. Roberts. I wouldn't want to see that," Timothy said with a cautious grin.

Her father chuckled as he walked down the hall and shut his bedroom door.

"Do you want to sit down?" Ava asked, pulling her sleeves over her hands and noticing his damp hair, the clean spice scent of soap or maybe shampoo.

"I need to . . ." He turned and pushed on the door that was already closed, clearing his throat. "I uh . . . Are you sure you're okay?"

"I am." She touched his arm then pulled away. "Sorry I missed your game. I really wanted to be there."

With a tight smile he faced her for a fraction of a second, then shifted his gaze to his hands. "It was really loud. It's a good thing you stayed home. You know, your head and all. You probably have a killer headache." He shook his head and cleared his throat again.

Ava could see his nostrils begin to flare, his chin tight. Slowly taking his hand in hers, she hurt for him. Did he even know how much she truly cared? He thought she lied to him.

Timothy squeezed her hand, his weight shifting as he inched toward her. "I want to tell you . . ." He dropped her hand and wrapped his arms around her, pulling her against his chest. "Thank you," he said, his voice cracking, "for not giving up on me."

"Never." She pressed her cheek to his chest, feeling the release of her own harbored anxiety.

He kissed the top of her head, swiped at the moisture building in his eyes, and ran his hands down the side of her shoulders as he stepped back. "I have to go. I don't want to see your dad in his man briefs."

"You can't unsee that," she replied, her eyes fixed on his, not wanting him to leave.

"I'll see you later, okay?" He pulled the door open, letting in a rush of cold air.

"Yes, I'd like that. Timothy, it means a lot to me that you came over." She followed him onto the porch, her hands tucked up to her chin.

Eyes downcast, he shuffled to face her as if he'd dropped something. "Ava . . . *you* mean a lot to me." He leaned in and gave her a quick hug, pinning her arms, then turned away and jogged across the street to his pickup.

Ava watched him leave until his taillights disappeared. She could have worded her promise better. Timothy practically asked if he could still see her. But did that mean see her as they passed in the hall or see her like she'd like to see him?

This Isn't Healthy

CHAPTER 22

At school Monday morning, Rochelle glared at Ava with a long, hard stare. "You didn't fall against the lockers."

"Where'd you hear that?" Ava asked.

"If you would call me, I wouldn't have to get secondhand information from the T.A. in the front office. How many times are you going to do this?" Rochelle's concern seemed to border on anger.

"Do what?" Ava asked as they walked down the hall.

"Make excuses for Timothy. You're a wreck every other day and then you're back together with him. I'm worried about you. This isn't healthy. It's not, Ava."

"You know what, you're right." Ava took her friend's arm in hers.

Rochelle, her closest friend, witnessed Ava's entire emotional roller coaster with few facts to filter her observations through. Had Ava been in her shoes, she might have come to the same conclusions.

Rochelle pulled her into the empty choir room. "Right about what?"

"I didn't fall against a locker; I smacked my head on a urinal when I tried to attack Timothy in the boy's bathroom." Ava faced her with an exaggerated smile as if she were joking.

Rochelle cocked her head and crossed her arms. "That's not funny."

"There's a lot I haven't told you. Please trust me on this. Timothy is in no way trying to hurt me. I'm trying to help him, but it hasn't been easy. He's having a hard time dealing with his brother's death."

"His brother's death?" Rochelle wasn't going to let her off the hook that easy.

"Honest. I'm not going to lie, I like him, but he has far bigger problems than girlfriend issues. Don't tell anyone, but he has an eating disorder. Pukes everything up."

Rochelle dropped her arms. "He does? Is there anything I can do to help?"

Ava assured her she'd been helping her all along by being her friend.

* * *

Due to Timothy's apologetic insistence, Ava spent very little time with him for an entire week. She ate lunch with Rochelle and the freshman girls. Seated at a table across the room, he'd catch her eye and smile, leaving her to wonder if he missed her as much as she missed him. At the end of every school day, she and Timothy exchanged small talk for a few minutes, him fidgeting and her avoiding eye contact as she skirted around the things she wanted to talk about but knew not to; things off limits, at least for now. Maybe this was the see-you-later he had in mind. Nothing more—ever.

At the end of classes on Friday, Ava made her way across the parking lot for their five-minute ritual, dodging old cars with new drivers. As usual, she found Timothy waiting, leaning against the driver's-side door of his blue Dodge, a sympathetic smile lifting one side of his face as she walked closer.

"Hey. How you doin'," he asked.

"I'm good." She leaned back beside him and bumped his side with her shoulder, mimicking his half grin. They stood quiet for a few seconds, watching the commotion, horns honking, kids shouting over the fifty-plus cars maneuvering through the parking lot.

"'Sup, Gray," One of the guys on the JV basketball team yelled as he drove past them, an arm out the window.

Timothy pointed and waved as the car passed, then shifted a pebble between his feet. "I'm seeing a counselor."

125

A dozen questions surfaced but remained unspoken, his telling her about the counselor already approaching an understood off-limits line. "That's good, right?"

"I don't know. I guess." He reached over and tugged on her coat sleeve. "Are you doing anything this weekend?"

She wanted to say, *yeah—thinking about you every minute of the day*, but she knew better than to distract him away from the help he needed, a rescue and healing she alone was not equipped to provide regardless of how desperately she wished she could. Space and time, the two things she could give him, she did. "Just hanging out at home. Nothing too exciting. You?"

"I uh . . . Ava I . . . did you play basketball in P.E. today?"

The way he looked at her, tender, vulnerable . . . oh, he asked her a question. "In P.E.? Yeah, basketball. I mean, yes, we played basketball. I made a few free throws since I am expertly trained, and—" She froze, the intensity of his stare leaving her speechless, her mouth half open as if she were in some kind of cosmic pause.

"Expertly trained, huh?" He tapped the side of her foot with his.

Her mother pulled into the parking lot, the car idling slowly toward them.

Ava took a step away from Timothy, the cold February wind blowing her hair over her face. She turned into the breeze and gathered wild strands, securing them with a hand at her neck. "I should go." What she wanted to say was *we can make this work.*

"You know I miss you, right?" He leaned toward her, pulled hair away from her eyes and tucked it down by her hand, brushing his fingers over hers, then stepped back, his attention shifting to the waiting car.

"I miss you, too, Timothy. But I'm not going anywhere. I'm a lowly freshman, remember? I'll be here for another three years, and you'll—." She'd said too much. With a weight in her chest, Ava stepped away from him. He'd move on. Without her.

He waved, his smile apologetic. "Can I call you?"

She nodded a reply, her grin forced, and reached for the door handle. It was a nice thing to say, but he probably wouldn't call.

Timothy stepped back and slowly waved until she could no longer see him.

* * *

"What are your plans today?" her mother asked.

"Don't have any." Ava picked at her scrambled eggs, fork in a slow spin between two fingers.

"A free Saturday. What are we going to do with ourselves? Dad had to go schmooze potential clients at a lunch in Walla Walla. We could go shopping. Maybe go to lunch?"

Not exactly excited, Ava agreed to the plan. Shopping wasn't Ava's favorite thing to do, but it was better than being bored at home.

As they were backing out of the driveway, Ava's phone buzzed in her pocket. A text. "It's Timothy!" He wanted to know if she'd like to go ice-skating with him in Spokane at Riverfront Park.

Her mother gave her a knowing look, pulled back into the driveway, and turned off the car.

Ava read the text again for the fifth time. "I could go with him after lunch, if you want to shop for a few hours first."

Her mother shook her head. "You go. Spending the day with Timothy trumps shopping with Mom. We'll go another time."

Ava thanked her for understanding, then replied with a quick, "*Yes, I'd love to,*" and apologized again for ditching her.

"Oh, poor me," her mother teased, "I'll have to suffer through the new remake of Pride and Prejudice I downloaded. It's my Valentine's gift to myself. Four hours of cinematic torture."

"I thought today was the twelfth. Are you sure it's the fourteenth already?" Ava asked pushing the car door open.

"Yes, it is. Looks like Timothy gets a break from his restricted schedule. Imagine that, he wants to spend Valentine's Day with you. Weird, huh?"

With an unsuppressed grin, Ava turned to face her mother. "Best day ever!"

* * *

The drive to Spokane with Timothy felt like a first date. Ava admired the scenery, both inside and outside his pickup, as he entertained her with reenactments of the latest if-people-were-cats videos. Ava couldn't help laughing, appreciating the freedom they now had to get to know each other, neither of them having anything to hide.

When they were half way to Spokane, Timothy grew serious, told her he thought his counseling was helping, and thanked her for attacking him in the bathroom. But he didn't want to spend any time discussing his issues. He wanted to have fun and enjoy the day with her. Ava agreed to comply, suspicious that he was following orders rather than setting fun-day ground rules.

"You might regret this," Ava warned. "I might need to hang onto the wall the whole time."

He encouraged her, promised to help her. Told her she'd be able to skate backwards by the end of the day.

* * *

Their skates on, they stepped onto the Ice Ribbon at River Front Park. Sun out and air still, it felt warmer than the forty-one-degree temperature scrolling on the digital sign across the street. Timothy held her hand, pulling her along the lazy-river shaped rink.

"I won't let you fall," he said. "I promise."

A young boy in hockey skates tumbled in front of her. Not sure how to stop, Ava tried to turn but suddenly skated along as if hooked to a clothesline, her coat pulled up tight under her arms. Another clothesline skater fumbled forward on the other side of Timothy, the young hockey player scooped up and ferried along in Timothy's other hand. He let go of the surprised boy and loosened his grip on her coat.

"Are you good?" he asked trading her coat for her hand.

Certain that she would have plowed into the boy, she eagerly agreed when Timothy offered to go over a few basics. Hand in hand, he led her to the side of the ice. Ava listened, enjoying his coaching enthusiasm as much as being his student. He showed her the toe pick on the front of her skates, how to stop and turn. She must have been having too much fun, because he squinted at her and asked her what was so funny.

"You're a good coach." She grinned and looked at her skates.

Timothy stood and pulled her arm closer. "How is that funny?"

"It's not funny, it's . . . nice." She stole a glance at him.

Judging by the gleam in his eye, he didn't mind her opinion of his coaching skills. He spun around and faced her. "Want to try skating backwards?"

"No!" She grabbed his arms. "I can barely go forward."

"You can do it." He held her waist and spun her around to follow the flow of traffic.

She wobbled, feeling awkward while maintaining a death grip on his arms. "Remember, some people are hard to coach."

He chuckled at the reference to their fun day of street hockey, but after showing her how to push her skates, his expression grew serious.

"Am I doing that bad?" she teased, wanting to support his fun-day directive.

"I wish all of our memories could be like today. No cracked heads or, you know, regretful things said. Mean things."

"Fun day, remember?" she said with a pat on his arm. "We need to have lots of days like this one, then those others will fade away."

Staring at her for several long seconds, his expression softened. He pulled her closer. "I don't deserve you," he whispered.

Tempted to take the we're-much-more-than-friends approach, she instead replied with a squeeze on his arms.

"I'm turning you around," he warned.

Ava felt a twinge of disappointment. She liked the closeness. Maybe it was too much for him.

"Ready?"

A weak bob of her chin gave him the go-ahead, her skates angled for the move. Timothy kept her close as he helped her turn, wrapping an arm around her waist. Not what she expected. She loved skating.

For another hour, they moved along the course, keeping their conversation light and away from regrets. Without warning, an amateur skater, apparently intent on improving his speed, plowed into the back of them. Ava felt the momentum swing her into a long arc toward the edge. Timothy followed, sandwiching her tight between him and the wall, while a pile of disgruntled skaters exchanged words with the careless Olympic wannabe.

"You okay?" he asked, pushing his hands against the wall to give her room to breathe.

"Is that called a body check?" she asked, fixing her hat.

Timothy seemed amused, his smirk and one raised brow suggesting otherwise. "If anyone checked like that in hockey, they'd get punched."

A warm flush and wide grin claimed her face, prompting Ava to look over her skates. "Well, I'm not going to hit you."

"No? Good to know." He took her hand, pulled her away from the wall. "We better get something to eat," he said with a satisfied smirk and a pat over his heart. "Don't want to have too much fun."

* * *

Ava polished off a burger piled high with cheese and pineapple and was working her way through an order of steak fries when she noticed Timothy watching her. "What?"

"You seem . . . hungry," he replied with a playful expression.

"I am. We've been skating for over an hour." She glared at him in mock offense. "Are you saying I'm a pig?"

"No. But I've never seen you mow through a meal like that." His eyes sparkled as if hoping for a rebuttal.

"If that's your idea of flirting, you need to try something else," she said cocking her head and taking another bite of a thick fry dripping with sauce.

"Flirting?" He scrunched his eyes and flashed his broad toothy smile.

Ava tossed the fry back in the basket, looked away. "I swear, you can—"

"Can what?" he whispered leaning in close.

With a liar's grin, she told him she forgot what she was going to say. What he could do was leave her speechless when he looked at her like that. The way he snickered at the exchange suggested he knew exactly what had her tongue-tied. She loved every taunt and tease. Loved being with him. Loved him.

Timothy excused himself to go to the restroom, reassuring her that it was for natural processes. When he came back, his pants were partially unzipped, t-shirt sticking out through the zipper.

"Timothy—your pants." Ava looked away, embarrassed for him.

"Oh good, you noticed. I wanted to make sure you knew why I went in there."

"You're crazy." Still turned away while he fixed his pants, Ava noticed a disapproving glare from an elderly woman a few tables away, whose husband was laughing.

* * *

Full and satisfied for multiple reasons, Ava leaned her head against the pickup window as Timothy drove home. An old Steven Curtis Chapman song, *All Things New*, played on the radio while she watched the sunset on the horizon, palettes of coral, pink, and deep blue stretching across the sky beneath layers of wispy clouds.

"Isn't that beautiful?" She said, "God does good work, doesn't he?"

Timothy glanced over at her, then back at the road ahead. "Yeah, he does. And the sunset isn't bad, either."

Turned his way, she mirrored his warm smile, a wordless agreement on what they both knew. They were more than friends, but for his sake, they needed to act like they weren't. This was a perfect day. "Thanks for teaching me to skate. I had a lot of fun." The ride home was turning out to be the highlight of the entire trip.

"You're welcome. Thanks for agreeing to go on hundreds of other dates with me." Timothy kept his eyes on the road, a smug grin speaking for him.

"What? Not that I don't want to, but I don't remember talking about that?"

"Those weren't your exact words. I think you said, 'We need to have lots of fun days like this one.' You know, that's totally the same thing."

"Totally," Ava agreed.

* * *

Timothy seemed conflicted when he walked Ava to her front door. He smiled, but she sensed a sudden uneasiness about him, his eyes down, hands pushed deep in his pockets.

"Maybe we could go on another adventure, you know, since we have so many to do," he said, looking at the ground.

Why did he seem so uncomfortable? "I'd like that. Is there something else?"

He jerked his head up. "Is it that obvious?"

Ava pulled one of his hands out of his pocket and laced her fingers in his. "If there's something you need to tell me, just say it."

Something over her shoulder drew his attention. "I'm not supposed to get . . . get too . . ." He bit his lip then breathed through his mouth and turned away from her.

She wouldn't finish it for him, but *serious* seemed to fill the blank.

Timothy slowly pulled his hand from hers, his brow pinched and eyes vacant.

"It's okay," she said, her hands clasped behind her.

Ava took a step back, but Timothy suddenly closed the distance between them and pressed his mouth over hers. Is this what he wasn't supposed to do? If it was, she wasn't about to stop him. Reaching up, she ran her hands behind his neck, pulled him closer, kissing his soft lips, her fingertips trembling as she framed his jaw.

Timothy leaned back, then looked down at her as if he'd broken a cardinal rule, his chest rising and falling as if in need of air. He wrapped an arm around her shoulder, the other around her waist, and held her tight against him, his chin pressed against her ear. "I have to go," he said, his voice raspy. As soon as he released her, he nearly jumped off the porch and ran to his pickup.

Still holding on to the front-door handle, Ava felt a little light-headed, her feet unsteady as she went inside. Ava didn't wonder why. Who wouldn't feel a little light-headed after a kiss like that?

* * *

"Do you want to give dinner at my house another try?" Timothy asked her on Monday as they walked to the parking lot after school.

"Sure. Maybe I'll stay this time." She poked his side. They'd definitely crossed the just-friends line but there remained a distance between them. The fact that she knew about his inner demons could have been reason enough to slow the romance thing. Whatever it was, she'd let him work through it without demanding an explanation.

"I'll have to put a tracking collar on you as soon as you get there. Is that going to be a deal breaker?" He put his hands around her neck, leaving his ribs exposed for her to jab.

The plan was set for Saturday evening, but unlike last time, both his parents would be there. More than once Timothy had insinuated a strained relationship between him and his father. In few words, he'd told her that his father hadn't forgiven him for his brother's death. Ava still wasn't sure how Billy died.

For the past two weeks, Timothy saw a counselor. The fact that he went was all she knew about it. She wouldn't pry into counseling details but hoped his sessions provided the help he needed.

Ava had a dilemma of her own, but she wouldn't expect more from Timothy than he already offered. On his cue, she'd dialed back the flirting, wanting to help him focus on things more important than her, but the harder she tried to support him, like a good friend would, the more he distanced himself, the flirting on their ice-skating excursion, the kiss, all but forgotten. No more rides home from school or private conversations. And, for the rest of the week, they ate lunch with their own friends, only spending the last few minutes of every lunch hour and school day saying hello or goodbye. The whole shift in their relationship was hard on her. And confusing. He would text her every night, usually a meme or a shared video, but never a personal message.

The kiss he gave her, almost a week ago, hadn't exactly suggested a platonic relationship. Timothy seemed conflicted, even afraid when she kissed him back. It was difficult being attracted to him while some unseen force wedged itself between them. Then again, if this forbidding force helped him more than hindered, she'd do her best to respect it. By Friday, she wondered if he regretted inviting her over, but at the end of the day he mentioned their Saturday dinner plan as if nothing had changed between them.

* * *

A little nervous to meet Timothy's father and somewhat embarrassed to face his mother after her last hasty exit, Ava watched out her dining room window, scanning the hill for Timothy's blue pickup. The anticipation of spending alone time with him hitched up

133

her pulse. They'd gone to Spokane together one week ago. A week that felt more like a month.

"Be a good girl and try to keep your hands off him," she whispered as she watched the road.

"What was that?" her father asked as he joined her in the dining room.

"What?" Ava replied, still facing the window.

"You look like one of those dogs watching the sliding doors at the grocery store. You can get them to look at you unless the doors slide open. Their favorite person is inside and that could be them now."

"So, you're saying you've put some effort into getting their attention?" Ava asked with a smirk, still watching the road.

"What else am I supposed to do while I wait for your mother?"

Chin up, Ava smiled at him and walked over to the door. "My favorite person is here."

"You can wait right there for dream boy. If he's your favorite person, I need to keep a closer eye on him."

"Dad, don't embarrass me."

Ava opened the door, and after a quick greeting and discussion with her father over the expected time of her return, she and Timothy were finally together again—just the two of them.

CHAPTER 23

"I'm glad this worked out," Timothy said as they pulled out of the driveway. "I need to warn you though, my mom's going a little overboard."

"What do you mean?" Ava asked, noticing how nice he looked in his sweater. Caramel . . . good color on him. Maybe she did need to be reminded to keep her hands to herself.

"Earth to Ava?"

"Oh, uh, can you repeat the question?" Ava chewed her lip and grinned an apology.

He side-eyed her, a knowing smile turning up the corners of his mouth. "Ava—I didn't ask you a question."

"I guess I didn't hear you," she replied, fiddling with the pocket flap on her coat. "Sorry."

"I was telling you that my mom made too much food. I didn't want you to feel obligated to try everything. But now that I think about it, I do recall you wolfing down that burger last week. So maybe . . ."

Ava crossed her arms and looked out her window with pretended offense.

Timothy laughed, put his hand on her shoulder. "You're so fun to mess with."

They teased each other for a few minutes, then rehashed their day in Spokane, recalling the young boy she almost fell on and the speed skater wannabe that plowed through half a dozen people. She praised Timothy again on his coaching skills. He pointed out that she was easy to coach. The only thing they didn't mention was the kiss.

* * *

As they walked up to Timothy's house, Ava asked if there was anything she should know.

He seemed sheepish, as if she might know something he wasn't telling her. "My dad does have an eye on his forehead. Just act like it isn't there. My mom will ask you to do some ritual singing and dancing before we can eat. You know, with fans and stuff. Other than that, it's pretty normal."

Ava scowled at him. "You're so helpful. Do your parents have any pet peeves? Things not to talk about? Does your dad have anything against real estate brokers?"

His arm draped over her shoulder, Timothy assured her she had nothing to worry about and opened the door.

Only one step inside, Ava wished she'd worn a dress rather than a sweater and jeans.

"Hello, Ava," Grace nearly sang as she joined them in the entryway. "I'm so glad you could come."

Ava thanked her for the invitation, not missing the tender emotion evident in the tears building in Mrs. Grays eyes.

Timothy's mother stood quiet for an awkward, few seconds, shifting her attention from Ava to Timothy and back again. "Oh, can I have a hug already?" Grace gave Ava's shoulders a tight squeeze then apologized for being overwhelmed. "Ava, it's nice to see you again. So very nice."

"Mom," Timothy said, his voice slow and deliberate. "Why don't we all go to the living room?"

"Yes, of course. I'm sorry. Where are my manners? Here, let me take those coats for you."

They shed their coats, then Timothy grabbed Ava's arm and hurried her into the hallway. "I take back the comment about everything being normal," he whispered.

"I like your mom. She's sweet. At least *she* gave me a hug after not seeing me for a while." Ava peeked at him, hoping the insinuation hadn't crossed any lines.

"You brat," he said, locking his arm around her neck and pulling her tight to his side.

"I can't help it if I missed you," she whispered.

"I know. Sorry about that." He didn't offer an explanation but took her hand and led her down an impressive tiled hallway lined with art and tropical plants. Large arched windows offered a view of a fenced courtyard with leafless, dormant shrubs bordering an empty fountain.

"This is really nice. Did you say your dad built it?"

Timothy shrugged. "Yeah. It's his thing, building stuff."

Mrs. Gray's quick steps tapped along the tile behind them. "Timothy, why don't you introduce Ava to your father? He's in his study. And tell him dinner is almost ready."

His smile as fake as George Washington's teeth, Timothy took her hand and shuffled down the hall to a paneled double door, one side sliding into the wall with the touch of a button.

"Dad?"

As they made their way into his father's study, Timothy's grip tightened on her hand. Apparently, he wasn't fond of this room, or more likely, its occupant.

A large man with a thick build and the same sandy blond hair as his son, stood in front of a digital drafting table. "Well hello there. You must be Ava," the man said, turning and looking at her over his reading glasses.

"Ava, this is my dad, William. Dad, Ava." Timothy released her hand and took a step back.

"It's nice to meet you," Ava said, shaking Mr. Gray's offered hand.

"The pleasure is all mine, Ava."

Timothy's father had a pleasant expression, but the lines around his eyes suggested weariness. Mr. Gray set his glasses on a side table and took one last look at the print in front of him, possibly reluctant to interrupt his work.

"Dinner is almost ready," Timothy said, his voice flat. He then curled his fingers around her wrist and turned to leave.

"Take a look at this, Ava," his father said, scratching the back of his neck. "I could use a fresh pair of eyes here."

"Not normal," Timothy whispered in her ear and followed her to the drafting table.

"See this." Mr. Gray pointed to an impressive image of a commercial building. "I'm assuming you're neither an architect nor an engineer."

"Right—neither." She smiled at the man, curious to know why he would care for her opinion.

"Look at the beams extending beyond the roofline. What do you think of them? Timothy, I want your opinion too," his father said, stepping back to allow them both ample space to consider his question.

Bracing himself with a hand on the edge of the table, Timothy cocked his head toward the image. "It's a building. Can we please go eat now?"

Inspecting the beams, Ava noticed they were progressively curved like a wave but they seemed out of order. "That one looks like it's in the wrong place," she said, pointing at the beam over the entrance. She turned toward Timothy, thinking he might validate her opinion.

He moved closer, his bored expression replaced by a hint of interest. "Yeah, it does. The beam over the door doesn't fit the curve. The pitch of the angle is too steep."

"That's exactly what I thought," his father agreed. "Unfortunately, asking an architect to change their design doesn't go over well. Somewhat akin to asking Michelangelo to use different colors."

Mrs. Gray came into the study, requesting that the conversation continue in the dining room.

* * *

Enough food for a dozen people sat on the table. A roast with carrots and potatoes was arranged on a large platter surrounded by sauces and salads. Several small dishes held something Ava couldn't identify, and a basket of warm rolls filled a cloth-lined basket.

"You've been busy, Grace," Timothy's father said, looking over the table.

She insisted it looked like more work than it was, then explained the contents of the side dishes, claiming them Timothy's favorites.

"You need to come over more often," Timothy told Ava. "I had mac-n-cheese and a nuked hot dog last night."

His mother reminded him that he'd turned down an offer of leftover casserole and warned him to stop making her look bad.

He clarified that his mother was an awesome cook and then surprised Ava by asking her if she was ready to do her dance for them, a hand over his mouth, mischief in his eyes.

"Timothy," Ava replied with a self-conscience glare, "what about your special song?"

His mother put down her fork. "Son, I thought you didn't want Ava to know it was your birth—"

"Mom," Timothy protested, his face flushed, "It's not important."

"Wait. Today is your birthday?" Ava felt both uninformed and fortunate to be his guest of choice. "That's a big deal. You're eighteen today, right?"

His attention on his empty plate, Timothy mumbled something about making a fuss over nothing. "Can we eat already?" He side-eyed Ava like a grade school boy unable to deny a crush.

Without a word, both parents took in the exchange, their silent stares shifting from their plate-inspecting son to her. Lower lip in her mouth to school a goofy grin, Ava also opted to inspect her plate.

Clearly entertained by the exchange, Mr. Gray chuckled, then offered to pray, thanking God for the food and the hands that prepared it.

* * *

On the way back to her house, Ava told Timothy she liked his parents and thanked him for inviting her to his secret birthday dinner. He apologized for not telling her but admitted he wasn't sorry for the dance comment—that it was worth the look on her face. She scolded him, taking advantage of the opportunity to touch his arm, the gesture disguised as a disgruntled push. This was what she wanted, a sense of normalcy.

Ava mentioned the blueprints his father asked them to inspect, hoping the nonthreatening comment might foster a kind word for his father.

"Not sure what William was up to," Timothy said, before changing the subject.

After a few minutes of easy conversation, an awkward silence began to build when he turned to drive up the hill. The closer they got to her house, the more uncomfortable the silence became. She tried to think of something to say but was distracted when she noticed his hand fisting the front of his coat.

"It sure is windy," Timothy said, keeping his attention on the dark road ahead.

"It's not too cold, though." Ava could tell something bothered him but wanted their time together, for once, to end without challenging his demons.

An unseasonably warm wind picked up, churning the trees and sending an empty garbage can rolling across the street.

Timothy did a U-turn and parked on the road in front of her house.

"I think my dad's home already," Ava said, thinking he might be concerned about blocking the driveway. Would you like to come in? We could nuke some hot dogs if you're still hungry."

It was getting darker, but she thought she detected a faint smile on his shadowed face.

"I better get back. Let me get that," he said, pointing at her door.

When he pushed his own door open, the wind rushed against it like an open sail. He hurried around the front of the pickup and pulled her door open, grabbing the edge of it to keep the swirling wind from slamming it back on her. Holding her hand, Timothy guided her to the front porch, her long hair stirred into a tangled mess.

Thankfully, the porch offered a degree of protection, allowing her cyclone of hair to fall over her face.

"Here, let me help." Timothy brushed a strand away from her eyes, tried to unwind another.

"It doesn't always pay to have long hair," Ava said, pulling another strand from her mouth.

"I like your hair." Timothy avoided her eyes but kept brushing strays back into place. He took a step closer, blocking the porch light. His face shadowed, he continued to comb through her now tangle-free hair.

As if a switch flipped, Ava took in a quick breath. Timothy stood motionless, his fingers woven through her hair. Slowly, he began to trace her ear, her face cupped in his hands. The wind subsided; air quiet.

He swallowed hard, then gathered her hair into a ponytail and laid it over her shoulder.

Her eyes locked on his shadowed face, but he looked away. Why did he seem so conflicted? What was he thinking? Torn between wanting to kiss him and knowing she couldn't, she reached up, took his hand, and pressed it against her cheek.

Timothy gently pulled his hand away and stepped back, then reached out and trailed a finger across her forehead . . . down the side of her face. "Your hair, missed some right here. Are you ready to go in?" He swiped the back of his hand over his open mouth.

"No," she whispered. With trembling hands, she took hold of his wrists and pulled him closer.

When he turned aside, light reflected in a glistening sheen rimming his eyes.

"Please tell me what's wrong?" Ava reached up as if his hair needed attention and gently ran a fingertip over his ear. "Timothy . . . please talk to me."

His chin down, he grabbed her hand, pulled her close, encasing her against his chest, his heart thumping against Ava's cheek.

"Timothy, it's okay."

"No, Ava, it's not," he whispered, one hand combing over her hair. "The things I said to you, really crappy things. And now I—"

She leaned back enough to face him. "But I know why. We're past that, right?"

He shook his head and ducked away from the porch light. "It's just . . ." His unfinished thought hung in the air like a lead balloon.

"I know you care about me," Ava said, resting her hands on his chest. "And I care about you."

Timothy blew out several long, nervous breaths and wiped at his eyes. "Ava, wouldn't it be easier for you if we *were* just friends?"

Her throat tight, she took a step away from him. "Is that what you want?" Why was he doing this? Didn't they have this relationship thing figured out?

The back of his hand to his mouth, he cleared his throat. "No." he choked out.

"Would it be easier for you? . . .Timothy? . . .Would it?"

"Ava—I love you." He rocked from one foot to the other, slipping further away from her, creating a breach between them. He then reached for her hand but stopped short of touching her. "There's nothing easy about this, but I'm a mess." He took another step back.

"Timothy?" The streetlight behind him blinded her from seeing his face. No, this doesn't make sense. She heard him sob as he shuffled backwards. He loves me? Why is he leaving like this if he loves me? "Wait—No!"

"I'm sorry, Ava." Timothy turned and ran to his pickup.

She watched him for a few panicked seconds. "Timothy, stop!" She leaped off the porch, sprinted toward the street. She wouldn't let him leave. Not like this. Grabbing the far corner of the tailgate, she launched herself around to the driver's side and yanked his door open.

Timothy jerked his hands up, dropping his keys. Ava snatched them off his leg and sent them sailing into a dark clump of trees next to her house.

"Ava—"

He leaned forward to get out, but she had other plans. She grabbed his neck and covered his mouth with hers. For a split second he froze, and then gently pushed her, not letting go of her arms.

"No." she sobbed, taking a step back as he got out. "Don't do this!"

He didn't reply as he turned her into the light.

"Say something," she pleaded, pulling against his grip on her arms. Was he afraid she'd lock her hands around his neck again with no intention of ever letting go? Actually, not a bad idea.

Timothy bent down and kissed her, let go of her arms and kissed her again. Not a passionate kiss, a goodbye kiss. An apology. Probably a last kiss.

"I told you, Ava, I'm a mess. You wanted to help me and you did. You really did."

"Can you help *me* then . . . with just one thing?" she asked, realizing things weren't going to go her way and knowing they shouldn't for reasons beyond attraction.

"How?" He pulled her into his chest and kissed the top of her head.

"I'm in love with this guy, he's amazing by the way, and I know it's selfish, but I want to keep him. To keep you, Timothy. What should I do?"

Resting his chin on the top of her head, Timothy let out a long, deep sigh.

"And," she added, "you're friend-zoning me."

"It's not like that," he said, his voice laced with apology.

She wrapped her arms tighter around him, the battle already lost. She wanted to plead, assure him she could maintain the distant-girlfriend routine without interfering, but knew she shouldn't. Her selfishness wouldn't help him.

"Ava . . . there are things I need to work through. My counselor said it would be better if, right now, I wasn't in a serious relationship."

"I hate your counselor."

"Ava—" He nudged her shoulders back. Faced her with pleading eyes.

"Sorry." She gave his back a pat and let go, putting a few steps between them. "I understand. I don't like it, but I do understand. Completely. I do. Really."

Leaning toward her, he ran a hand down the side of her arm. "Friends then?"

She forced a half-smile. "Yes . . . friends."

"We need to talk about this attacking thing, though. If we're going to be friends, you'll have to curb that."

It was like him to distract her in an effort to diffuse tension, but like he'd said already, there wasn't anything easy about this. She responded with a weak chuckle, as he stepped past her and slid behind the steering wheel.

"Ava, I need to go."

Both hands in the air, she swung to look at the dark, thick patch of shrubs next to her house. "Your keys! I'm so sorry!"

Timothy reached under the seat. "It's okay." He held up an extra set, looked at her as if she were the one pushing him away, his wounded expression begging her forgiveness.

"Do you think we can really be friends?" Ava asked as she stepped back so he could close the door, but he didn't close it.

"Yes, I do." His gaze grew painfully soft. "When is older better than new?" He took her hand, pulled her closer and kissed the back of her fingers.

Chin down, Ava felt this new distance in their relationship already wedging between them. "I don't know." What she did know, he was doing the right thing.

"Love is. When new love is put to the test, it often fails. Love that's been tested, you know, seen a few troubles, that's the real thing." Before releasing her hand, he kissed it again.

"You won that one," Ava said, a light wave of dizziness prompting her to grip the door. "We'll have to start a new game." She slowly pushed his door shut. "I love you."

"I love you, too, Ava," he replied over the rumble of the engine.

This wasn't just a relationship speed limit, a test of immature affection. It felt more like goodbye.

* * *

After Timothy drove away, Ava slipped into the house, surprised that her father hadn't heard her yelling and come to her rescue.

"Mom?"

Her mother leaned out of the kitchen. "Everything okay?" she asked with a sing-song voice, eyes too wide for a mother that's been minding her own business and grinning like a toddler caught with a handful of cake.

"Where's Dad?" Ava walked into the kitchen, a hand on the wall to steady feet that grew more stable with every step.

"I don't know. He's here somewhere." Her mother refolded the hand towel hanging on the stove handle.

"Mom, where's Dad?"

"Found 'em." Her father sang as he came in the back door.

"Dad!"

"Ava—you're home." Mr. Roberts walked into the kitchen, a hand stuffed in his pocket, hair tangled and littered with pine needles.

"Were you outside?" Ava took a bold step toward him.

"When?" He looked at her mother and shrugged.

Lola shook her head. "Sorry. Can't get you out of this one, Eric."

He threw his hands up. "Babe, when you yelled at Timothy, I thought he was attacking you. By the time I got outside, you nearly pegged me with his keys. And when *you* attacked *him*, I wasn't sure who to save."

Ava slumped against the counter. "Did you hear what he said?"

Her father pulled Timothy's keys out of his pocket. Set them on the counter. "No. When he pushed you away, I started feeling around for these and asked God to keep an eye on you two."

Ava brushed her hand across the counter, scooped up the keys. "I think everything's going to be okay. We're just going to be friends."

"Yes!" Her father pumped his fist, then quickly crossed his arms. "I mean . . . I think that is a very, very wise decision. Very wise."

Ava scowled at him but couldn't suppress a tired grin.

"You know, Lola," her dad said, grabbing his wife and dancing around the kitchen island, "I really like that kid."

Without You

CHAPTER 24

Sunday night, Ava heard her phone ringing in her bedroom and ran from the kitchen to answer it. The caller ID flashed with Timothy's picture. She took a deep breath, a finger swiping over the screen. "Hey."

"Ava, I need to talk to you."

"Is everything okay?" She closed her door and sat on her bed.

"Um . . . I'm leaving."

"Where are you going?" Ava pulled her pillow onto to her lap.

"Spokane. I won't be able to see you for a while. It's a treatment center."

Ava pushed off the bed, paced across her room. Weren't things getting better for him? "Okay. For how long?"

"It all depends. A few months maybe. Or longer."

"You don't want to finish basketball?" He was himself again, wasn't he?

"I can't. There's a few things I need to figure out."

Trying to keep her voice steady, she asked about school. She wanted to protest, but he wouldn't be going unless he needed to, and she wouldn't make it harder for him to leave.

"Got school covered." He sounded resigned, like someone tasked to dig a mile-long ditch. "Already switched to online classes."

"Timothy . . . I'll miss you." She rubbed a hand over her shoulder, hoping he could still call her. "Will you have your phone?"

"My counselor said something about that. Might not have it at first, but as soon as I can, I'll call you. Ava . . . I leave tomorrow."

"Tomorrow?" How long had he known? "Can I see you before you leave?"

"No, I'm sorry. I really am. I wanted to tell you last night, but you know. I couldn't."

"Then I'm not sorry I attacked you." She wiped a tear off her cheek and laughed that laugh that says *this isn't at all funny.*

"You know you're braver than I am. Ava . . . you've been good for me. You have no idea."

"I'm still here for you. I'll always be here for you." It was a promise. Not a hasty one, one she meant to keep.

"Listen to me, Ava. I want you to remember that we're friends now—okay? Go to the dances. Do things. You know, go out with someone if you want to."

Unable to reply, Ava swallowed over a building lump. She couldn't imagine it.

"Ava?"

She cleared her throat in an effort to steady her voice. "I heard you. You want me to do life." She wanted to add—without you.

"Exactly. Do life. I'll call you as soon as I can. It might be a few weeks. I'll try to keep you in the loop if that's okay. If you're up for that."

"Yes! Of course. Oh my goodness, of course I want you to call me!" She wasn't ready to say goodbye. "Wait, Timothy, I have a confession. Don't real friends tell each other stuff?"

"Maybe. You've surprised me a few times." He sounded relaxed, humored, his voice less strained.

A palm pressed on the dark window in her room, she tried to see through the northern shadows, imagined Timothy sitting in his room. Why was his live-cam blocked? "I went to your JV games to stalk you."

"You're stalling, Ava. You know I love you."

Shoulders heavy, she pressed a thumb into the corner of her eye. "Will you please . . . please say that one more time?" she asked, her voice cracking.

"Ava—" He coughed, cleared his throat, coughed again. "I love you, Ava."

A deep breath pulled in, she slowly exhaled. "Timothy—are you still there?"

"I am," he replied, his voice only a whisper.

She had to let him go. "I love you, too. Goodbye."

"Bye, Ava."

She waited to make sure he hung up. "Timothy?"

He was gone.

Face wiped on her sleeve, Ava found her mother working in the den. "Mom, Timothy is leaving."

Lola stood, closed her computer, and walked toward her with open arms. Ava's head on her mother's shoulder, the floodgates opened, releasing unrestrained sobs. Ava tried to talk. Tried to tell her mother that Timothy was leaving. "It's a hard thing . . . but a . . . good thing," she forced out between hiccups and gulps of air.

Her mother held her, patting and rubbing her back. "It is a good thing, sweetheart. I heard about it. Grace called me today. It's going to help him. He wanted to go. That's the best thing, right? Timothy wants to get better."

Ava hugged her and stepped back to lean against the desk, her last huffs of air settling into controlled, quiet breaths. "It's good, but I'm really going to miss him."

"I know you will. And I'm sure he'll miss you too."

* * *

The first week of Timothy's absence was the worst. At school, some people stared at her as if she were the cause of all his trouble. Rumors made their rounds, trickling from mouth to ear. Crazy stories. Rochelle attempted to quell all rumors within her earshot. Ava ignored them as best she could, offering no explanation when pressed for information. Carina blamed Ava for interrupting Timothy's healing process, something Carina claimed to be a part of until *a certain freshman girl* threw herself at him. Some rumors were harder to ignore than others.

At the beginning of the second week of his absence, the office called Ava out of her fourth period class. Someone was there that wanted to speak with her. The teacher told Ava the office didn't give a reason. "It's not an emergency," her teacher assured her. "That's all they said."

She loaded her backpack, classmates watching her with questioning looks. Was she in some kind of trouble? Empty hallways echoed the tap of her steps. A security guard leaned out from his post, chair creaking, then reclined back to face the monitors displaying entrances and exits. They exchanged nods as she walked past the checkpoint.

A school counselor met her in the breezeway outside the office, told her that an advocate from Timothy's recovery center was hoping to visit with her. "The advocate, Emily, spoke with your mother earlier today. Your mother called the school and gave permission for you to speak to her, but you have the right to deny the interview or refuse to answer any questions you're not comfortable with."

"Why would I deny it?"

The school counselor went on to explain school protocol and personal privacy rights. Since Ava's mother agreed to let the advocate speak to her, Ava chose to agree as well.

"I can go in with you if you'd like."

"That's all right. I'm good." Ava made her way through a maze of doors. She passed Jase Shoemacker who smiled and gave her a thumbs-up as he left the conference room, the gesture somewhat calming her nerves.

The advocate stood as she entered the room, a tall woman with a ready smile. Maybe in her early thirties. Striking, really, which surprised Ava given the fact that the woman was completely bald, huge gold hoops dangling just above her shoulders. They exchanged greetings and sat down. Emily filled Ava in on what her role was at the recovery center and why she was there. "Timothy's treatment is, how shall we say, is very regimented." She went on to explain that his contacts needed to be vetted, interviewed to ensure they would contribute to his recovery.

Ava leaned in, a hand on the table between them. "Contacts? I get to see him?"

Emily offered an apologetic half-smile. "When I say contacts I'm referring to phone calls."

Not what Ava was hoping for but better than nothing. She leaned back in her chair, ready to prove herself the most trustworthy contact known to man.

The questions started out easy then gradually delved into personal territory; had he ever threatened her, pushed or hit her, made her feel unsafe?

"No! None of those!" Ava wondered if the rumors about her and Timothy had influenced this line of questioning. "Someone thought he did but she was way wrong. Not even close."

Emily nodded as if familiar with the information. "Would you say you've exchanged heated words with Timothy? Misunderstandings maybe?"

This lady must know a lot about her and Timothy. Not accustomed to an open-book personal life, Ava shed all reservations. Whatever it took to help Timothy was worth it. "We've had some misunderstandings," she said with a shrug, "We've moved past them. Figured things out. It's not a problem anymore. Wait, what I meant is that yelling at each other was never a problem. He's not like that." She scooted her chair in and leaned on her elbows. What if she wasn't a good contact after all?

The advocate told her she understood, then asked if Timothy was ever angry with her.

Ava bit at her thumbnail. "Yeah. One time I think he was more worried than angry . . . except the time he thought I was lying about liking him." She pulled at a thread on the cuff of her sleeve. "Even then he wasn't like mean angry. I think he felt stupid. He definitely knows I like him now. I kind of made it obvious." Arms tucked tight to her sides, Ava grimaced as if poked by something sharp and glanced at the advocate.

Emily wore a knowing grin that seemed to lean more towards *isn't that cute* than *you just blew it, baggage-loaded girlfriend*. "Did Timothy mention anything to you about your relationship?"

"He did. Told me we needed to keep it a friend thing. I can respect that. For real, I can."

"I believe you. Well, thank you for talking with me. It was nice to meet you, Ava."

Her things collected, Ava made for the door. That went well. At least she thought it did. What if it didn't? She stepped back into the room. "When will Timothy be able to call me? He can call me, right?"

The advocate told her she couldn't say. His counselor would make that determination. "I'll say this, though: he's blessed to have a friend like you."

Her insides in an instant flutter, Ava wanted to ask if Timothy was getting better but instead offered a quiet thank you and left the conference room.

* * *

Almost two weeks, the middle of March, and still no call. Ava began to adjust to yet another new normal. Why couldn't she be content with the fact that Timothy was where he needed to be? Not knowing anything made contentment impossible. If she could talk to him, hear his voice, have him tell her that he's happy where he's at, it would make things so much easier. As if her life was what mattered right now. She scoffed at her own selfishness and shuffled to the car.

"What's going on in that mind of yours?" her father asked as he drove her to school. "I can hear the wheels spinning. This isn't a pout about us not letting you stay home alone, is it? I know you're old enough to be on your own for the weekend while your mom and I are gone. I trust you, I do, but I'd rather you stayed with Rochelle. It's for me. A dad thing. Isn't Rochelle excited about it, having you over and all? You can go shopping, put paint on your fingers, do girl stuff. Yeah? Do up your hair, and talk about . . . clothes. Right? Fun, huh?"

"Dad, I'm okay with going to Rochelle's."

He turned at the base of the hill, bottom teeth working over his top lip. "Oh. Well . . . that's good."

"I just miss Timothy. Thought they would let him call me by now." She drew a line in the condensation on the window. "Not knowing anything about anything is the hardest part."

"Love is no cakewalk. I mean, not that you're in love. It's just a saying. A good friend, same thing. Being a real good friend—that too has its challenges."

"Don't you mean piece of cake?" Ava asked him.

Her dad pulled his chin back, his signature did-you-just-challenge-me move. "No."

"You said cakewalk. That's not a thing." Ava crossed her arms, their mental sparring game a welcome distraction from unanswerable questions.

"It most certainly is, miss correct-opotamus. Have you never heard of a cakewalk?"

Ava watched the yellow light as they approached the intersection. "You just ran that light?"

Her dad scoffed at the reprimand. "It was light red. Anyways, no one was coming. Don't you ever do that."

"I see how it is." Tongue rolling in her cheek, she stared at him until he questioned her with a raised brow. "Being an adult must be a walk with cake, right dad?"

"No, babe. Trust me; it's called a cakewalk. It's a game. People buy a ticket, walk in a circle, and the winning number gets a cake."

"Right. They just get a cake for walking in a circle?"

They pulled into the school parking lot, her dad embarrassing her by honking at a crowd of kids blocking the parking space he'd apparently deemed his own. At least he waved at them.

Car door open, she thanked her dad for the ride and the misinformation.

"Obstinate youth. Getting through to you is no *cakewalk*." He blew her a kiss as she turned to shut the door.

"You made it up. Love you, Dad."

Unusually early, Ava took her time going through the temperature scanner and the security line, letting those around her funnel down to the single line in front of her. Her thoughts shifted to her father who had a way of distracting her into a cheerful mood. Maybe that was a dad's job, to cut up and tell bad jokes until their kids stop pouting. He definitely rose to that challenge.

A few minutes to spare before class, Ava added a few pictures to the collage inside her locker, syncing her phone with the digital frame. She touched the image, expanded it, and added a heart on the corner. Timothy leaning against his pickup stared back at her, eyes bright and full of mischief. Prince charming in loose jeans and a hoodie.

"Oh good, you're still here," Rochelle said as she emerged from a river of students. "I have something for you." She showed Ava a magnet. Held it up and waited for her to read it. *Friends are like four-leaf clovers, hard to find and lucky to have.* "Today's St. Patrick's and all. It's totally true, though. For you."

Ava thanked her. "I'm the lucky one." She put the magnet on the inside of her locker next to Timothy's picture.

For nearly two weeks, Rochelle had been keeping her busy. Really busy. After the first week, Ava stopped protesting when Rochelle wanted to go to the movies, hang out with her at the golf course, or go shopping. It wasn't helpful to stay home alone and wallow in loneliness. In all honesty, she enjoyed spending time with Rochelle. It was the get-up-and-go that didn't come easy.

Rochelle looked at Ava as if intending to apologize for something, then told Ava that Jase Shoemacker asked her to go golfing with him on Saturday.

It was like Rochelle to be sensitive. Her friend had to be crazy excited. Ava wasn't about to rain on her parade. "Are you kidding me? That's awesome!" Ava added with a smirk that Jase might make golf worth playing. Ava then remembered the plan, to be with Rochelle on Saturday while her parents celebrated their anniversary in Leavenworth. That wasn't going to happen. In no way would she let Rochelle cancel her first date with Jase. Maybe she could say she'd like some time at home on Saturday. Catch up on homework.

"You're not going to believe this, Ava, but I thought he was like, asking for free game passes. The course has only been open for two weeks. So, like a newb, I told him I'd have to ask my dad. Get this—Jase says, 'shouldn't I be the one to ask for his permission to go out with you?' Can you believe it?" Rochelle hugged the notebook she pulled from her locker, red curls dancing as she bounced on her toes.

Genuinely happy for her, Ava insisted she wanted to hear all about it.

Rochelle's elated expression made a wild shift, eyes wide, mouth open. "I totally forgot! Ava, I'm so sorry." Her friend stood there, a hand fanning gritted teeth.

"No, Rochelle, really, it's not a problem. I've got this report in Vocab and Comp. I'll stay home on Saturday. Then I can go to church with you and you can tell me all about it. Let's do that." Ava moved toward her locker as if the plan was already set.

"Not a chance," Rochelle shot back at her. "I tagged along on your date, Ava. You owe me. You're going golfing. Yep. That's it. Jase will get a fourth and we'll hit the green."

"No, Rochelle. I'm not going. You go with Jase and have a good time. I don't want to double with anyone. Really, I don't."

"Rochelle ignored her and tapped away on her phone."

"What are you doing? Don't make a plan."

Rochelle continued to tap, paused for a few seconds, then tapped again, her smile growing wider by the second.

"I'm not going golfing."

Rochelle nodded at her phone and slid it in her pocket. "It's settled. Jase is bringing his little brother, Jude. He's a sixth grader. Great little golfer. I don't think he'll try to put the moves on you."

That actually sounded fun. "Are you sure? Does Jase really want his little brother to tag along?" Or her.

"Totally. They're buds. And my dad will be stoked. He doesn't think I'm ready to date but agreed to it, after some pressure from my mom, since he'll be working at the course shortly after we get there. This is going to be awesome!"

Due to circumstances determined to be out of their control, their third-period teacher no longer allowed them to sit together.

* * *

As Rochelle gave her a play-by-play of Jase's invitation and their altered plans during the lunch break, Ava's phone buzzed in her pocket. Rochelle looked at her with eager eyes, but Ava shook her head when she saw the caller ID. Michael Azar. Ava didn't recognize the name and almost deleted the message but wanted to make sure it didn't have anything to do with Timothy. She opened the text, revealing a row of dancing hearts and waving flowers with a message that read: "*Don't respond. Not my phone. Breaking the rules.*"

"It's Timothy!"

She showed the phone to Rochelle, who made a huge deal out of it. One little message had Ava on top of the world for the rest of the day.

That night Ava got another short text. This time the caller ID flashed Timothy's name.

"I can call Sat. night @ 7 p.m."

She replied, telling him seven worked for her, and hoped he would respond again. There were no more messages. In twenty-four hours, she would finally get to talk to Timothy.

Do Life

Chapter 25

The anticipation of Timothy's call made Saturday feel like Christmas. Phone charged and snug in her jacket pocket, Ava helped Rochelle prepare for her date with Jase. They both dug through Rochelle's closet in search of the perfect casual yet flattering outfit, the forecast promising a sunny day with a high of fifty-six. When Jase arrived, Ava stayed in her friend's bedroom while Rochelle answered the door and introduced her date to her father. Seconds later, a rose-faced Rochelle returned to her room and huddled with Ava while Rochelle's father put the fear of death in Jase. Rochelle's mother slipped into the room and assured them that all was well and that fathers often have more bark than bite.

"Well, Dad has killed people, so there's that," Rochelle added.

"This isn't a war," her mother said, "It's golf."

Rochelle's father called down the hall announcing it time to hit the green.

Ava, relieved to find Jase survived the interrogation, followed Jase and Rochelle to the car, joined a waiting little brother, and headed for the golf course.

With swings, shanks, and hacks, the four of them played the first two holes. Ava tried to encourage Jude to play ahead of Rochelle and Jase, the date an awkward mix of third-wheel and younger-brother distractions. It didn't take long for Ava and Jude to fall into a brother-sister routine, him trying to instruct her on her golf swing and her telling him to respect his elders. Jude shared personality traits with his older brother, both full of themselves, full of life, and very attentive to their golfing companions. The four of them on their way to the tee box at the third hole, Jase informed his little brother that Ava was too old for him and to stop flirting with her. Jude responded with a red face and a wild swing at his brother's arm that missed the target.

In all truth, Ava found the day fun. A little cold when the wind kicked up, but worth it. By the fourth hole, Rochelle and Jase started conversing without clowning around. They were still loud, but they started talking about their interests and things they had in common. By the fifth hole, Ava and Jude were fifty yards ahead of them, challenging each other with every swing.

"On this swing," Ava said, "I bet I can hit over the creek."

Jude adjusted his ball cap and appeared to size up the challenge, a hand resting on the top of his club. "Maybe, if you don't shank it. I bet I can drop my hit two trees father than yours. At least."

"The two tree challenge, huh?" Ava gave him that you're-on look and drove her ball straight into the creek.

Jude's ego got a boost on that one, not that his ego was in short supply. Being an only child, Ava didn't know what it was like to have a brother or sister. Within a few hours of hanging out with Jude, she could see how special that sibling connection might be.

By 6:30, the four golfers were full of pizza and still reliving every detail of their day—Jude, Ava's new sidekick, loud and proud. At 6:45, she moved her phone from pocket to hand and drifted away from their corner in the clubhouse, both Jase and Rochelle giving her a nod of confidence.

"Jude, stay here," Jase said. "Ava has an important phone call. Hang with us, bud."

Ava headed for the path along the ninth hole, knee-high lights casting bright circles along the serpentine pavement. Sun down and air crisp, she pulled a sleeve over chilled fingers.

An older man shuffled toward her with a purpose in his step, his winter cap shielding his face as he tapped his walking stick in a steady rhythm. "You better zip up that coat, missy. You'll catch your death." He slowed his pace, his cap tipped as she slid the zipper pull tight to her chin. "There's a smart girl. Wish my grandson listened half as much as you do. You may know him. He's 'bout your age."

Ava checked her phone: 6:55.

"Name's Shoemacker. Jase Shoemacker. A name I'm partial to, since it's mine as well."

Ava gestured toward the clubhouse. "I do know him. In fact, we were—"

"And your name is?"

Perhaps the older man was hard of hearing. "Ava. Ava Roberts."

"Nice to meet you, Eva. You say you know Jase? I thought I saw his car here. Not at all unusual. When this place opens up, he's here more often than not. You see, his mother, that's my daughter, Kayla, maybe you know her. Anyways, Kayla tells me Jase has an eye for the manager's daughter. Maybe you know her. Michelle, maybe?" The older man placed both hands on the top of his walking stick and widened his stance. "No, that's not it."

"Rochelle?" She glanced at her phone, 6:56, and slowly edged past him.

He pivoted around his stick. "Sounds about right. What are you doing out here, anyway? It's time to head in. Gonna be a cold one before too long. And kids these days; I don't see a one of you wearing a hat. It's a wonder your ears don't freeze. And that coat of yours is half what it should be for this time of night. Why don't you join me? Could us some company on the trek back to the clubhouse."

Hands clammy, she took another step toward the dark course. Phone switched to sleeve-covered fingers, Ava swiped her palm over her waist. "I'm sorry," she said with a shrug, phone held up for emphasis, "I'd like to, but I'm expecting a call."

Without another word, the man offered a wave and trudged off toward the clubhouse. She hoped he believed her, the I-have-a-call claim a common way of saying I'm done with our conversation. Why did he have to be Jase's grandfather?

6:59 on the screen, Ava leaned against a tree and pushed all thoughts from her mind except Timothy. She began to feel dizzy, then realized she was holding her breath. "Don't pass out now." At exactly 7:00, her phone buzzed for a millisecond before she tapped the screen.

"Hi, Timothy." Light headed, she could barely talk. She wanted to see him, but the live-call camera only showed a picturesque scene of snow-capped mountains. Given where he was, it made sense.

"Miss you, Ava. I'm sorry, I've got to make this quick. Only have a few minutes." He told her he was allowed two non-family calls a week and asked if he could call her every Saturday.

"Of course—that's perfect. Can you tell me how you are or where you are, or no?" Ava wanted to ask him all kinds of questions but wasn't sure what was off limits.

"I'm okay. This place is in Spokane, probably four, maybe five blocks from the hospital."

"Timothy, really, how are you?" Fingers combing through her ponytail, she shifted to face north, as if to draw him closer.

"Fair to middling," he said with chuckle. "Honestly, my whole body hurts so bad I can hardly move."

Ava slid down the tree and sat on her heels. "Why, what happened?"

"Nothing to worry about. I have this personal trainer, more of a mentor really, that's trying to kill me. I think he wants me to be totally wiped out every night so I'll crash the second my head hits the pillow. You know, no down time at all."

"Is he mean to you?"

"No, no, not at all. He's more like a hammer of encouragement. Tell me about you, Ava. What have you been up to?"

"Me?" He probably couldn't talk about his treatment. "Well . . . Jase asked Rochelle out."

"That doofus. About time. Jase has been talking about her ever since we went to that movie. If they get together that's gonna be one loud couple. Good on him, though."

It was true. Both of their friends seemed to have an internal volume set on high.

"We're all actually at the golf course right now. A double date."

"Oh . . . I can let you go."

"Not even maybe. Nothing is more important to me than talking to you. By the way, I'm doubling with Jude."

"Jude? Jase's little brother? The kid's a clown. I mean a clown in a good way. What is he, sixth grade?"

"Yeah. We had a lot of fun today. Sure wish you were with us." Ava bit her lip. What could she say that wouldn't discourage him? "Does Jase know where you are?"

"He does. His brother-in-law is the trainer I told you about, the hammer of encouragement. Jase clued me in on this place. I thought I'd give it a try. And I'm sorry I can't tell you stuff. You know, rules."

"That's okay, I understand." Ava wanted their conversations to be as easy on him as possible. "I got this mystery call the other day."

"Anyone I know?" he teased, the bright tone of his voice like music.

"A really good friend," Ava replied, her throat beginning to tighten.

"Thank you for saying that. I have to go, but I want you to know, Ava, you've really helped me with some crazy . . . stuff. A crazy bunch of stuff. You're one seriously stubborn girl. And that's a compliment."

"Is it? Just remember you said that when you're done there. Do you know when you can come home?" The question didn't seem too invasive.

"I don't, but I know it's a good thing I got here when I did."

Ava felt the weight of his reply. She knew better than to meddle in things he wasn't ready to tell her. "I pray for you every night. Have you ever heard the verse that says, 'My help comes from the Lord'?"

"Yeah. That comes up here every once in a while. Starting to believe it. Love you, Ava."

"Love you, too, and loved hearing your voice. Bye, Timothy."

Ava stood in place and stared at her phone. Tears stung her eyes. Happy tears.

* * *

Monday morning on the way to school, Ava noticed flowers pushing out of the thawing ground, a handful of daffodils with bright yellow and orange trumpets blooming along the road. If it weren't for the stress that winter put them through, they would never be so beautiful.

"How are you doing over there?" her mother asked, as they turned onto Main Street.

"I'm all right. Since Timothy called, I don't feel so . . . I don't know, anxious. Things are getting better for him. It's not like I don't miss him, though."

"That's a healthy attitude. I know you miss him."

"I do. A lot." As they passed the pizza parlor she could almost smell the fresh-baked bread, see Timothy's wide grin as he asked her if she was looking for a man with a real job. "It's kind of weird, though," Ava said, as they waited at a stoplight. "I think not being able to see him makes me like him even more."

"That's not weird," her mother said. "Timothy is gone, so you're thinking about him all the time."

Ava smiled, acknowledging the obvious. "The whole distance makes the heart grow fonder thing?"

"You got it."

* * *

Ava moved through the first half of the day in a melancholy fog. Not depressed, just feeling the length of days before Saturday. At lunchtime, she sat at the freshman table of girls without Rochelle. Her friend was sitting with Jase. Although they asked her to join them, she didn't want to be the third wheel. At least not yet. As she picked at her salad and fake chicken, Ava fielded a few questions about Timothy, informing inquiring minds that she didn't have any details on his treatment, but she thought he was in a good place. One of the girls wanted to know if they were still together.

"We're friends," Ava replied, paying more attention to her lunch than their curiosity.

"So . . . I know someone who has the hots for you," Crystal said with a sly grin. "And since you're available, wanna know who?"

"Not really." Ava glanced across the cafeteria at Jase and Rochelle. Both of them wore those silly grins that seem to be the official insignia of a new crush.

"You don't even want to know?" Crystal seemed offended.

Not only did Ava not want to know, the information source hadn't always proved reliable. But more than that, she wasn't available. Available for what? Did she have a boyfriend vacancy?

161

No. There was no room available for a boyfriend. Timothy had encouraged her to date if she wanted to. She didn't. "I'm not available," Ava announced.

"What do you mean?" Crystal asked, "I thought you said you weren't going out anymore."

"I'm not, but that doesn't mean I'm available." Ava looked over the five confused girls staring at her and waiting for an explanation.

"Someone we don't know about?" the girl next to her asked.

"No. I don't need a boyfriend just because I don't have one. What if you get stuck with a dud because you were in a hurry to hook up? Why hurry? What's wrong with being friends?"

"That's lame," Crystal scoffed, then changed the subject.

Ava glanced back over at Rochelle and Jase. They weren't rushing things. That didn't mean Rochelle wasn't attracted to him, but Rochelle told her that getting to know Jase as a friend was all she could commit to until she knew him better. If Jase wasn't interested in being a friend first, then she wasn't interested in him. It sounded more like advice from her parents. Rochelle had plenty of guys that liked to talk to her, clearly in favor of her attention, but they rarely ventured beyond the ranks of friend-at-school-only. The fact that Rochelle's father used to be a sniper in the Marines might have influenced Rochelle's relationship status.

Ava wished Timothy was there. They could be friends. They could even be only-at-school friends, the decision easy now since she didn't have a choice.

Not disappointed that lunch was over, Ava stood up to leave, but the room suddenly went sideways. She plopped down and took a few deep breaths.

"You okay?" Crystal asked.

"Head rush. Got up too fast." Ava put her hands on the table, slowly stood up. Better, but a little nauseous. "I'm good."

By the time she got to her locker, the reason for her vertigo became painfully apparent. A whopper of a migraine stabbed at the side of her head. Doubled over, Ava pressed one hand over her ear, her eyes closed, teeth clenched, one arm wrapped tight to her gut. As much as she could, she hid behind her open locker door, hissed out quick breaths as students hurried down the hall. Oh no—I'm gonna throw up!

"Ava?" Rochelle grabbed her arm. "What's wrong?"

"Help me to the bathroom."

Rochelle wrapped an arm around her waist and practically carried Ava across the hall. Stooped over the trashcan inside the door, Ava brought up her lunch. That helped her stomach, but her head felt as if it were in a vice.

Knees giving out, she ran the back of her hand over her mouth and pointed at the floor.

Rochelle held onto her arm to steady her. "I'll be right back," her friend said as she helped her sit on the cold tile. "I'm getting the nurse."

Ava pulled her legs in, head on her knees. The lights were too bright, voices in the hall too loud . . . she could see two of everything. This was by far her worst migraine ever.

Legs began to materialize around her, girls asking questions, some curious, some concerned.

"Migraine," she whispered, hoping they'd all be bored with the truth and leave her alone.

The bathroom door opened again. Rochelle marched in, announced there was nothing to see. The legs shuttled away; the show over.

"What's going' on, Ava?" the nurse, Mrs. Jackson, asked as she knelt down beside her.

"Bad migraine."

"Okay, sugar, can you open your eyes for me? Have you had a migraine before?"

Ava opened her eyes, but she couldn't seem to focus on Nurse Jackson's face. "A few."

"I'm gonna call your mother." The nurse pulled a cell phone out of her blazer pocket. "Can you give me the number?"

"Um . . . 289 . . . 4 . . ."

"Here, I got it," Rochelle said, handing the nurse her phone. "It's ringing."

"Hello Mrs. Roberts, this is Jamila Jackson at the high school . . . Yes. Ava's not feeling' so good. Looks like a migraine. If I were you, just to be sure, I'd go ahead and take her on up to the doctor . . . The entrance by the ball field . . . You're welcome."

Ava tried to move, but the pain paralyzed her.

"Hold still, Ava," the nurse said. "Just relax, now. Your mother is on her way."

Ava heard Rochelle ask if she could stay with her. Nurse Jackson must have agreed, since Rochelle sat on the floor next to her.

"I'm praying for you, Ava," Rochelle whispered.

Ava couldn't say anything, a flash of pain rendering her mute. Couldn't open her eyes. She held out her hand. Rochelle wrapped hers around it and didn't let go.

* * *

"Hello, Ava," The doctor said as he approached her bedside. "Feeling a little better now?"

"Yeah. Kind of floaty."

"Perfect. Floaty is what we're shooting for," he said with a wink, then the doctor informed her that she wasn't to operate any heavy machinery for the rest of the week.

Ava offered him a lazy smile. Asked where her mother was.

"I'm right here, honey." Her mom moved to her side and rubbed her arm.

"You hang out here and take it easy for a while, all right?" the doctor said before turning to her mother and saying something about going over scans when her father got there. "Can I get you anything, Ava?" the doctor asked, "A new car, trip to Hawaii, a warm blanket? You can only pick one."

Ava slid a lazy tongue over dry lips. "Car."

"It's your lucky day. Today and today only, the code word for warm blanket is *car*," he replied with a goofy grin.

Ava giggled and watched the doctor leave. "He's funny, huh Mom?"

"Yes, Ava, he's funny," her mother agreed—but Lola wasn't laughing.

* * *

Lola sat at the table with her husband and the doctor in a small conference room, staring in disbelief at the highlighted area on the monitor—a cross section of Ava's brain.

"The good news is Ava's tumor is likely non-cancerous," the doctor said as he pointed to the highlighted mass on the MRI scan. "Mrs. Roberts, when we spoke earlier you mentioned that Ava has been having problems sleeping, along with headaches and dizziness for about eight months, and lately starting to have migraines. This meningioma pressing on her pineal gland is the likely culprit. We were able to get a copy of her earlier CAT scan and can see two things. Because the tumor shares the same cell structure as the lining of the brain, and was very small at the time, it went undetected in the first scan ordered by your sleep specialist. What we can now see, by comparing the two scans, is that the mass is quickly growing."

"If that's the good news," Eric asked, his leg in a fast-paced bounce, "what's the bad news?"

"Ava needs emergency surgery. Because of its size and location, the removal of her tumor is imperative, to keep from damaging the gland it's impinging on and to relieve the pressure on these vessels on the interior side," he said, pointing with a stylus. "Because of its size and location, the mass will begin to deteriorate brain function as well. There are, however, significant risks involved with its removal." The doctor slid a tablet across the table.

Lola's husband put his arm around her as they read over the possible side effects of a surgery deep inside their daughter's brain. Lola was in shock. Surgery wasn't optional; it was the only choice, but the consequences could damage Ava for life.

"We have a helicopter waiting to make the transfer to Sacred Heart. All we need is your consent and we'll get her up to Spokane."

Eric jerked his head forward with one decisive nod and tapped his thumbprint on the screen, but Lola continued to stare at the life-altering side effects.

"What is Ataxia?" Lola asked, fearing the answer.

"Ataxia is more or less limited coordination," The doctor replied, and then explained that the procedure would not be the open-skull surgery she might be assuming. "The surgeon will insert a robotic endoscope through a small keyhole incision behind Ava's left ear." On the MRI, he traced the path the scope would take to access the deep-seated tumor in her daughter's brain.

Lola felt a little better knowing the operation wasn't as invasive as she first thought, but the possible side effects still scared her.

"You can see Ava before she goes into surgery," the doctor added. "They'll want to start pre-op early in the morning, by 6:00 a.m."

"Can I see her now?" Lola asked, "Before they take her away."

The doctor stood and swept a hand toward the door. "Of course."

Lola's hands trembled as the harsh reality of the situation began to sink in. They were going to take Ava, her only child, and operate on her brain. What would they do if there were complications? Would their daughter have to live the rest of her life with the coordination of a drunkard? Please, Lord, no. She stood, her purse falling from her lap, dumping on the floor.

Eric collected her things, zipped her purse, and tucked it under his arm. "Lola . . . sweetheart, they need your print."

She brushed a hand over her ear. "My what?" Nothing made sense.

Her husband pointed to the tablet with the consent form. "Your fingerprint." We'll see Ava now, then drive up to Spokane as soon as they leave with her." Eric's steady voice helped her focus, but she noticed the tightness of his lips and the worry in his eyes.

"I can't, Eric. My hands—" She held them up, unable to still the quivering.

The doctor assured her the signature ID would still record an accurate print.

Feeling as if she were signing her daughter's life away, she reached over and tapped the screen.

Fifteen minutes later, Lola watched the changing sky, praying as they drove past Steptoe Butte, shadows crawling in and out of rolling hills. *Lord, Ava is up there . . . somewhere in the sky . . . on her way to Sacred Heart. You know how hard it was to bring her into this world. The endless specialists. The miscarriages. I love her with everything in me. Please be with Ava.* Lola fiddled with the small emerald in her ear. *Please, Lord, keep her safe.*

CHAPTER 26

With his elbows on his knees and forehead pressed into his hands, Timothy sat across from his grief counselor, Mr. Gonzales. He should have been prepared for this session, since he'd been given the questions about his letter three days ago, but he wasn't. To make it easier for him, the counselor asked him to summarize what they'd already talked about, starting with the relationship he had with Billy.

Timothy always wanted to be just like his older brother. Billy was confident, talented, responsible. Though three years older, Billy always let him tag along. When the counselor asked if they fought, he replied with a nod and confessed that he'd been talked into trying pot when he was in the seventh grade. He'd gone to the park across from the school, but Billy caught him and punched him in the mouth, splitting his lip. They agreed not to tell their parents about the pot or the real cause of the split lip. Never did tell them.

"I didn't hold it against Billy. He was looking out for me. You know, didn't want me to be stupid. I never tried pot again. Billy told me he'd do the same thing if he ever caught me drinking. And I didn't, until after . . ."

"After he died?" the counselor asked.

Timothy nodded. "My dad caught me."

Timothy got the alcohol from home. His parents didn't drink, but they kept it for company that did. His father had been given the liquor as gifts. Russian vodka from a golf tournament, other bottles of wine and hard alcohol from construction supply houses and business associates. A year after his brother's death, Timothy started taking a few shots along with over-the-counter sleeping pills. He'd refilled the empty vodka bottles with water. The deception worked for two years. Wine was usually the drink of choice when the liquor cabinet was opened, so he didn't get into those. Company came over for New Year's. That's when his father figured out what he'd been doing. An investor tossed down a stale water shot. Needless to say, his dad was beyond mad but also claimed responsibility for its easy access. Timothy didn't get in as much trouble as he thought he would.

"What did you expect your father to do about it?"

Timothy didn't really know. How could he be more of a disappointment than he already was? "Maybe kick me out. Or threaten it. Take away my keys."

"Do you believe your father when he says he doesn't blame you for Billy's death?"

Timothy shifted in his chair, shook his head.

"Can you tell me why?"

When his father first found out how Billy died, his dad came unhinged. It was too senseless for his father to accept.

Timothy cleared his throat and took a drink of water from the cup on the coffee table in front of him. "*Why didn't I stay with him? That's what he asked me the night it happened.*"

His father later apologized, repeatedly, but the blame was already etched on Timothy's conscience. The truth hurt. It hurt deep. If only he'd stayed at the party, Billy would be alive.

"When faced with the death of someone they love, do you think people can say things they don't mean?"

"Yeah."

Timothy was familiar with grief blaming. They'd all met with a family counselor for a month, after his mother first caught him purging. None of the explanations or excuses seemed to make any difference. All he knew was the guilt and pain he felt, and he did whatever it took to make it go away.

"Do you think your father wants you to take Billy's place?"

His father wouldn't let him quit basketball. His sophomore year, his father told him quitting wasn't the answer. Tried to threaten the will to succeed back into him. When Timothy asked the coach to bench him, his father stopped going to his games, until he started trying again. Even then, his father still didn't talk to him about it.

"I can't be like Billy." Timothy ran a hand over the arm of his chair.

Mr. Gonzales asked if he thought the sessions they'd started having with his father were helpful. Timothy wasn't sure. Maybe they would be.

"Can you tell me when you wrote the letter?"

Timothy looked at the crumpled envelope on the coffee table between them. "I wrote it to Billy on Christmas Eve." The letter was kept in his closet under a pile of dress slacks that no longer fit him. Both the envelope and letter showed signs of wear, evidence that the letter had been handled a number of times.

"This past Christmas Eve?"

"Yeah."

"Is that when you started purging again?"

"No . . . started a few weeks before Christmas. Maybe in November."

He'd stopped after his second surgery, but the alcohol and sleeping pills weren't enough. After a few months, he started purging again.

"How did you feel after you wrote the letter?

"Relieved . . . kind of. You know . . . felt good to talk to Billy, even if he wasn't there." Timothy finally said what he'd been thinking since the night his brother died, but was afraid to admit.

"Did you think you were bound by what you wrote, like it was a promise you had to keep, or was it enough to write down what you were struggling with?"

Timothy huffed out an agitated sigh, fingertips tapping together. He didn't know how to answer that question. Or didn't want to.

"Timothy?" Mr. Gonzales pressed; the man's tattooed arm relaxed atop the cushion beside him.

"I don't know," he replied, hands pushed into his sweatshirt pocket.

His counselor shifted the focus away from the contents of the letter and asked him how he felt when his mother found it.

"Angry . . . ashamed."

"Why do you think you felt angry?"

Ava came over for dinner that day. She said something to his mother about his purging and found out he'd lied to her. He thought his mother's reaction was more to blame for Ava's panicked flight out of his house than his lies. When he couldn't find Ava right away, more than fear, he felt rage. He was mad at her for doing something so stupid, something that could hurt her. If anything happened to her, it would be his fault.

"Why didn't she even think about that? I would have taken her home. She didn't need to run away."

"Do you think you were mad at Ava for the same reason you're mad at Billy?"

Timothy swallowed hard and flexed his jaw. He didn't like the question. "I'm not mad."

"Do you think your brother made a choice that cost him his life, leaving you to blame for his death?"

Grabbing the back of his neck, Timothy jumped up and paced the room. "Why didn't he go back inside? If Billy hadn't stayed out there, he wouldn't have froze to death."

The coroner's report suggested Billy tried to empty his stomach, based on the vomit inside his coat sleeve. They found the purging evidence thirty feet from where he'd passed out.

"Why didn't he go to the bathroom to throw up, like everybody else?" He was mad at him, even though, days after he died, Timothy learned that Billy hadn't been drinking. His brother still should have known better. "Even drugged, he was smart enough to figure out what was going on. Why not call for help? His phone was right in his pocket. 911, how hard is that? I don't get it."

Mr. Gonzales told him not to feel guilty for his anger. Being angry at Billy's choices didn't mean he loved his brother any less. "In fact," his counselor added, "dealt with in the right way, anger is a healthy, coping emotion, not something to deny or suppress."

Standing at the window, Timothy pushed a tight fist into his hand. "I punched him."

"Yes, we've talked about that, but can you tell me again why you hit Billy?"

"I thought he was being stupid. I was mad . . . didn't know what was going on."

"Did Ava know you were mad at her?"

Timothy nodded, looked at the floor.

"Did you hit her?"

Timothy jerked his head up. "No—never! I would never hit her!"

"You told me you love Ava. Is that true?"

"Yes, I do." Another thing he'd screwed up big time. She'd be better off without him.

"Why did you hit your brother and not Ava? Didn't you love your brother?"

"That's a dumb question," Timothy replied with a smirk.

Mr. Gonzalez nodded, an easy smile curving his thin mustache. "Maybe it is, but can you explain why it's dumb?"

He told the counselor the reason was obvious. He and Billy were brothers; brothers hit each other sometimes. "You know, when they're really mad—when they want them to stop the crap they're doing."

Mr. Gonzalez took a drink of his water, then with a slow swipe of his thumb, cleared condensation from the base of his glass. "So that kind of anger, while not considered a healthy way to express one's opinion, is, in this particular situation . . . let's say, justified?"

Timothy understood the man's point. Even though his mother always told him and Billy to use their words instead of their fists, punching each other usually led to a lightning-fast peace agreement—generally, him agreeing with Billy. As they got older, more adept at expressing opinions with words, fists rarely flew. "Justified? Yeah. Maybe."

"But you wouldn't hit Ava?"

"No! Never." Why was his counselor even asking him that? Did someone think he'd hit her? Was the cut on her head listed in his school file? Hurray. Now people think he's beating up girls. "I would never hit a girl. Especially not Ava."

"I didn't think you would. However, when you hit your brother, could it have been because you cared about him, regardless of why he appeared to be drunk? Maybe Billy understood why you did it—before he died."

Timothy dropped down in his chair. "I guess he could have."

"It might not be what you want to remember as your last words to your brother, but had he lived through that night, he would have understood. Do you think Billy might have punched you if he thought you were the one drinking?"

Timothy replied with a smirky huff. "Definitely would have."

"Let's go back to the letter. What happened after you took Ava home?"

He told the counselor that he went to practice. Couldn't wait to get out of the house. But while he was gone, his mother tore his room apart.

"Did she know what she was looking for?"

"No. Just anything. Probably drugs."

When he got home from practice, he could hear his parents talking. He knew they were frustrated, disappointed in him for lying, but he wasn't ready to face them. Went straight to his room. When he opened his bedroom door and saw everything from his dresser piled on his bed, things pulled out of his closet, he lost it and threw his sports bag across the room, breaking the closet door.

Timothy leaned forward and rubbed his hands over his legs.

"So, you were mad at her for going through your things?"

He told the counselor he was mad at first, until his parents came to his room. When his mother took the letter out of her pocket, she grabbed onto him as if she couldn't breathe, tried to say something but could only gasp for air. It scared both him and his father. When she could finally breathe again, she couldn't stop crying.

"Is that why you felt ashamed?"

Timothy tucked his chin. "Yeah."

That night his parents pleaded with him to understand how much they loved him and wanted to help. They felt the same loss and pain he did over Billy' death, mourned the fact that they weren't able to help his brother, but they were there to help him if only he'd let them. Timothy never wanted to hurt them or anybody else. He wanted to feel better. Feel anything other than the way he felt.

"When you wrote that you'd see Billy soon," Mr. Gonzales said, pointing at the letter, "why did you think ending your life was the only solution?"

Timothy stood up and walked back to the window. It would have been easy. Once he turned eighteen, a quick trip to one of the Life Choice clinics would have numbed the pain forever. Could have ended it all with a simple signature, complete with soothing music and a quick injection. For people eighteen to twenty-five, the *choice* didn't cost anything. Sign a donor card and they'd kill you for free. That wasn't Life Choices' exact motto, but it meant the same thing.

He'd visited the clinic's website more times than he cared to count, always remembering to delete his search history in case his parents checked up on him. Even drove by the clinic three months before his birthday. A girl, not much older than him, was headed in when he passed the place. Looked like her parents were with her. Flowers on her lap, dad pushing her wheelchair to death's open door. All of them crying. The truth, the scene made him sick to his stomach.

Beyond the window, Timothy could see the hospital up the hill, full of people fighting to live or preserve life.

"Timothy?"

"Yeah, I heard you. Honestly, I didn't really think about solutions. Just wanted the pain to go away."

CHAPTER 27

Eric didn't see the Grays, Timothy's parents, come into the waiting room until they sat down across from him and Lola.

Before he could acknowledge them, Grace Gray had her arm around his wife. Given all that had happened over the last few months, Grace and Lola quickly became confidants.

William offered Eric a half smile and held out his hand. "Hello, Eric. How you holdin' up?"

He shook Timothy's father's hand, knowing the man was no stranger to heartache. "The waiting is tough."

"Bet it is. Mind if we stay for a few minutes?" William asked.

"No, not at all." Eric leaned back in his chair and tapped a thumb on the armrest. "We should hear something before too long. Ava's been in surgery almost four hours now. We were told it could take eight or more."

Grace took Lola to get something to eat in the cafeteria, after Eric encouraged Lola to go. He promised to call if anyone came in with an update. His wife had said she didn't want to go, but she hadn't eaten for twenty-four hours, Lola's low blood sugar evident in her trembling hands.

Their wives gone, Eric asked William how Timothy was doing. Ava's father didn't want to pry, but he was genuinely concerned. "We sure hope things are going well for him."

Eric knew very little about William Gray. They'd seen each other at a few of Timothy's games. When Timothy seemed to be making progress, Eric and Lola wanted to support Timothy's efforts by going to the few home games he played in before he left for treatment.

William leaned forward, hands rubbing together. "It's awful nice of you to ask, Eric, given what's already on your plate."

"I'd like to hear how your son's doing, if it's something you don't mind sharing. Did you know I had a talk with Daniel Thatcher?"

"With coach? I didn't." William's attentive stare made it apparent the man wanted to know more.

Eric ran a hand over his stiff neck, stretched out his legs. "I played basketball with ol' Dan in high school. He was always a pretty good guy. Anyways, Ava was still worried after things started to cool off between her and Timothy, so I called Dan and asked if he could meet me for lunch. Ava doesn't know about it."

"Thatcher coached both boys when Timothy was a freshman," William added, "Before Billy died. Timothy didn't want to play basketball after his brother's death. I made him play. Had it in my mind that giving up on the small things would lead to bigger problems. You know, a full-scale checkout on life. Coach Thatcher didn't feel like he had the right to push Timothy, so when my son refused to apply himself . . . basically stopped trying, Dan had no option but to move him to the Junior Varsity Squad."

Eric asked what Timothy thought about the switch.

"Made no difference to him; said it didn't matter what bench he sat on." Timothy's father huffed out a defeated chuckle. "Thought my son was just acting up to spite me. Figured he'd come around soon enough. You know, get over the blame thing. Get on with life. I figured wrong." William leaned his elbows on his knees, pulled on the back of his neck. "Coach was there the night Billy died."

"Dan was there?" Eric asked, leaning forward in his chair.

"Yeah. He took it pretty hard. Almost gave up coaching over it. He'd given all the players an out if they ever got in a situation they knew they shouldn't be in. It was a no-questions-asked policy. You know, like coaches always do. If a kid was in a bad way and called him, he'd go pick 'em up. And Billy called him."

Coach Dan had mentioned he was too close to Billy's death to push Timothy, but Ava's father hadn't realized how close.

"Dan didn't tell you, did he?" William asked.

Eric shook his head. If this was too much for Timothy's father, he would let the conversation steer a different direction.

"Dan went to the party to get Billy but couldn't find him. A girl that had been with him told Dan he'd already left, so Coach went back home and called Timothy to make sure Billy was there. But he wasn't. That's when Coach and Timothy went back to Pullman to find Billy. The party had been over for a while. They thought he might've gone home with a friend."

William shifted, pulled his shirt away from his chest as if the thermostat needed adjusting. "Are you sure you're up for hearing this?"

"I am if you're up to telling me." Eric replied, figuring Timothy's father might benefit from the explanation.

"So then . . . uh . . .where was I?" William asked, swiping the back of his hand over his brow.

"You mentioned that Timothy and Dan went back to the house."

"Yes. Timothy didn't want to leave without checking around. Coach had a flashlight in his car. It was well below freezing . . . still snowing. There were tracks in the snow behind the house, leading away from the back door. That's when they found him." Mr. Gray rubbed a knuckle over his mouth. "He was already gone." A handkerchief pulled from his back pocket, the man wiped his face and blew his nose. "It's been hard for Timothy. Harder than Grace and I realized."

"I'm sorry, William. That's got to be tough. Can't even imagine."

"Sorry, Eric. I didn't mean to unload on you like that. You have enough on your mind right now."

"No need to apologize." Eric leaned back and tapped the edge of his chair. "I wanted to know, to understand Timothy's struggle. Thank you for telling me." He still didn't know exactly how Billy died but wouldn't ask.

William's expression made a sudden, drastic change from melancholy to wonderment. "Your little Ava, she's something else."

"Yeah . . . a pretty special kid." Eric looked down the empty hall through the glass doors of the waiting room. Still no news.

"She sure is. I thank God every day for putting Timothy on her radar. And, you know what, Eric, she just might have saved my son's life. God's little game changer, that's what she is."

Eric grinned and tried to process William's claim. Why doesn't God intervene for everyone? This man lost one of his sons but trusted God to save the other? Where does that kind of faith come from?

"I need to ask you something, Eric. Grace and I . . . well . . . we don't know how to tell Timothy about Ava's operation. We're afraid he'll want to be with her and won't finish his treatment program. He's at a tough place right now. However, he'd be upset with us if we didn't tell him. He'll find out about it one way or another. Lord knows I'd grab at any chance to gain his trust."

Eric rubbed over his whiskered chin. "You could ask his counselor. They'd have a better idea on how to handle that, but as far as I'm concerned, he's sure welcome."

"I appreciate it, I really do."

Eric gave William his phone number. "Go ahead and give me a call if Timothy can come see Ava."

Grace and Lola returned to the waiting room with wrapped sandwiches. Eric tried to eat just to please Lola, his stomach cramping after a few bites.

A surgical nurse pushed the door open, capturing everyone's attention. "Mr. and Mrs. Roberts?"

"Yes! How is she?" Lola stood and stepped closer to the nurse.

"Ava is doing fine. The operation is progressing as expected without any complications."

Lola wanted to know if they'd removed the tumor yet. The nurse informed them that they were still in the extraction process, but the surgeons were optimistic they would be able to remove the entire mass with little to no damage to the pineal gland.

When Lola pressed her for more information, the nurse wasn't able to make any assurances beyond what she'd already told them. They thanked her for the update and let her return to surgery.

Eric closed his eyes and rested his head on his hand. He didn't get much sleep the night before. Fatigue was beginning to catch up with him. When he woke twenty minutes later, the Grays were gone.

* * *

Lola hovered over Ava, unable to rest until her daughter regained consciousness and proved the surgery hadn't debilitated her with any of the possible side effects. A bandage covered a baseball-sized patch behind Ava's ear. Lola considered the shaved area beyond the bandage, glad for her daughter's sake that she still had most of her hair.

"I'm right here, Ava." She kissed her daughter's cheek, knowing she wasn't supposed to wake for another twenty minutes or so.

Mr. Gray called. Lola could hear Eric talking to him in the hallway.

When he came back to the recovery room, her husband told her he'd given permission for Timothy and his counselor to see Ava, after she was moved to the ICU.

"They'll be here in a few hours." He also told her about William's earlier concerns. They needed to assure Timothy that Ava was going to be fine.

Lola pulled him away from Ava's bed. "What if she isn't?" she whispered. "We don't know anything yet."

"She is." Eric moved to his daughter's side, rubbed his hand over the white blanket covering her silent frame. "She has to be."

Lola prayed, begging and bargaining with God to grant their only child a full recovery.

* * *

Ava heard people talking, her eyelids heavy. After some effort, she forced them open. Looked around the room. "Dad?" Her lips felt heavy as well.

"Ava, hey babe. How you feelin'?" He kissed her cheek and squeezed her hand.

"Tired." She squinted at the hazy blue walls flanking her bed.

Her mother leaned over her . . . seemed fuzzy, but after a few seconds, Ava could see her clearly. Her mother began to cry.

"Mom . . . what's wrong?"

"Nothing, honey. Everything is fine."

"Where am I?"

178

Rubbing her arm, her father told her she was in Spokane at Sacred Heart Hospital.

"Mom."

"Yes?"

Ava could feel her mother's warm breath on her ear. "What's that sound?"

"What sound, honey?"

"Clocks. Lots of clocks . . ." and then she didn't hear anything.

* * *

"Ava, can ya open your eyes for me, dearie?"

Who was that? It sounded like a man, but it wasn't her father. She turned toward the voice but couldn't open her eyes.

"Come on, Ava. Try to open up those eyes."

"Mom?" she slurred, struggling to comply. She felt a hand on her face, then a finger slowly lifted one eyelid, then the other, flashing a quick point of light in each eye.

"She's comin' round. You can expect her to fade in and out for a spell, as the anesthesia wears off. We'll be keepin' a close eye on her. She'll be a bit groggy, to be sure, but she should be all together within the hour."

Ava heard her father thank someone. Doctor McDavin? The doctor sounded like the guy on those new, vintage soap commercials . . . Irish clean . . . It's magically delicious. No, that's not how it goes. She must be dreaming.

* * *

Lola turned to a light tap on the door.

"Hello, Mr. and Mrs. Roberts," Timothy said quietly, holding a vase of pink roses. He stared past them at Ava. "This is my counselor, Joseph Gonzales."

After greeting each other with whispers, Lola told Timothy the surgery went well, but Ava had gone back to sleep only minutes before they arrived.

"Is it okay if I touch her hand?" Timothy asked, the concern in his expression bordering on panic.

"Of course," Lola replied. "Timothy, she'll be fine. They were able to remove the tumor through a small incision behind her ear. It's amazing what they can do now." She glanced out the window over her left shoulder and then smoothed a crease in Ava's pillow.

Mr. Gonzales briefly looked at her with a raised brow before shifting his attention to her husband.

Earlier, when Ava regained consciousness, it was true that she appeared to be fine, but it was too soon to rule out possible side effects.

Timothy set the vase of flowers on the counter and moved close to Ava's side. He gently slid his large hand over hers and stared at her face. Lola noticed Timothy's pinched brow, which prompted her to cast a do-something look at her husband.

"Ava will be glad to hear you came by," Eric told Timothy as he took a seat in a chair by the window. "She'll wish she'd been awake to see you."

"It is so nice to see you, Timothy." Lola added. You look good." She glanced at his counselor for any sign that her comment was pushing a boundary, but Mr. Gonzales only smiled at her, nodding in agreement.

"How long will she be here?" Timothy asked, without looking away from Ava.

"She should be home by the end of the week," Eric replied, scratching over the two days of growth on his jaw.

Timothy turned to his counselor and asked if they could come back when she was awake. Mr. Gonzales apologized that they couldn't, but reminded Timothy he could talk to Ava on Saturday.

Timothy slumped his shoulders and rubbed his thumb over the back of Ava's hand. "Thank you for letting me see her." His brooding expression changed to a grimace. "I know I haven't made things any easier for her."

"There's nothing easy about a life worth living," Eric replied, pushing out of his chair. "You hang in there, son."

Lola noticed that Eric's reply drew Timothy's attention away from Ava for a second. Timothy smiled at Eric then looked at Ava as if willing her awake. His counselor told him it was time to go.

"We look forward to seeing you again," Lola said with her arms out, not looking at the counselor for permission to hug the troubled young man.

Timothy bent down, hugged her, and then reached out to shake Eric's hand. Eric hugged Timothy with a solid shoulder-to-shoulder squeeze and pat on the back. Timothy looked confused with their reaction to him and stood in awkward silence as Eric shook the counselor's hand and thanked him for bringing Timothy.

"We'll be sure and tell Ava you were here," Lola promised as Timothy followed Mr. Gonzales out of the room.

* * *

A heavy ache built in Timothy's chest as he trailed his counselor through the parking garage. The sight of Ava lying there, so small and frail, broke him. He ran two fingers over his mouth. This telling him what to do routine wasn't going to work for him anymore. "I want to come back."

Mr. Gonzales rounded their van and unlocked it with a wave of his ID card. His counselor, as calm as he was irritating, waited to reply until they were both in the van and headed down the ramp. "Timothy, we bent the rules to let you come here today."

"Screw the rules." His conscience needled him. It wasn't his counselor's fault that his life was a mess. He apologized to the fount of wisdom in the driver's seat. Drummed his fingers on the door handle. "What good would it do to keep me from her? I'm going to worry about her constantly. Every minute. That's not healthy. It's not."

His counselor reminded him that he wasn't being held against his will. He could leave at any time. But, if he wanted to focus on his recovery, he needed to trust the program. Including the rules. "Yes, Ava is important. Your parents made that clear when they asked if you could see her."

"See," Timothy challenged, "the rules aren't set in stone."

Mr. Gonzales told Timothy it wasn't about the rules. "You still have some important work to do. Things to sort out, no?"

Timothy slumped against the door. "Whatever."

"Come on. You know I'm right." His counselor turned into the alley behind the center and parked in the carport. Van plugged in, they both waited at the back door until the sensor recognized the ID card with a loud buzz. "You bolt now, Timothy, when you're so close to figuring things out, and it could cost you everything you've gained. Believe me; I've seen it time and time again. These dudes, they come in here with all their life baggage then leave before they got their crap figured out. I don't need to tell you what happens to most of those that bolt."

Timothy leaned against the door to his room, arms crossed. "But you're going to, aren't you?"

"You know it. Alcoholics, addiction, broken families. They can't keep a job, can't keep a wife. You hearing this? A number of them, they end up on the street or worse. I'd hate to see you give up now."

Timothy scuffed a shoe into the carpet. "How is going to the hospital a few times going to land me on the street?"

"You don't have the energy to focus on anything but your recovery right now. Any distractions will set you back. You'll still get to call her. You can talk to her every week. Ask how she's doing. It will be enough to keep you going in the right direction, yes?"

"How is a call different than talking to her in person?"

Mr. Gonzales gave him a narrowed-eye smirk. "You gotta be kidding me, right? I saw the way you looked at her. Some friend, huh?"

Timothy wasn't interested in losing his talk time with Ava—his close *friend*. "Okay, okay, you win. Did I already say this sucks?"

"Probably. Believe me, I've heard worse. In fact a lot worse. Now, to get that toxic energy burned up, why don't you go see Azar."

His head thrown back, Timothy pushed hands through his hair. "You're killing me. I think a nap would clear out all my distractions."

"Get changed and go see Azar. Let's get back on schedule."

Timothy slumped forward as if inspecting his knees and blew out a resigned huff.

* * *

Ava woke to new surroundings.

"Hello, sunshine." her father said, scooting the rolling stool close to her bedside.

"Still in Spokane?" she asked him.

"Yep. You were moved to another room. We're still at the hospital."

"Timothy's in Spokane," Ava mumbled, then heard someone chuckle.

Her mother brushed a hand over Ava's forehead. "Timothy's parents are here, William and Grace."

"Oh. Can I say hi?" Her tongue felt funny, as if bigger than usual.

"Hello, Ava." Mrs. Gray stepped closer and touched the back of Ava's hand.

"Hi, Grace. How's Timothy?" Ava looked around the room, hoping to see him.

"He's doing well, Ava. Thank you for asking," she replied, dabbing her eyes with a tissue.

"Is he still at . . . that place?"

Timothy's father patted her hand, and then put his arm around Grace. "Yes, Ava. He's still there."

"Oh." She wanted to visit with everybody, but her eyelids still felt heavy.

"We'll see you later, Ava," Grace said.

"Okay. . . . See ya." Ava heard Mr. Gray say something, but she was so tired.

CHAPTER 28

Ava woke to the smell of bleached linens and antiseptic, vaguely remembering something about William and Grace Gray. It took her a second to focus on the person sitting in the chair next to her bed. "Rochelle?"

"Hey, you're awake." Putting her tablet down, Rochelle moved closer, hugged her like one might hug a ninety-year-old granny. "How you feelin'?"

"Kind of groggy." Groggy? Why did that remind her of Irish soap? "How long have I been asleep?" Her eyes cleared, the fog of confusion beginning to lift.

Rochelle told her she didn't know, that she'd been in Ava's room for less than an hour. "You've probably been sleeping on and off for most of the day." Rochelle tilted her head and looked at her with a tender grin. "Your parents are here. They're downstairs getting something to eat." Her friend tapped out a quick text and put her phone down. "You scared me to death. I can say that 'cause you're okay now."

"I scared you? Why?"

Rochelle leaned on her bed. "Don't you remember anything? Leaving school or the ride to the hospital?"

Ava tried, but she didn't. A total blank.

"You passed out." Rochelle tapped the screen on the tablet next to her bed. "Wanna look at new hair sty—"

Ava grabbed the handrail. "Oh, no! What day is it?" She pulled herself up, scanning every table and tray for her cellphone.

"Wednesday. Why?" Rochelle loosened the tension on Ava's drip-line.

"When did I get here?"

"Monday." Rochelle looked concerned, shifting her gaze from one eye to the other, as if her examination could determine Ava's mental state.

Leaning back on the raised bed, Ava breathed out a sign of relief. "Good. I didn't miss his call." She turned toward Rochelle and giggled. "You thought I was losing it, didn't you?"

"Maybe," her friend said with a smirk. "Don't you think Timothy would understand if you just had brain surgery? Good grief, infatuated much?"

"I'm the one worried about it." Ava replied, noticing the growing collection of flowers on the counter. She thought she remembered someone telling her Timothy had been there. Maybe she dreamt it. "Was Timothy here?" Ava pointed to the flowers.

"I don't know." Rochelle went over to the counter by the window. Looked through several cards.

"Check the pink ones. Is there a card?"

Rochelle picked up the vase and inspected the arrangement. "Yeah, there's something in here." She brought the flowers to the bedside and pulled out a rolled paper tucked into the greenery.

Ava took it and slipped it under the covers.

"Are you kidding me? You can't wait to read that. You don't have to tell me everything it says, unless you want to."

When Ava hesitated, Rochelle rolled her eyes and stomped both feet on the floor. "I have to go to the bathroom. I'll be right back," she mumbled.

"You don't have to go to the bathroom just so I can read the note."

"No, I really have to. I'll go down the hall. I need to stretch my legs," Rochelle said as she backed out of the room.

Ava mimicked her scowl. "Love ya."

As soon as Rochelle left the room, she pulled the note out and unrolled it:

Ava, hope you can read this. I wrote it in the car on the way to see you. I think about you every day and wonder why you refuse to give up on me. You really are Ava Interruptus—my new, favorite

superhero. Get well so we can go on those hundreds of fun
adventures still waiting for us—Love, Timothy.

Rochelle peeked around the doorway. "So?"

Ava held it out for her. "You can see it."

"Someone has twinkle eyes," her friend said as she took the note and leaned against her bed. "Oh," Rochelle cooed, a hand to her chest, "he is way sweet! Ava Interruptus, I like that." She thanked Ava for letting her be a snoop and handed the note back. "Can you believe Timothy was here?"

Ava looked out the window at the sun-washed buildings lining the street below. He was so close. "Wish I could see him."

* * *

Timothy's father sat next to him in the conference room and thanked Mr. Gonzales for the exception made on his son's behalf. The counselor agreed that seeing Ava was the right thing to do. He then reminded them both that this session would be difficult but necessary so that Timothy could move on in his treatment.

For a week, Timothy knew he would recount the night of his brother's death in the presence of his father. He'd gone over every detail with his counselor, the painful revisit helping him learn to grieve Billy's loss in a healthy way. Reliving that night again, with raw honesty, wasn't going to be easy. He'd given statements to police and investigators. Went over the events of the night a dozen times with his parents, but he'd never shared his most guarded wounds with anyone, until Mr. Gonzales unearthed them.

"Timothy," his counselor began, "I'd like you to describe the night of Billy's death starting with the conversation you had with your brother before you left for the party."

He nodded, a hand raking through his hair. The room felt crowded with his father there. "Mom and Dad were in Coeur d'Alene for the weekend. Billy wanted to go to a party in Pullman. He told me to stay home, but I wanted to go. Billy said there'd be alcohol there. Warned me not to touch it or I'd be kicked off the team. Antonio, his friend that graduated a year earlier, was a freshman in college, no longer had the threat of coach or parent propping up his self-control. But Antonio respected Billy. Wouldn't pressure him to drink. Normally Billy wouldn't even go to a college party, but Kandy was there." Timothy glanced at his father who knew all about Kandy and how much Billy liked the older girl.

"When we got to the party, around 10:30 p.m., the house was already pumping. There were tons of people we didn't know. When we went in, the place reeked like spilt beer and pizza. One of Billy's friends grabbed his shoulder and gave Billy a hug with one hand while balancing a cup full of beer in the other. Antonio saw us come in and yelled for someone to get Billy a pop. Then Kandy pushed her way in front of us and handed Billy an open can."

Timothy took a few cleansing breaths, rubbing his palms together. "Some kind of pop. She said someone just gave it to her, but she hadn't taken a drink of it yet. Billy took it. Followed her around for a while like a puppy in love, so I went to the basement and played pool for about, I don't know, twenty minutes. When I went back upstairs to see what Billy was doing, I found him in the kitchen flirting with Kandy." Timothy stood up and walked to a window with a view of the freeway. "I thought for sure he'd been drinking."

"Why did you think that?" his counselor asked.

Noticing his father's heavy expression, Timothy swiped his brow with the back of his sleeve. "Billy's eyes were droopy . . . stumbled when he turned to walk toward me, then laughed like an embarrassed drunk. I was mad, really mad. He was supposed to be the responsible one, watching out for me, his brother's keeper, but he was stupid drunk . . . I thought. I told him we needed to leave, but he wouldn't go with me."

"What?" his father said. "You never told me that."

Timothy shifted his focus to the floor. "Didn't think you'd believe me."

"Son—why not?" His father stood and took a step closer but stopped short of touching him.

"Because I'm not him." Everything in Timothy ready for this get-together to be over, he resisted his typical shut down and tune out reply to any question asked by his father, but that wasn't an option. Not this time. "I'm the irresponsible one. The one that should know better, but never did. It's true. Billy was my moral compass for as long as I can remember. Sure, we went to church and all, but my life goal was to be like my brother. When he was gone, I felt lost, empty, like I didn't have a soul. I couldn't remember every detail at first, but after a few days, everything that happened that night began to loop in my mind, an endless movie in slow motion. Dad, I thought you'd think I was lying. You would have, if I somehow miraculously remembered I asked him to leave." Timothy swallowed hard to relieve the tightness building in his throat, his focus still on the floor. "Billy had it together, made the right call, took the high road. Not me."

His father leaned against a bookshelf, a hand cupped over his mouth.

"Timothy," Mr. Gonzales said, "can you go back to your reaction in the kitchen? What happened next?"

"I grabbed his arm. Tried to force Billy out the door, but he pushed me away. Said he wanted to stay. That's when I punched him. He just laughed and told me to leave if I wanted to. Threw his keys at me. Said he'd get a ride home. I could drive, but I didn't have my license yet. I thought he'd cave and come with me when I reminded him how much trouble I'd get in if I got pulled over. When he said it was time for me to grow up, I left. Drove home like a maniac. I wanted to get in trouble so he'd regret sending me home without him, so I drove his Mustang ninety miles an hour between Pullman and Colfax, and then ran every red light in town. But there wasn't a patrol car anywhere. I couldn't believe it. That's not normal."

"It's not," his father agreed.

"How long were you home before you tried to call him?" Mr. Gonzales asked.

Timothy left the window and sat back in his chair, palms pressed over his knees. "About an hour, but he didn't answer. It was 12:33 a.m. when I left him a message. Told him I wrecked his car. I wanted him to call me back. He never did. Coach called me around 1 a.m. to see if Billy made it home, or if I knew where he was. When I didn't, he agreed to take me back to the party and look for him. Someone must have called Thatcher to tell him Billy was drinking. A few days after it happened, someone told me coach had been there looking for him earlier that night."

"Billy called Coach—from the party," his father added, looking at Timothy as if confessing a lie. "I should have told you, son.

Thatcher was so broken up about it. He asked me not to tell you. We shouldn't have kept it from you. I'm sorry."

"Dad—" Timothy sat tall on the edge of his chair. "Billy called coach? Did the police know?"

"They did, but not until after they'd already given a statement to the press. Your mother and I were afraid you'd blame your coach for Billy's death. We were wrong to do that. Keeping it from you did far more harm than good."

Timothy stood up and paced the room. "Billy called Coach to pick him up?"

His father nodded. "Just before midnight. When Thatcher got to the party, Kandy told coach that Billy had already left, but she wasn't sure when or with who. Coach tried to call Billy, checked around in the house. When coach returned home, he tried to reach Billy again. That's when he called you."

Timothy slumped back in his chair, hands on his head, fists full of hair. "Billy was already outside when coach was there. Dad—he was still alive!"

His father nodded and pulled a handkerchief out of his back pocket.

"Timothy, what are you thinking right now?" his counselor asked.

"I'm . . . coach Thatcher could have saved him. I could have saved him. God could have saved him. But nobody did. He just lay in that ditch . . . by himself . . . and froze to death." Timothy's voice broke. He cleared his throat. Snatched a water bottle off the coffee table and took several long swallows. "Why would God save me . . . when I wanted to take my own life, but not Billy when he didn't have a choice?"

The counselor stretched an arm toward his father. "William, want to respond to that?"

His father wiped his handkerchief over his eyes. "Son, life and death, it's not something we can control. When given the choice, we always choose life, but we're not always given that choice. You know I struggle with your brother's death. It's not easy. Especially when we found out it was a date-rape drug meant for someone else that made him pass out. Remember how badly we wanted to find out who put the Ketamine in the pop Kandy gave him? I had this anger I didn't know what to do with. I needed to blame someone, but when they couldn't give us that target, I fired those blame bullets in every direction. Your mom and I blamed ourselves for being gone. I blamed you for leaving him, and Kandy for handing him that dang laced pop, even though it would have killed her if she drank it. I blamed God for not watching over Billy, Antonio for having the party. I even blamed Billy for going in the first place. But he died because he was drugged and passed out where no one could see him. So many what-ifs. He would have lived if it hadn't been so cold, but it was. And Billy died. That hurts, but we learn to grieve. And through that grief we understand how precious and fragile life really is. Your life, too, Timothy. It's so precious. Your mother and I desperately need you to understand that. You are precious to us. We love you and we'll do anything to keep from losing you. Anything, son."

Timothy stood, tears streaming down his face. He leaned on the wall a few feet from his father. So badly he wanted to believe him but his heart felt empty, a living corpse, as if God had already given up on him. "What about God? Why does He get a pass?" This question remained unresolved, a raw wound resisting what he'd believed until Billy's death. Did God care about him? Did God care about Billy?

"Timothy," his father said, clearing his throat, "God knows what the death of a son feels like, knows the pain of grief. But he'd do anything to save you and me, and anyone else willing to accept his forgiveness. I had no idea how powerful forgiveness was until I thought I was losing both you and your mother. I couldn't let it go. I pleaded with God to help me forgive. And it wasn't a one-time plea, believe you me. The hardest person to forgive wasn't who I thought it would be. It wasn't the boy that drugged his soda. It was me. I couldn't forgive myself."

Timothy startled, quickly shifting his full attention to his father. "You? . . . Dad, why you?"

"Because I was failing you and your mother. You were all I had left, but instead of facing Billy's death, grieving with my family, I tried to power through it. Worse than that, I expected you to do what I couldn't. I buried myself in my work, until we found your letter. I'm not losing you. I can't lose you, Timothy. We can get through this together. You can't buy back Billy's life with your own. You don't owe your life to anyone but the Lord who gave it to you. His is the only death that purchases life. When I let the Lord into my sorrow, only then could I forgive. Begin to heal. It's hard to forgive, to let go and trust God to get us through it, but he does care. He cares for Billy and for you.

Hands rubbing over his arms, Timothy wanted to believe him. He was wrong about his father, but he still couldn't forgive himself.

"Son, this isn't a perfect world. I still have unanswered questions; but I know God grieves when we grieve. I believe that and rest in the hope that I will see Billy again someday. You know your brother chose to live in the watchful arms of the Savior, and still lives even now." Timothy's father turned and reached for him.

Without hesitation, Timothy launched at him, fell on his father's shoulder, his chest heaving as he clung to him, sobbing as if he were a long-lost child finally rescued. Since the day his brother died, he desperately needed his father to reach for him.

Ugly Pictures

CHAPTER 29

Driving home from the hospital late Saturday afternoon, Ava asked her parents about Timothy.

"He looked really good. Don't you think so, Eric?" her mother said. "I mean—really good. Healthy . . . maybe a little heavier, or bigger."

Ava caught her father watching her in the rear-view mirror and couldn't keep a sheepish grin from owning her face.

"Yeah," he said with a wink, "I think you would approve, Ava. His guns were loaded. I'd say that boy has been spending some time in the gym. Gave him a man hug. Kid felt like a slab of granite in a coat."

She wanted to know every detail. They told her about Timothy's counselor, Mr. Gonzales, and that William and Grace Gray had been there several times before bringing Rochelle up with them.

By the time they arrived home, Ava needed to rest. She lay on her bed, the afternoon sun streaming through her window, warming her face. Like a nervous nurse, her mother shuttled into her room, set the pink roses next to her bed, fussed with the things in her backpack and the clothes she wore to the hospital, then walked over to close the blinds.

"It's okay, mom. The sun feels good."

Blinds left open, her mother asked if she could do anything else for her. "Do you need some water?"

Ava pointed to the water bottle already on her nightstand. After insisting on fussing over pillow and blanket placement, Ava told her she loved her, that everything was fine, and promised to let her know if she needed anything. When her mother left her alone, Ava shifted her thoughts to Timothy's phone call. In five and a half hours she'd hear his voice. His note pulled from her pocket, she read it a dozen times before tucking it under her pillow, eyes tired and wanting to close.

* * *

"Ava, honey, I'm sorry to wake you, but I think you'll want to take this call," her mother said, handing her the phone from the kitchen.

"What?" Ava glanced at the clock: 7 p.m. She'd been asleep for hours.

"Hello." She tried to sound wide-awake as she slowly sat up in bed.

"It's just me," Timothy said, "Did your mom wake you? I called your land-line so I wouldn't disturb you if you were sleeping."

"No worries, Timothy, I'm so glad you called. It's the total highlight of my week. See how special you are?" She leaned back against the headboard, her knees up. "I heard you came to see me at the hospital. Was I drooling?" She closed her eyes and focused on the sound of his voice.

"I wish I could have come back when you were awake. Sorry I can't be there with you, Ava."

"Don't worry about me, I'll be fine. The doctor said I'd probably sleep a lot for a few days. Before I left the hospital, they did some tests to see if everything worked like it was supposed to. Now I have proof that my brain is fully functioning."

"We'll have to test that," he teased. "Ava . . . are you really okay? Tell me the truth."

She sat up straighter. "Yes. Honest. Other than a patch of missing hair, I'm fine. By the way, thanks for the flowers—and the note."

"You're welcome, Ava Interruptus."

After a second of silence, Ava asked how he was doing.

"You know, I'm making progress. My dad . . . well, things are better between us. There are some guys here that have been through stuff that's hard to imagine. I'm not supposed to say anything about it, but if they can make it to the other side, anyone can. Tough stuff—really tough stuff."

"You're probably good for them, too. You and your giant grin. I bet you were born smiling."

"Not true. I was an ugly baby."

"I don't believe you."

"I was. My mom has the pictures to prove it. I looked like a catfish."

Ava giggled. "I'd have to see it to believe it. Maybe I'll visit your mom and take a peek at your baby pictures."

"I'm warning you, there are some things you can't unsee. I have to go. Love you, Ava. Don't ask my mom to see those pictures."

"I'm not making any promises, except that I love you, too, and I miss you. Bye, Timothy."

* * *

Timothy set the phone on the side table, the call timer on his phone clicking to zero. What he wouldn't tell her was that he was having recurring nightmares. He couldn't find Billy, couldn't find Ava. Woke up almost every night in a cold sweat. Eight hours after his call with Ava, he proved to be a creature of habit, waking in a panic, heart pounding, jaw tight. His mental image of himself screaming at Ava was the worst part, unloading everything he could never say to Billy onto her. Like a scene from some horror movie, eyes wild, hands clawed, spit spraying with every rapid-fire accusation. Was he some kind of animal? He pushed his covers off and sent a hurried voice text to Azar, his trainer. This was the post-nightmare protocol.

His phone chimed a second later. Maybe Azar never slept. Maybe he's a machine or at least half machine. A chimera? That would explain a lot. Timothy fought to still the tremor in his hands so he could clearly read Azar's message. A song link followed instructions to stretch, shadow box, stretch again, and do fifty push-ups. With enough experience to know that Azar wasn't trying to kill him, he sunk an earpiece in his ear and synched it with his phone. Song link selected, he stretched, then boxed the air to warm up his chest and shoulders. A band called *We The Kingdom* sang about holy water, the chorus catchy and the rhythm well timed for push-ups.

Over the course of the next two weeks, his nightmares took less out of him. The music and exercise brought relief from the tremors. By the third week, the nightmares were sporadic and less vivid, but still there.

* * *

Since Timothy started calling her, a melancholy slump clouded Ava's Sundays. Each day that inched closer to Saturday, closer to another call, the slump shifted to anticipation.

Lunch plans made before church, Ava collected toppings and veggies and arranged them on the counter. As soon as her father came home, he would fire up the grill and barbecue burgers. Real burgers. And not only real beef, but bacon as well. Her father had a connection with what he called the pork underground. Some pig farmer tucked away in the Palouse hills sold unregulated chops and bacon, street merchandise, to willing carnivorous customers. Not only did her father buy street merch for himself, he also bought it for friends. Maybe there should be a meme that says good friends buy you bacon.

Table set for lunch, Ava wandered down the hallway toward the clicking in her mother's office. It sounded as if her mother was setting some kind of word-per-minute record. "What are you working on?"

Her mother waved her to sit down in the chair beside her desk, grinning like a child anticipating their birthday cake. "A representative from a school in Virginia just sent an email."

"From Virginia? Why?"

"You know that website project you worked on with Rochelle?"

"Yeah."

"Well, your teacher entered several of those projects into a tech competition. I gave them permission months ago."

"I remember. Did we win something?"

"You could say that." Her mother stood and paced around the desk. "They want to offer you a scholarship!"

"Mom, you helped us on that project. It's your skill that got their attention."

"No, no, no. Listen to me, Ava. I enabled you to design and code with skill. You designed, you coded. I did not do it for you. It is your skill that got their attention."

"What about Rochelle?"

"I was informed that they were impressed with her part in the project, but the scholarship was being offered to you. They said you had the unique approach they were looking for."

"Really?"

"Yes, really." Her mother turned her monitor and waited while Ava read it. "What do you think?"

Unfamiliar with the name of the school, Ava skimmed the email for significant facts. "Are you sure this isn't a scam? You didn't give them any information, did you?"

Her mother laughed, but Ava missed the joke.

"Honey, when I talked to them earlier, they predicted your hesitance. I spent hours making sure they were the real deal, as did your father from his office. He put feelers out to several of his military friends. It's not a scam."

This didn't all go down over the last half hour. When did you talk to them *earlier*?

"About that," her mother replied, a finger swiping dust from a bookshelf. "You were in the hospital when they first called with the news that you were in the running. At the time, it was a low priority. Your father took the information and answered several questions. They said they'd stay in touch with us and that we should keep the first weekend in June free for potential travel."

More confused than excited, Ava stared at the screen.

"Honey, if you're interested in this, we'd move to Virginia. You'd finish high school there as well as attend college. They want to fly us to Chantilly for a visit. What do you think?"

"I've never even heard of Chantilly, Virginia." Ava jumped from her chair. "Mom, that's Timothy's graduation! There's no way I'm going."

Her mother made a face like people do when they open the bathroom door on someone. "That is bad timing isn't it. He'd understand. Probably be excited for you."

Ava wondered if her mother was from a different planet. "I don't care if it's the President of the United States offering a private tour of Air Force One. Nothing is more important to me than being there to see Timothy graduate. Nothing."

Her mother sat in her chair, elbows on her desk, lips twisted to one side. "Ava, Timothy may not be home for his graduation."

"He might be." Ava had no way of knowing. Why not hope for the best?

"You don't want to think about it?"

"Mom, no. Not even maybe. If they think I'm worth it, they'll give me another chance some other year. I'm not going. And please message dad so I don't have to go through this with him, too. I know he'll be even more disappointed than you are. I agree it sounds interesting, even a great opportunity, but it's not something I can make a decision on right now. In fact, I don't want to move. I want to graduate here."

"Ava, Timothy won't be here next year. He'll be away at college. Don't be too quick to reject the offer."

"I really don't want to go. I like it here."

Her mother offered her a weak smile and a nod, which prompted Ava to give her a hug. "Thank you for being proud of me."

"Ava, just one last question, and I'll drop it, I promise. If you did have a chance to see Timothy, not just talk to him, would you give it a second thought? I'm not asking for a commitment to move. Scholarships like this don't come around every day."

There was no harm in agreeing to her mother's plea. It wasn't going to happen. "If it works out, sure."

No Guilt

Chapter 30

With one hand subconsciously running over the inch-long hair behind her ear, Ava set her backpack on the kitchen table and searched the pantry for a quick snack.

"Mom," she called down the hallway, "don't we have anything good to eat?"

Her mother came into the kitchen and leaned against the refrigerator. "Good as in not good for you?"

"Exactly. Dad used to hide his junk food on the top shelf. You know, the stuff you can still buy in Idaho."

A finger on her chin, her mother scanned the kitchen for potential hoarding sights. "Maybe above the microwave."

Ava pulled a barstool next the cooktop and climbed up to reach the potential stash. "No way!"

"What's he got up there?" her mother asked.

Ava filtered through a stash of baked goods, brightly colored bags of salty chips, and candy bars. "Everything. Want something?" Ava held up a few calorie-loaded choices.

Her mother pointed at the candy. "I'll take the chocolate bar."

Both sharing in a guilty giggle, Ava handed it to her. "I feel like a pirate pilfering loot."

Her mother shook her head. "I don't feel guilty one bit. We're doing him a favor. Your father shouldn't eat all that junk food. It's not good for him."

Ava closed the cupboard and put the barstool back before biting into a chocolate-covered donut rolled in toasted coconut. "Yeah. We're eating this because we love him."

"You do sacrifice for those you love." Her mother took another bite of her candy bar and faced Ava with a lifted brow.

"What?"

"Did someone ask you to the prom?" her mother asked with a sheepish grin. "It's a small town. Word gets around."

Dropping her chin, Ava fumbled with the plastic sleeve of mini donuts. "I didn't feel like going."

"Without Timothy," her mother added. "Rochelle's mother told me. Want to talk about it?"

Ava twisted her lips to the side. "It's not a big deal."

It was at first. In fact, it was beyond humiliating when Devin came into the crowded cafeteria with a guitar. She told her mother that a friend of Devin's recorded the lunch-table serenade, while the girls sitting with her watched her with wide-eyed surprise. Devin wasn't exactly a gifted singer or guitar player. When he couldn't manage a chord change, he cut the song short. She felt bad for saying no but assured him that another girl would appreciate his efforts more than she did, since her heart was already spoken for.

"That's what you told him? Your heart was already spoken for?"

Ava covered her mouth to suppress a grin. "It rhymed, sort of, with his unfinished song: '*I should go with him fer shore.*'" A poorly timed bite of donut threatened to exit in a spit-spray of giggles. A hand providing a barrier to any potential projectiles, Ava added, "It was a country song. Kind of." She swallowed hard, faced her mother who looked as if she were trying not to laugh.

"Oh, honey, I hope you didn't hurt his feelings. Poor kid."

"No." Ava waved back and forth while attempting to clear thick frosting from her throat. "I asked the other girls at the table if anyone wanted to go. Three of them offered, and Devin just stood there like he didn't know what to do. He ended up asking if all three would go with him. He totally got a three-for-one upgrade. Everyone seemed happy. To top it off, his video had over a thousand hits by the end of the day."

An approving smile stretched across her mother's face. "A country song, huh? I'd like to see that." Lola folded her empty candy wrapper as if it were something she intended to save. "It's okay to enjoy yourself while Timothy's gone. You don't need to feel guilty for having fun."

"I know," Ava replied, tipping her head to the side as she pushed away from the counter. She reached for the wrapper in her mother's hand. "I'll take care of that."

An offer remained open for her to join Devin's entourage. Maybe she would go.

Ava tossed the wrappers, then lugged her backpack to her bedroom and left it on the floor, the closet door inconveniently closed. Even without the bag of notebooks, both digital and paper, she continued to feel weighted. Timothy wouldn't be calling her for another six days. She retrieved her phone and set it on her cluttered dresser. It didn't need to be charged, since she rarely used it anymore. Rochelle was doing something with Jase. Maybe Rochelle would call her after dinner.

At least Ava's room seemed cheerful. She smoothed a crease on her new floral comforter and rearranged the yellow-printed pillows leaning against the headboard. The yellow and red colors were a welcomed change. Dried-pink roses hung upside-down on the wall above a picture of Timothy prominently displayed on the nightstand.

She picked up the picture she'd taken of him at River Front Park, admiring his happy face. A twinge of nerves surfaced as she contemplated how he might have changed. Maybe his feelings for her were different now, or maybe they would change when he came back. She'd try not to expect too much. Of course, he'd need to adjust to being home again. He'd been gone so long. Every time he called her he seemed careful not to insinuate anything more than friendship.

The rest of the week was as exciting as watching puddles dry, but the earth kept spinning and Friday finally gave way to Saturday.

* * *

"You should go," Timothy said. "Devin is a good guy."

Ava couldn't tell if Timothy was pressing her to be interested in other guys or encouraging her to have fun. "I might go, but I wish you could go too."

"I know you do. Tell me about the video. I can't watch it here."

She told him about the goofy lyrics and the bungled chord progression that cut the song short. Hearing Timothy laugh sent a soothing warmth clear to her toes. They both agreed that Devin probably knew how bad it was but loved the attention anyway. Ava left out the part about her heart being spoken for, not wanting to be left with an awkward pause that might haunt her. After she hung up, she tried to push a nagging reminder aside. Her heart was not spoken for. Not by Timothy.

Breaking Point

Chapter 31

"Wake up, Rocky, we are going on a road trip." Azar flicked on the light, assaulting Timothy's senses with enough ultraviolet light to change the color of his skin.

"Except for I'm blind now. And I'm not a boxer."

"Get up, Mr. Timothy Gray. Running shoes, clothes. Snap, snap."

"You probably like this taskmaster thing, huh? Is it really therapeutic to exchange physical torture for mental torture?" Timothy slid his feet to the floor. "How is this helpful? Maybe a little sleep-in time is in order. It is Sunday, right?"

"Yes, Sunday. You, not so lucky."

"What's this? It's a miracle." Timothy stood, felt over his chest, then turned his hands as if seeing them for the first time. "I think I'm healed!"

"You get dressed, wonder boy," Azar ordered. "That might work on your girlfriend, but not on me. Be in the kitchen in five."

"As in minutes? Don't I get to eat first? Breakfast isn't until seven. Then there's chapel at nine. I'm looking forward to a good sermon. Mr. Gonzales, that man can preach."

Azar left him without a response. Nothing rattled his mentor. Tired and disappointed, Timothy couldn't find the goatee man's limit. Not that he disrespected Azar. He had loads of respect for him. It was more of a challenge, like father-son banter, although Azar wasn't old enough to be his father. The man had to be used to the jabs, working in a place like this. And Jase probably gave Azar the brother-in-law business. Everything a challenge, everything a race.

There's no way Jase cut Azar any slack. Rooster talk, that's all it was. Jase really liked Azar. Now Timothy understood why. Jase and Azar were responsible for getting Timothy to agree to come to this place. He hadn't realized how much he needed it, and he hadn't come a day too soon.

Timothy smiled at the thought of Jase. Like Ava, his friend never gave up on him. Whenever Jase thought things were going south, his friend would say, out of the blue and for no apparent reason, *Do you wanna fight?* It didn't make sense. Jase didn't care. His friend had a peculiar way of dealing with things. *Put 'em up cowboy*, Jase would say with a slur, then he'd hop around like a drunken boxer, yelling at the top of his lungs, *Come at me, bro!*

It was nice to be able to talk to Jase. Talk about home to help cut through the loneliness. Talk about school, the basketball team, and Ava's friend. Jase was still afraid of Rochelle's father, but he was determined to win the man over. Timothy had suggested the drunk-boxer routine. That set off a round of laughs that used up too much of their call. It was worth it. Crazy Jase. The laughter felt good.

Shoes and shorts tied, t-shirt on, and a hoodie tied around his neck, Timothy made his way through a carpeted corridor toward the kitchen. A few of the residents were shuffling the other way, their round of kitchen duty completed. Each sleepy-eyed troubled teen offered a high-five as they passed him.

Inside the kitchen, Mr. Goatee stood waiting, a pack at his feet and a hat in each hand. Azar pointed at a slurry of green sludge capped with foam. "Drink that. It is your breakfast."

"Yay. Breakfast of champions." With enough protein shake in his stomach to satisfy a calf, Timothy accepted one of the hats and followed the Persian behemoth to the alley door. "You know, I'd like some breakfast I could chew. The solid kind made out of meat. You've heard of that, right? Bacon, sausage. My teeth could go soft from lack of use."

Azar chuckled. "Well now, if that were true, your jaw should be in fine shape. No lack of use there."

Timothy scoffed at the clever reply. He had it coming.

"Cat got your tongue, huh, Timothy?"

With a smile that accepted defeat, Timothy asked him where they were going. His trainer told him he would see soon enough and to simply enjoy the ride.

Headed south on a familiar stretch of highway, Timothy watched the landscape change from evergreens to cultivated fields shrouded in muggy gray skies, the outline of Steptoe Butte in the distant haze. Day trips were usually a nice break from the walls of the center, but not when they included Billy's gravesite or the place of his brother's death. No amount of music could calm those demons. When Azar turned off the highway toward Steptoe Butte, Timothy relaxed, stiff fingers bending again, the back of his neck not as tight. Sunday outings often involved a vanload of day-trippers, not just him and Azar. But there was nothing on these back roads that posed a threat.

Azar pulled over at the gate at the base of the Butte, dark clouds moving in from the south.

Timothy pointed at the horizon. "It's going to rain."

"Likely. Won't hurt us any," his mentor replied.

"Looks like the park is closed." Timothy, having stated the obvious, gestured at a sign informing all visitors that the butte would be closed for two days to repair the road.

"Not for us. Come on."

Out of the car, Azar, a pack clipped to his shoulders and back, slid his ID in front of the gate reader, the latch clicking, gate-cam flashing a picture.

"Is there anywhere your ID doesn't work? I mean, can you get into concerts with that thing? Or that room at the airport, you know, for first-class travelers that don't like sitting with commoners?"

"Not exactly." Azar had Timothy drink down a few electrolyte-laced swallows of water, then tucked the bottle back in his pack.

Steptoe Butte was impressive, but it was small potatoes when it came to hiking. One could take the straight-up approach rather than follow the circling roadway. Maybe that was the plan. Not a big deal, really. It was Sunday. They usually took things easy on Sunday.

After one circle of picturesque strolling, the wind kicked up and the sky began to rumble. Azar quickened the pace to a slow jog. "Stay in front of me."

As they jogged along, Timothy asked Azar where he went when he wasn't at the treatment center. "I mean, besides home. Do you have another job? Are you special ops? SEAL team six? Just tell me, I can keep a secret. Clearance all the way up to the Pentagon?"

Azar told him he watched too many movies and quickened the pace. The road was steeper and longer than it appeared from the bottom of the butte. Halfway up, a gust of wind peppered Timothy's face with dust and grit. Lungs burning, he slowed to a stop. "Come on. I'm dying, here." Between gulps of air, he asked his trainer if his parents stopped paying the bill.

Mr. Azar passed him a water bottle. Thirst quenched, his taskmaster allowed him a twenty-yard walk, then stayed on him like a drill sergeant.

A third of the way from the top, the clouds cut loose, drenching them in sheets of rain. Legs burning, Timothy dropped his pace to a heavy-footed trudge, his chest aching.

"Let's go, Gray."

"It's Sunday. Day of rest ring a bell?"

Azar pointed up the road. "You have more in you."

"No I don't!" Timothy shot back. "I've got nothing in me. Nothing! I couldn't even pee if I wanted to."

Azar's eyes widened slightly. Without raising his voice, his mentor told him that he could still run if he had the energy to yell. "Get going."

"Why?" Timothy challenged. "So I can have a mountain top experience? Forget this!" He turned downhill and headed for the car. They didn't have a ride down the butte. Why prolong the torture?

Azar blocked his path. "What are you afraid of, Timothy?"

"Nothing. I'm afraid of you—you psycho. Looking for some CPR practice? Maybe I'll break my leg and stop breathing. First aid and CPR. Two for one." One shoulder back and his weight on his toes, Timothy stood nose to nose with the man who'd been on his heels the whole time with no sign of fatigue. Why didn't Azar punch him? Just once. He had it coming. Timothy reached out to push the man and experienced the involuntary swing-around of centrifugal force.

"You don't want to do that, Timothy. We're close to the top. Let's go."

Timothy swung back with a left hook that connected with nothing but rain, sending him in a stumble to regain his balance. "No! I'd rather you beat me to a bloody pulp than take one more step! I can't burn enough energy in a lifetime to chase away my demons. I'm ruined! I don't want to live like this. I can't run up a hill or pump iron every time my brother comes to mind. I don't want to go to sleep. I don't want to be awake." Both hands in a swipe over his face to clear both tears and water, he longed to know why the breakthrough with his father hadn't changed things in his mind. Why couldn't he be who his parents needed him to be or who Ava and his friends thought he was? Timothy dropped to his knees and sobbed out that he was done. "I'll go home if I have to. Whatever. I quit."

His mentor gripped his arm. "Two weeks to go and you're going to quit? You have PTSD, Timothy. You can't control some of your responses to trauma, but you can reroute them. Override them, and learn to cope. Give yourself a chance. Giving up is not an option. You won't believe you can do it until you push yourself beyond what you think you're able. Only then will you trust the strength that is beyond yourself."

"Is this a God thing?" Done with that, too, Timothy didn't want to go there.

Azar stepped back, Timothy's arm freed from the man's iron grip. "Everything good is a God thing," his mentor said. "He created us to benefit from our own body's chemistry. And from relationships and hard work and commitment and personal achievement and creativity. And loss."

Hands pressed on his thighs, Timothy faced him, the rain slowing to a steady trickle. "What? You had me until that last part."

Azar waved him to move up the butte, thankfully at a walkable pace. "Your feelings of loss are evidence of love. Without love or the sense of loss, how would our hearts feel pain? And it is real pain. Affects everything about you. If loss is not dealt with in a healthy way, it can become a monster that drains you emotionally, spiritually, and physically. If there is a monster, let us admit it. Only then can you build its cage."

On the southern horizon, slivers of sunlight broke through distant clouds and inched toward them like spotlights on a grand stage. His mentor hung back, a yard or two behind him, while Timothy trudged up the last and smallest circle to the butte's top. Far below, swaths of yellow canola cut through a sea of green that stretched out in all directions for miles upon miles. "I think you just met my monster."

"Well," Azar said as he leaned on a nearby bench, "at least he has a wild swing."

Timothy rewarded the jest with a weak chuckle. "Sorry about that." In search of a throwable rock, he bent down and sifted through a pile of pebbles on the steep side of the road. Projectile selected, Timothy stood and threw it as far as he could, watched it arc and fall to the ground.

"Why don't you name it?" Azar asked him.

"The monster?"

"Yes, the monster. A coping mechanism. When this thing you do not want controlling you starts to take over, you separate yourself from it. Reject its hold on you. It is an emotional and mental reroute. You could name it something simple like . . . Ed. What do you think?"

"No. Not Ed." Timothy sat on the other end of the bench, elbows on his knees. "How about bindweed? It's a farmer thing."

"Yes. Bindweed. I like it. Let's get going. We will walk down to save your shins. Timothy, you should know we are not going straight back to the center. We are going into Colfax."

Timothy felt Bindweed make his first named appearance. That didn't take long. "The grave?" Beads of salty sweat trickled down his forehead and stung his eyes.

"Yes, Timothy. We are going to Billy's gravesite."

* * *

By late morning, rain clouds skirted around the eastern side of the valley, the bulk of their storehouse unloaded on higher ground north of Colfax. In no hurry, Ava held her orange umbrella overhead as she wove through headstones and flower-lined paths. Along the road dividing the cemetery, spent daffodils yielded their seasonal show to lilac trees and red tulips.

Closer to her destination, she saw the irises still hanging next to Billy's grave, perched inside a plastic cone hung on a shepherd's hook. At the base of the headstone, wilted, cellophane-wrapped roses suggested another visitor. Ava pulled a faded blue petal from the flowers she'd placed there. Yesterday she and Grace picked the irises out of the Gray's courtyard, along with full, white peonies. Hundreds of white petals now lay strewn across the grass, dismantled and dispersed by the wind. In a week and a day, the cemetery would be full of flowers and flags, people remembering those they loved.

Timothy mentioned Billy during last night's call. He didn't elaborate. When Ava told him Jase wanted to take Rochelle and her to a pro soccer game, Timothy said he remembered something from earlier days. Nothing important, he claimed. Things he and Billy had fun playing when they were young.

Under the impression that Billy was not an approved topic of conversation, Ava didn't know how to respond. When she told him she placed flowers on Billy's grave, Timothy seemed hesitant, claimed it a nice gesture, and then asked her why she liked to walk among the graves. Other than the view from the top of the hill, she didn't have a ready answer. After their conversation, his question continued to linger in her thoughts.

Why did she like coming up here? Maybe she wanted to understand what Timothy was going through. What did it feel like to mourn the dead so deeply that it threatened the living? She moved slowly past a row of markers, reading the inscriptions. Fathers, sons, and husbands lost in war, decades of life etched on some, others only days. Too young to understand loss when her grandparents passed away, she'd never felt the sting of death. Ava bent down and brushed over an image of a lamb on a small marker. So many people die before an acceptable age.

"For how many centuries, and how many times, Lord, have you been asked *why*? How do you comfort them?" She prayed that Timothy would accept the Lord's comfort, even if she didn't fully understand where it came from.

Air clean and sun breaking through the clouds, Ava pulled in one more lungful of rain-filtered freshness and headed for home, umbrella under her arm. Without a goal in mind, she dawdled on the front porch. Fixed to a post rail, their stars and stripes slowly tipped and twirled as it rode a gentle breeze.

Chapter 32

Almost to Colfax, Timothy asked Azar how many residents make a full turnaround to a healthy future. "You know, a full recovery?"

"About forty percent," Azar replied.

"Forty percent? That's a straight-up F."

Goatee man wagged a finger at him. "You choose what to do with the skills you're given, my friend. Once you leave the center, you can use them or lose them. Four out of ten, give or take a few, will continue to use what they have learned after a few years. It is the sad truth, but that forty percent makes all this worth it. Some will come back a second or third time. Some will die in an alley with nothing but an empty needle stuck in their arm."

They fell in behind a pilot car trailing a trio of tractors and sprayer booms folded to accommodate the width of the road. After a silent, slow-going mile, the convoy turned off the highway onto a muddy dirt road, freeing the line of cars behind them.

Timothy didn't care for that needle in the arm scenario. "What about the government? Won't they pay to euthanize a street junkie at one of those clinics? You know, if a guy wants to off himself. They don't have to die in a dark alley."

"No, that is not the way it works," Azar replied. "Most of those clinics are only interested in marketable merchandise. Drug free. The younger the better. Medical research, they like to call it. Whatever makes them appear sympathetic to the rights and needs of humanity yet keeps them profitable. Ironic, really, since they are deemed non-profits. Bloodthirsty dogs dealing in body parts. They don't want pickled livers and hepatitis in those chop shops. Except in Southern California and some of the eastern states. The beaches are not cleaned up down in L.A. because all their homeless people found a job and bought homes. No, they're fertilizing palm trees along Hollywood boulevard. Very earth friendly.

"That's disgusting."

"Yes, but nothing new. They've been composting people for years." Azar rubbed his chin tuft and claimed a need to tell Timothy something off the subject.

His trainer and mentor then informed him that not all residents at the center went through the same program. "Our approach to treatment is tailor-made for each person's needs according to their past and what we learn in interviews and profile analysis. Everybody gets gym time, but few get Azar's fantastic path to pain and wellness."

"Fantastic? Really? Lucky me. Looks like my inside connection isn't granting me any favors."

His mentor said nothing but wore a knowing grin as they turned down a long, steep decline into town, the electric car barely whining under the stress on the engine.

Timothy shared his opinion of the car, preferring the throaty rumble of internal combustion to the near-silent drone of tires on pavement. "We still have two real gas stations in Colfax. These farmers around here aren't ready to trade in their old trucks that can keep running day and night for Teslas or self-drivers anytime soon."

Azar agreed and shared a glimpse into his private life: a passion for motorcycles, the faster the better. His wife, however, did not share in that passion. Azar confessed to a promise he'd made to his wife. He'd stick to vehicles with doors when the two of them became three.

Timothy took in the familiar sights as they drove up the other side of the valley. Parked at the north end of the cemetery, he felt Bindweed's unwelcome arrival. Like a constrictor on his insides, his mental nemesis trailed an invasive vine through Timothy's chest. At least the fatigue from the jog up the butte had stalled a full on panic attack. Probably part of Azar's fantastic plan.

Released from the confines of the car, Timothy drifted west, hoping to catch a glimpse of Ava over the rise. Bindweed allowed him a few easy breaths since his inner monster was no longer the center of attention.

"This way, Romeo. I know who lives over there. By the way, do you think it is a coincidence that a young lady, who you initially did not know, sets her mind on you like a magnet to metal? Come on, my friend. Here is a thought: Ava followed a trail of heavenly breadcrumbs. Between God and Ava, you did not stand a chance. I don't know if you even needed my expert training skills."

"Expert, huh?" Timothy knew better, and he knew Azar knew better as well. Mr. Goatee was as much a godsend as Ava. And it wasn't a stretch to think of Ava as a miracle. "Maybe God moves people to do things all the time . . . we just don't realize it."

Azar patted his shoulder. "You are starting to see clearly, my enlightened one."

"Great. Is this where you go back in the lamp for another thousand years? Maybe I should hold the car keys."

"Careful, smarty mouth. I could still punch you in the nose." Fingertips together, Azar offered a slight bow. "Now, let us do what we came to do."

They walked over to Billy's grave, Timothy's pulse quickened but manageable. He bent down and ran shaky fingers over wet, faded blooms on the ground. People hadn't forgotten Billy. He recognized the blue irises, his Mother's flowers. Maybe Ava brought them.

"All jest aside, how are you feeling, Timothy?"

"Uh . . . keeping it together." But would rather be anywhere than here.

Azar told him he was going for a stroll to dry his clothes a bit. "Take as long as you want, Timothy. I am in no hurry."

* * *

Ava stood on the back deck, watching the cars trickle along at the end of town. Two more weeks to go and Timothy would be back in Colfax. She wished those days could flash by like lightning. Not likely. Back inside, she picked at some chips and veggie dip on the counter, then wandered toward the front window. Someone was walking up in the cemetery. She couldn't tell who, just that it was a man with a stride that didn't seem to have a destination in mind. A white car sat at the north end. She didn't recognize it. Not that she knew all the local cars in town, but the cemetery had its regulars. She nibbled at a corn chip and watched the man stroll in and out of view stopping here and there to read a headstone. Every so often, he'd turn back and look her way, but not directly at her, as if expecting someone. Seemed odd. Looked like a man dressed for a hike, but he wasn't moving very fast. Something on his arm caught the sun for a split second. A wrist phone maybe or a monitor of some kind.

"What are you watching?" her mother asked, a manila envelope tucked under her arm as she balanced chips loaded with dip. "Want some?"

"Already had some. Thanks. There's someone at the cemetery. Seems to be aimlessly wandering. Makes me curious. Shows how bored I am. Walkers usually chuck along with purpose. Sightseers carry a camera. I don't know. Thought I'd spy on him for a while."

"You are your father's daughter."

"What do you mean by that?"

Her mother waved off the question. "Nothing. Just mumbling."

Ava would have pressed her mother for an explanation, but an older woman in a camo raincoat shuttled past the front window, a Lab puppy fighting its leash at her side. Not something one sees every day. Both Ava and her mother waved at the elderly neighbor who had never before walked clear to the end of the street. The road steep, it wasn't an easy climb. At least not for someone in her eighties.

Ava's mother wondered aloud about what the older neighbor might be up to. "And doesn't that seem like a lot of puppy for Ethel? Hope she doesn't fall. She needs one of those little yappy dogs."

Ava agreed but thought Ethel looked particularly excited with her pet choice.

Her mother leaned toward the window and looked up the hill. "I see the guy. Looks like one of those weightlifter types." Lola popped a chip in her mouth and told Ava that she needed to go to the attorney's office and leave something in the drop box. "I'll be back within fifteen minutes."

The front window still providing more entertainment than anything online, Ava waved at her mother as she left, then continued

212

to watch the cemetery man and Ethel with her puppy. The man seemed to recognize Ethel, offering her a low wave as if some kind of rendezvous was in the works. He hurried down the hill, hat pulled too low to see his face.

"Ethel? . . . You've got to be kidding . . . Are you seriously buying street merch?"

Expecting a packet of bacon to exchange hands, Ava watched the man take the puppy and remove its collar, then stuff it in his pack. "What?" Ethel seemed pleased, as if she'd just won bingo night. The man then skirted the hill like he was on a S.W.A.T. mission, cresting the top with the same slow meandering pace as before. Ethel stood where he left her, raincoat held at her neck with both hands, as if the sun wasn't shining.

* * *

An arm resting on his brother's headstone, Timothy brushed a pile of flower debris aside and sat on the wet ground. He knew Billy wasn't there, but something about a person's final resting place made it seem like the closest one could get.

The gray granite in front of him reduced his brother's lifespan to a short dash, a chiseled line between a first and last breath. He read over the epitaph, considering every word. *Blessed are they that mourn, for they shall be comforted*, the Bible reference engraved below to prove its validity. Timothy didn't believe he was at the blessed stage yet, but hope was not lost. He was stuck at the end of the second line with *they that mourn*. Didn't feel blessed or comforted. Earlier that month he'd been here with Mr. Gonzales and Azar. It didn't go well. Timothy hadn't heard and hadn't asked, but his parents probably got a bill to repair a dented van hood. The recollection embarrassed him. When panic moved in, he felt like a different person. It helped to name that nemesis Bindweed, give it its own identity. His was a problem beyond a lack of self-control. More like no control. He'd thought PTSD was something soldiers dealt with. It helped to have a reason for what he'd been going through. Healthy self-talk wasn't enough to snuff out Bindweed.

He leaned forward and traced a fingertip over his brother's name. "Miss you, Billy."

"Whoa!" Something wet nudged his arm.

A fat, blond puppy with floppy ears took up residence on his lap, intent on giving Timothy a full-face wash.

"And who are you?" Timothy sputtered and laughed, the back of his hand clearing slobber from his nose. "Where'd you come from, boy? Got away, didn't ya?" He rubbed the offered belly. "Happy about it too, aren't ya?" The puppy in a resistant twist under his arm, Timothy stood to see if someone might be looking for his new friend.

Azar strolled close by, hands clasped behind his back, oblivious to the visitor. When Timothy caught his trainer's eye, he held up the wriggling pup.

"What have we here?" Azar shortened the distance between them and gave the little runaway a scratch on the neck.

They spent a few minutes watching the puppy run and tumble, each energetic display ending with a flop on Timothy's shoes. The puppy then tugged at the hem of Timothy's shorts, tearing the dry-weave fabric easily with its sharp teeth, until forced to give up its mouthful. One hand on his waistband to maintain decency, Timothy wrestled the pup flat to the ground and told it not to eat his clothes. The reprimand resulted in a slobber-loaded lick on his chin followed by a snatch at his sweatshirt.

"No, no, you little rebel," Timothy said as he muzzled the dog with his hand.

"Did you hear that?" Azar asked.

"What?"

Over the hill, a faint voice called for *Sparkles*. The puppy didn't seem to care, its little tail whipping Timothy's knee.

"Sparkles, huh?" Timothy scratched behind a velvety ear. "No wonder you ran away."

They followed the voice to find an elderly woman in a camo raincoat, standing within twenty yards of Ava's front door, her hood still on even though the rain had passed. Azar offered to run the dog down the hill to her. From the top of the rise, Timothy watched his trainer wrangle the puppy into its collar and leash, then pass Sparkles to its grateful owner. With Azar occupied, he took advantage of the opportunity to study Ava's house for movement. If he saw her, not even the mighty goatee man could stop him from talking to her, at least not without causing a scene. But her front window offered no sign of life.

* * *

One of her father's forbidden snacks tested and approved, Ava headed back to the dining room to check on the Ethel situation. In a determined tromp past the window, the elderly Ethel again had the puppy in tow, her smile so big it appeared she might laugh.

Chocolate suspended in mid-chew, Ava leaned closer to the window. The white car was leaving the cemetery. Show over, she shrugged and shifted her attention to the candy.

Source of Strength

Chapter 33

    In the car on the way back to Spokane, Azar asked Timothy if he felt they'd made any progress. As rolling fields made the shift back to tree-covered hills and valleys, Timothy considered the question, joked about a punch that didn't land, and apologized for words he wished he hadn't said. "I take that wanting to be beat to a pulp back. I think we crossed that bridge. Kind of like my nose the way it is."

    Azar agreed to take the beating off his to-do list. Though Bindweed made a showing earlier in the day, Timothy admitted to leaving the cemetery with a sense of closure as opposed to anger or panic. For the rest of the trip back to the treatment center, his mentor asked him questions about his and Billy's childhood, playing hockey and basketball together, and working with their father. Happy memories. Memories he needed to focus on when a past he couldn't change attempted to overwhelm him. Those what-ifs weren't reality and offered no help to the wounded. Azar reminded him he had strength available beyond himself, heavenly muscle ready and waiting to kick in whenever he admitted a load too heavy to bear alone.

    Timothy quoted a verse he'd memorized at least a decade ago, "My help comes from the Lord, the maker of heaven and earth."

    Azar replied with a hearty nod. "And puppies," he added with a sheepish grin.

    "Puppies? You think you're funny, don't you, goatee man? I thought we were having a serious conversation here, you know, about Bible stuff. Then you throw *Sparkles* in the mix. I think I need to have a look at your credentials."

"How about next time we are in the gym, you put the gloves on and give that sissy left of yours another try. I'll show you my credentials, tough guy."

Timothy laughed at the challenge, realizing for the first time that Azar wasn't much older than Billy would have been. "You know, second thought, I'm good. I'll let you off the hook this time."

* * *

Seated in the chair across from Mr. Gonzales, Timothy eyed the pen and blank paper on the coffee table in front of him. He was to use them to complete this last assignment. An old-style letter, pen and ink, intended to chronicle his new resolve and answer the questions he'd asked in his first letter.

"You've come a long way," his counselor said. "I'm proud of you. But you need to remember, you'll still have bad days. Your brother's death isn't something you *get over*. Billy's birthday will be difficult. You'll see guys having a good time with their brothers. You'll feel cheated. Many things will remind you of Billy's death; Christmas, basketball, accomplishments you'll wish you could share with him. You won't get over Billy's death, but you can adjust to life without him. What will come and go is a desire to be with him. Expect those longings. Recognize them for what they are—love. Do you feel equipped to handle that?"

Fingertips tapping together in a steady beat, Timothy agreed with a slow nod.

"Concerning future accomplishments, do you feel free to pursue your own personal successes, even those things Billy might have done? Things as simple as turning nineteen?"

"Yes, I think I'm ready for that."

His counselor smiled, pointed at him with a two-gun, *I agree with you* gesture. "Now, as you continue to work through the grieving process, will you be able to resist the temptation to mask your grief?"

"I will." After three months of counseling, healthy coping mechanisms felt as if they'd been forever imprinted in both body and mind. In two days, he'd finally be going home.

"I believe you, Timothy, and I have faith that one day your grief will mature into wisdom." Mr. Gonzales pushed his sleeve up to reveal a large, fully-inked cross tattoo covering the inside of his forearm. "Beneath this cross is the shame of my own past, but I can no longer see what was once written there. All I see is the cross." He pointed at the blank paper. "Have you forgiven yourself?"

Timothy shifted his eyes to the paper. "I have." It wasn't easy, but when his father reached out to him, it opened the door to trusting his heavenly father as well. As he looked back over the last three years of his life, he could see God reaching out, offering the help he needed. He had allowed his guilt, pain, and grief to blind him while pretending it all didn't exist. Not anymore.

"This is our last session. Remember, Timothy, you choose where to fix your eyes, your thoughts. Are they on the storm, or on the one who can get you through it? After you write that letter, take it with you. When you're having a bad day, and you will, get it out and read it. If that's not enough, you have my number. I'll be happy to remind you where your strength comes from. And I know from experience, we all need those reminders from time to time. I'll see you at the open house. The Lord bless you, Timothy."

Before Mr. Gonzales left him to complete his final task, Timothy hugged his counselor's shoulder and thanked the older man for his help and encouragement.

Alone with his thoughts, he scooped the pen up, clicking it with his thumb as he stood and paced the length of the room. This letter would replace the one he wrote over five months ago, Christmas Eve, when he wanted to give up on life. He'd tell Billy how much he missed him, tell him things he wished he could have said, and then tell him goodbye. The rest of the letter would be to himself. His life was worth living. An endless reservoir of strength—far beyond his own—was available whenever he needed it. Always within his reach. All he had to do was ask.

My help comes from the Lord, he wrote as he recalled Mr. Gonzales explaining a Bible passage about God not letting us go through trials without providing a way of escape. The terms were nautical, in reference to a ship tossed in a stormy sea. The rise and fall of the waves didn't mean the Lord had left us alone, just that we needed to back away from the helm and trust him to bring us into a safe place, the harbor of his will. For Billy, that harbor is heaven, and one day he'd see Billy again. For now his own harbor is knowing that God loves him and reached into his life to prove it. It's what he needed most, from God and his father: to be rescued. To be reached for.

The same day Mr. Gonzales explained the ship tossed at sea, Ava told him that help comes from the Lord. He almost felt dogged by heaven's angels as he struggled to believe it. He believed it now. *The things I think about, dwell on, those are my choices*, he added to the letter. *My thoughts can bring me to a dark place only if I let them. I'm not alone in this. I never was.*

Timothy folded the letter and pushed it into his back pocket. Ava . . . he'd see her in two days. She'd never know how much she'd interrupted his plans. He thanked God that she did and asked God to bless her, his Ava Interruptus. He shook his head in an effort to dislodge a worry threatening to take root. After all this she might want to move on, a friend that made herself available when he needed her most. Maybe things had already changed for her, the way she felt about him. Their relationship would be different. They'd have time to talk about it in person. No rush. Wait awhile. Let her get used to having him around again. They'd figure it out.

Coming Home

CHAPTER 34

"How about that one?" Rochelle pointed to the short hairstyle at the top of the screen.

"I don't know if asymmetrical is really me." Ava had been parting her long hair on the side to cover the bald patch behind her ear, now covered by several inches of new growth. Ready for a new style to even things up, she scanned through the images to reveal another page of options. "This one's cute." Ava expanded the picture to get a better look.

Rochelle agreed. "Kind of Tinkerbelle-ish. I like the longer bangs, too. You can do a virtual try-on, see if you like the whole look." Rochelle took a picture of Ava and downloaded it onto the app, then inspected Ava's altered picture. "Oh yah. That's the one. I love it."

That afternoon, Ava watched what remained of her long hair fall to the floor. The stylist rubbed a dab of gel through her short hair, then tousled and dried.

Ava ran a hand up the back of her neck. "It feels so weird."

Rochelle insisted she looked better than the picture they'd shown the stylist. Ava's mother smiled, nodding in agreement.

"But will Timothy like it? I think he likes long hair." Ava tried to find a strand long enough to twirl in her fingers but unless she wanted to fiddle with hair in front of her eyes, hair twirling would have to be put on hold for a while.

"You don't have anything to worry about," her mother assured her. "Your hair is adorable. And I think Timothy will be thrilled to see you no matter what your hair looks like."

"This Saturday, right?" Rochelle asked with an excited grin, as they got in the car.

"Yes. Finally. Only two more days!" Ava could barely contain her nervous energy. Just the mention of seeing him made her heart race.

Timothy told her two weeks ago he'd be coming home. A plan was in the works to celebrate a successful end to his treatment, and he had invited Ava and her parents to the center's open house in Spokane. He'd been gone for three long months.

Rochelle mentioned that he'd be home just in time for graduation. "Jase told me he was walking with him on Sunday. How'd he finish school?"

"Timothy completed his classes online, along with several college-level courses he'd started before he left," Ava replied. "The center has someone authorized to proctor final exams, so he's not behind at all. In fact, he has a head start on college."

"Ava, you sound like a proud parent," her mother teased.

She was proud of him. He was coming home. After months of Saturday night calls, she would finally get to see Timothy.

* * *

Ava followed her parents into the treatment center, the large room buzzing with excited chatter. A dozen or so young men milled around in button-up shirts and ties, people laughing, hugging, older people dabbing their eyes.

"There he is," her mother said, pointing across the crowded room.

"Where?" Ava's hands began to tremble. "I don't see him."

"Geez Louise, the kid's huge," her dad said. "What the heck did they feed him?" Eric put a hand to the side of his mouth. "Glad I already got the tough dad routine out of the way."

"Oh my!" Ava stared at the guy hugging Mrs. Gray. "That can't be him. Timothy's neck is longer than that." She twisted and tugged at the front of her blouse.

Her dad leaned down as if he had a secret. "Ava, his neck isn't shorter, it's thicker."

"That's him, honey," her mother assured her. "Right there in the blue shirt."

Timothy seemed to be scanning the room until he found her, a broad grin spreading across his face.

"Mom," Ava squeaked, "I'm gonna pass out."

"Here he comes." Her mother held her arm. "Oh, Ava, doesn't he look marvelous."

Ava sucked in a few quick breaths. "Lord, help me."

Some giant guy with Timothy's smile swooped her into his arms and buried his face in her neck. "Thank you for coming. Oh man, Ava, it's *so* good to see you." He set her down and wrapped an arm around her shoulders without taking his eyes off her. "I like your hair. You look kind of . . . sassy." He tilted his head and stared at her as if he were committing every feature on her face to memory.

Ocean-blue. How can his eyes be even brighter? She wanted to say how happy she was to see him, that he looked like a new person, and if he kept looking at her like that she'd have to sit down, but her throat tightened. Not letting go of her, Timothy turned his attention toward her parents, thanking them both for coming. He then faced her again.

Hoping her involuntary ability to breath would soon kick in; she drank in the fullness of his face. His thick hair. "It's really you," she forced out, her voice breathy. "You look . . . different."

"I hope so," he laughed, his face electric with pure joy. "Not so pale. A little healthier maybe."

"Yeah," Ava's neck was as hot as a furnace. "That's an understatement."

"Why are you blushing?" he whispered in her ear. "Am I making you nervous?"

"Very." She swallowed hard.

"I am?" He pulled his arm back. Took a step away from her. "I'm sorry."

"No, no, don't be sorry." She grabbed one of his hands with both of hers. "It's just . . . Timothy . . . you look amazing."

He laughed and pulled her into his broad chest as if she were blinded by love. "So, you don't have a new boyfriend?"

"No!" If she did, it was him.

"I love you," he proclaimed boldly, obviously not caring who heard him. "Did I tell you how nice it is to see you?"

"You did." Fingers smoothing the short hair over the scar behind her ear, she added that this time she was awake.

He hugged her again and held her close to his side, his expression suggesting unasked questions. "Don't go anywhere. I need to catch someone before they leave. I'll be right back, okay?"

"I'll be right here." Ava leaned close to her mother when he walked away. "Could you please roll my tongue up and shove it back in my mouth?"

"He's pretty handsome, isn't he?" her mother replied.

"Yep. He is that."

"Lola," her father whispered, forcing his face between them, "Don't eat the sandwiches. You'll wake up as big as a horse."

Her mother nudged him with her shoulder. "Eric, shush."

Back pats, handshakes, and laughter continued to be passed from one to another. Ava watched as this new Timothy said goodbye to several young men who likely overcame tragic situations of their own. Not knowing him before his brother's death, she hadn't witnessed how Timothy's grief had changed him. How it had stolen his vitality. She continued watching as he introduced his father to a tall man that looked like the genie from Aladdin. Maybe he was a counselor or, judging by the man's physique, a physical trainer.

Timothy pointed toward her. The dark-skinned man turned and caught her eye with a wide smile. She fiddled with her skirt and asked her dad if he wanted another sandwich. When she looked back, Timothy and his parents were headed her way. Another round of greetings were followed by hugs. Mr. and Mrs. Gray thanked Ava and her parents for coming, then slowly separated off, taking her parents with them. The awkward they're-giving-us-space thing seemed to catch Timothy off guard. She and Timothy looked at each other as if meeting for the first time.

"Ava, I want to introduce you to someone." He took her hand and forged a path through the crowd. "This is Mishael Azar, a ruthless task master that believes in no pain, no gain. And this," Timothy said, sliding behind her and resting his hands on her shoulders, "is Ava Roberts."

"It's nice to meet you, Mr. Azar," she said, shaking the man's rather large hand.

"And you, Miss Ava," he replied with a deep voice, his ebony eyes shifting between her and Timothy as if they were puppies in a pet store. "It is a pleasure to finally meet Timothy's girlfriend. You two do make a lovely couple."

Timothy cleared his throat. "We're not *exactly* a couple."

"No?" Mishael rubbed a hand over the dark whiskers on his chin.

"We're friends," Timothy said, squeezing her shoulders, then leaned to the side, nudging her to look at him. "Did I tell you Mr. Azar is Jase's brother-in-law?

"Timothy, Timothy," the man scolded, "do not try to change the subject. Just friends, then?" Mishael raised dark eyebrows.

"Not *just* friends," Timothy corrected, "True friends. The kind your life depends on."

Ava leaned her head back against Timothy's chest. She liked the way he said that.

"I see. Then it is a pleasure to meet the truest of friends. And, I want an invitation if you two should ever seal that friendship for life."

Ava blushed at the insinuation, glad that Timothy had slipped behind her.

"You got it." Timothy promised, shaking Mishael's hand.

As Timothy led Ava from one side of the room to the other, introducing her to people that had changed his life forever, she wondered if this was the old Timothy, the one before his brother's death, or an altogether new person. How could someone go through what he had, a sea of grief, and remain unchanged?

She noticed the gold bracelet on Timothy's wrist, identical to the one Mr. Azar wore. While Timothy visited with a counselor, she pulled their clasped hands closer and spun the chain around to read the engraved inscription. *I can do all things through Christ who gives me strength.* Who would know that better than someone pulled from the riptide?

Reintroductions

Chapter 35

Her heart near to bursting, Ava sat in the high school gym, watching Timothy cross the stage to accept his diploma, the applause deafening. He looked her way, his broad grin bigger than ever as his gaze shifted from his parents to her. She formed a heart with her hands and gave up trying not to cry.

The school principal stepped to the podium. "It is my privilege and honor to introduce to you the graduating class of 2038."

After the ceremony, Ava hugged Timothy and stepped aside for a growing crowd waiting to see him. He kept looking over at her while he thanked people offering their congratulations. She soaked in the sight of his friends and teachers reacting to his transformation. Not wanting to distract him from visiting with people that cared about him, she promised to see him at his party. He and Jase were celebrating their graduation at the golf course, and Ava had agreed to help Rochelle with the food.

* * *

For three hours, Ava helped fill pitchers with iced lemonade. She and Rochelle stood in front of the fan while Timothy and Jase greeted several hundred guests. Every time another guest arrived, an eighty-degree blast of air rushed into the crowded room. After the first hour, the air conditioner wasn't enough to keep up with the heat.

As if he had an Ava time-out clock, Timothy found her every fifteen minutes to see how she was doing. He'd then go back to face the crowd again. He seemed to be holding up.

"Timothy so looks like Billy," Rochelle whispered. "I hope it's okay to say that, but he really does. It's crazy."

Remembering Billy's picture on the mantle, there were definite similarities, but Timothy had a uniqueness all his own. It might have been easier for people that had know Billy to make the comparison, but all Ava saw was Timothy.

"I don't want you to leave," he informed her during his next time-out, tie discarded, collar unbuttoned, and fanning his face with a paper plate. "Can I get you anything? Do you want some cake? Something to drink?"

She assured him she was fine hanging out in the freshman corner with Rochelle.

"Sophomore corner. You're not a freshman anymore." He wiggled his brow and planted a quick kiss on her cheek.

When he walked away, Rochelle fanned her face with her hands. "Whoa, it's getting hot in here." She elbowed Ava's arm. "Isn't it?"

"Like an oven," Ava agreed, elbowing her back. "Jase sure seems happy with all this. And with you. Guess he thought you were worth the risk to his life after all."

For the first time since Ava knew her, Rochelle stood there speechless, top teeth working over her lip.

"What is it?" Ava pressed. "Jase kissed you, didn't he? I can't believe you didn't tell me."

Rochelle held a finger to her mouth, eyes so bright they could light the room. "Did you see Jase's new puppy?"

"Puppy? Okay, I get it. Your dad didn't hear me. Go ahead. Tell me about the puppy."

With a bounce on her toes, Rochelle told her about Jase's grandmother. She'd given Jase a puppy but he had to keep it at his grandmother's house. "Two reasons. Well, really three: he can't keep a pet at the apartment, he's leaving for college, and his grandmother wanted to lock him in on daily visits before he leaves. Jase's little brother is stoked. Jude wants to say the puppy is as much his as it is Jase's since he'll be taking care of it when Jase is gone to college. It's sleeping in its crate in the office. Really cute."

"Jase or the puppy?"

Rochelle leaned into Ava. "Both."

The mention of Timothy and Jase leaving for college stole some of their joy until they both agreed to live in the moment. Ava locked arms with Rochelle. "Why be sad when there are so many reasons to be happy?"

* * *

It was after 10:00 p.m. when the party started to wind down. Ava helped Mr. and Mrs. Gray load Timothy's gifts and decorations into their car. Jase's new puppy, Champ, excited to be free from its crate, slowed her progress as it wound around her feet and tugged on her skirt. Back inside for another armload while Timothy said goodbye to the last few guests, she downed a few swallows of ice water, potential alone time with Timothy planting prickles on her skin. Ava's parents left an hour earlier, but she had driven her own car to the party.

"Hey, I need to talk to you." Timothy took the boxes out of her arms and set them in the back of his parent's car, then took her hand in his and led her around the clubhouse balcony toward the lighted path on the golf course.

A gentle breeze felt good as they walked over the bridge and turned to follow the path winding toward the river. The temperature had quickly dropped nearly twenty degrees. When Timothy asked if he could put his arm around her, she felt a surge of mid-day sun warming her from the inside out. His arm pulled snug over her shoulder, she laced her fingers in his. Did he ask because they were alone?

"Crazy day, huh?" Timothy said without looking at her.

Ava thought she sensed a combination of nerves and contentment. "You've got to be exhausted. You just got home, and then all this."

"It's a lot to take in. Things are different. Feels almost like time-travel. I've been released back into the wild. Should be able to make it. Maybe you could strategically place piles of food where you know I'll find it. Pizza, burgers, maybe some cookies, too."

Ava quietly giggled and squeezed his hand. "I'd be happy to boost your survival odds."

He glanced at her, then shifted his attention to the path in front of their feet as they strolled along a dark line of ancient evergreens.

"My face hurts from smiling so much. Really, it does," he told her in a tone that grew quiet and serious.

"You can frown at me if you want," she softly teased, leaning into his side.

Timothy pulled her to a stop and drew in a deep breath. Ava's heart responded by pumping enough blood to sprint a mile, but she stood perfectly still, her spine as stiff and as straight as a board. He pulled away from her, leaving her exposed as he turned to face her.

"I had this whole speech thing worked out and now I can't remember any of it. Ava . . . remember when I asked you if it would be easier if we were just friends?" He reached for her and took her hand in his, his feet in a constant weight-shifting shuffle.

"Yes, I remember." She wanted to add that she hated the idea.

"I know I just got back . . . and it's going to take some time to get used to me again, but . . . what I'm trying to say is . . . not that you owe me any kind of explanation, or, you know, things are going to take some time. We've got lots of time, right? You and me? I'm thinking we could stay in touch while you finish high school. That's cool, right?"

Ava started to respond, but he cut in, leaving her to think he was hesitant to let her answer.

"Don't even worry about it," he said, his hand trailing down her arm. "What's the rush, right? I just, you know, I missed you, Ava. A lot. But I understand if you're not ready for anything serious or more of a commitment kind of thing. I'm a patient guy. Good things are worth waiting for, right?" He stared at her for a few seconds, the lights behind him too bright for her to read his expression. "Did that make any sense . . . at all?"

Not wanting to assume anything, Ava moved him in a half circle so she could clearly see his face. "You want to stay friends because you're leaving for college?"

He looked at the ground and slid his free hand over his hip. "You know that's not what I meant, don't you? What I want you to understand, Ava, is that I've got it together. I have room for a relationship. With you. No more mind clutter. I know I said we were just friends at the open house. I didn't like the way it came out, but I was afraid to put you on the spot. I can handle more than that, but I don't want you to feel pressured to pick up where we left things three months ago."

There, he said it. Everything she wanted desperately to hear. "Timothy, don't worry about me. I'm so happy you're home. I can hardly believe you're standing here. With me." She fixed the roll of his shirtsleeve. Touched a button on his shirt and a tiny curl above his ear. "You're real." Her hand shifted to his chest as she attempted to clear the tightness building in her throat. "And I feel like I . . . like I need you in my life." Her voice broke, vision clouded. "And I'm so relieved that you're better." Ava's voice inched up to a barely audible squeak as tears let loose. "I'm so happy for you."

"Stop, stop, Ava, no. Don't cry." He pulled her tight to his chest, their clasped hands beneath his chin, his fingertips combing her short hair. Timothy gently rocked her from side to side like a couple on a crowded dance floor. "It's okay. Ava, listen," he whispered, his lips almost touching her ear, "Let's take this slow, okay? We have to. I kind of bungled things. Ava, look at me."

She tilted her head to face him. So close. So warm.

"What I meant to say is I love you, Ava. Let's get to know each other again without the mess." He rubbed his lips together, his gaze in a constant shift from her eyes to her mouth. "We don't have to rush the romance. Unless you want to attack me. We can put that back on the table," he said with a nervous chuckle.

The option already on her mind, Ava dabbed at a tear on her chin. "I can wait as long as you need to." She leaned back a little and locked onto his stare, traced his jaw with her fingertip.

He stood completely still for two long seconds then pressed his lips to hers, nearly squeezing the breath out of her. Her arms tight around his neck, he picked her up and turned a slow circle. Kissed her again. She wouldn't tell him she couldn't breathe. If she passed out, it would be worth it.

"I meant to wait a little longer than that," he whispered, still holding her against him.

She attempted to pull in a deep breath, her head at his neck, arms still locked in place. "We can do this. I'll confess I wanted that. And I didn't want to wait for it. You're right, though. We can take things slow. Take time for friends. That kind of thing." Ava wiggled her feet, realizing her suspicions were correct. Her feet were not on the ground. "Timothy?"

"Yes?"

"I, uh, can you set me down? I need some air."

He startled and lowered her as if she were made of glass. "Oh— I'm sorry."

"It's that Prince Charming kiss," she said with a quiet giggle. "Knocked me right off my feet."

"I think I'm more beast than prince," he told her as she straightened his collar, the edge of his hand tracing her cheek. With a reluctant grin, he told her they needed to go. Snug to his side, he held her close as they made their way back to the clubhouse. "We're talking years, Ava. Are you sure you want to sign up for that?"

"Yes! Without a doubt, I'm all in. Do you happen to have a pen?" Ava wrapped both arms around his waist. "I love you, Timothy. And thanks again for calling me every Saturday, and for the roses. Just . . . for everything."

He pulled on her shoulder, kissed the top of her head. "You're welcome. I love you, too. By the way, I'm planning on sending you a lot more of those. Got to keep you on the hook."

"I'd be okay with that." Looking back over the last seven months, Ava had no regrets. She'd be forever glad she had not minded her own business.

Four years later—

"This is going to cost me a fortune," Eric said as he filtered through envelopes on the kitchen counter.

"I'm not buying it." Lola kissed his cheek. "You're as excited as I am."

He plopped onto a barstool. "*I'm* buying it—steak dinner for five-hundred people. Why couldn't Ava and Rochelle get together on this, do one of those double things? Now the whole month of June is shot. Hey, I know, they could share dresses and all that . . . fluff." He poked a finger at his wife. "Right there, that's genius. And what's wrong with hot dogs? We could get organic ones. Now there's a good idea. Healthy, too."

"It's only two hundred people." With a tight-lipped smile, Lola tousled his hair. "After you take those to the post office, could you go to the store? We need eggs. Real ones."

"Love to," Eric replied, tucking the invitations into a paper bag. "Couldn't we send a group text? Do people even send paper invites anymore? What's the postage costing us, two dollars a pop?"

"Eric—"

"Yeah, yeah, I'm going. I don't know what the rush is on this. Ava's only one year into college."

"Hypocrite," Lola said with a tap on his nose. "We were both still in college."

He placed another stack in the bag. "We were older at their age. It's not the same thing. They're just kids."

Lola informed him that kids grow up. "Timothy has already graduated. Already has a job. Maybe he could build us a new house."

One elbow on the counter, Eric picked up the top envelope. "Who is Mr. Mishael Azar?"

"Sounds familiar," Lola replied. "I'm not sure. He was on Timothy's list."

THE END

Made in United States
Troutdale, OR
07/28/2024

21602172R00148